Jump Into...

DEATH SPINS AN INDIGO WEB

Ivy C. Leigh

JumpRope Chronicles

https://www.jerseypinesink.com

This is a work of fiction. Names, characters, businesses, places, events, locales and incidents are either the products of the author's imagination or used in a fictitious manner. Any resemblance to actual persons, living or dead, or actual events is purely coincidental.

All rights reserved. All rights reserved, including the right to reproduce this book or portions thereof in any form whatsoever.

Cover art— Dar Albert, Wicked Smart Designs

Interior design—River Cove Production

Copyright © 2021 Jersey Pines Ink, LLC

The publisher is not responsible for websites or any other such content not owned by the publisher

For information, address the publisher at: Jerseypinesink.com

ISBN: 978-1-948899-12-3

JERSEY PINES INK

https://www.jerseypinesink.com

To Bernice, my good friend, and in memory of her "Colonel Darling."

Jump into . . . the JumpRope Chronicles
by Ivy C. Leigh

Death Behind the Lilacs

Death Counts the Golden Coins

E-Book
Jump Into: Three Short JumpRope Stories

And look for the next in the
JumpRope Chronicles Series
Death Wears Pink Roses
Coming From Jersey Pines Ink
Jerseypinesink.com

JERSEY PINES INK

Little Miss Muffet, sat on a tuffet . . . along came a spider, who sat down beside her, and frightened Miss Muffet away.

Old Nursery Rhyme

"Will you walk into my parlor?" said the Spider to the Fly.

Mary Howitt (1799–1888)

Dear Readers,

It seemed to me that Alexander Fanshawe, who was mentioned in two previous JumpRope Township books, deserved attention.

So, here he is, meeting Solstice Windsor, and becoming involved in the dangerous secrets of her past.

I hope you enjoy the perils of their adventures as much as I enjoyed writing about them.

Best always,

Ivy C. Leigh

Death Spins an Indigo Web

Before Mar-see-ah Speaks

*G*uided by the spirit of the Native American wise man, Mar-see-ah moves the smooth river stones. Once again, she seeks to divine the life and loves of that dear little New Jersey Township with the odd name of JumpRope.

Mar-see-ah smiles. The lives of the townspeople weave such interesting tangles. One couple has found one another but has not yet made a commitment. And there—a woman who keeps herself alone. A patient man waits. Is she brave enough to accept what he offers?

Yes, Mar-see-ah thinks, *a harmless tangled web.*

The voice of Little Bird, the daughter of the wise man, comes to her. "A web of danger," says Little Bird.

Mar-see-ah catches her breath as she sees a vision of a spider's web take form. Caught in the strands is a young woman with a delicate, elfin face.

Alarmed, Mar-see-ah says. "Who is this young woman?"

"She is a stranger," says Little Bird.

"Who is the spider?"

"Hidden—a spider's nature," says Little Bird. "You cannot know until it is nearly too late."

"Nearly?" Mar-see-ah desperately seizes on the word.

"There is always hope," says Little Bird.

Chapter 1

It was the sort of brisk November morning when anything good or bad could get started and so it did.

Darlene Gage, the JumpRope Township property inspector, had an appointment with an investor who had purchased an unoccupied house to rent. Before he could move in tenants, he needed an inspection for a Certificate of Occupancy, but unless everything was perfect, he would get a Conditional Certificate. That meant fix the flaws and have a second inspection. When Darlene inspected, perfection was as rare as a welcome mat on a tombstone.

Clipboard in hand and wearing her ID tag, she approached the house, one of many with similar layouts but different facades, in the Pullen Farm development.

Darlene despised the town's two developments, Pullen Farm and Peach Acres. Neither offered the quality of older homes and the residents were always complaining about the flaws. Acer Wolfgang, who had illusions of being able to charm her, was planning a third development on the former Mather Farm. She didn't expect his efforts to be any better than the others.

She met the investor, Ron Barnes, on the narrow porch.

"You'll find this place is ready for occupancy," he said as he punched in the lockbox code and opened the door.

"Feels like there's a draft," Darlene said as she stepped inside with him.

"There shouldn't be," Ron said as he closed the front door behind them.

The air kept moving.

The two of them followed the draft through the house to the rear where a patio door hung open, the lock broken.

Ron grabbed his cell phone to call the police and report a break-in.

Darlene smelled an odor she didn't like. She stepped around the half counter that separated the family room from the kitchen.

"Ron," she said, forcing her voice to express a calm she didn't feel. "You'll want to report something more."

"What?" Phone in hand, he moved around to her viewpoint.

"Get hold of Chief Parkerson," Darlene said. "I think there's been a nasty fight." She indicated overturned bar stools at the breakfast bar, broken glass and dried blood.

A lot of blood.

Chapter 2

That evening, Slim Parkerson, JumpRope Chief of Police, off duty and in casual clothes, was disgusted by the lack of evidence at the Pullen Farm house. No fingerprints, no clues, just a busted door, overturned furniture and blood. A forensic team had come over from the Melton County Prosecutor's office to investigate. They took blood samples, but without somebody to match it to, the samples would sit forgotten.

He strode his long-legged way into the barroom of Teddy Bear Bar and Grill and took a seat at the bar. The establishment included a popular restaurant with spacious dining spaces for groups and events. It was owned by Theodore Baird. He not only used his nickname for the place but by making his emblem a teddy bear jumping rope, he had tied it in with the name of the town. The mural behind the bar showed a bear jumping rope and reading a newspaper, giving the room the name, the News Room, a.k.a. the Booze Room, an aptly named late-night hang-out for a gang of *Melton Monitor* reporters.

Slim noted a few others nearby; faces that were all shades, all colors, most with local family histories, some from far away. His people, his town. He gave them an all-inclusive nod. They nodded or waved back.

There were no bids for conversation, which suited him fine.

The worst had happened between him and Lana. She'd broken off their engagement. He hadn't said anything yet to his best pal Holly, a guy he could always tell his troubles to. Right now, he only wanted to brood. He plunked down a bill for Loy, the bartender, to run a tab.

He and Holly, now the township mayor, had been buds since grade school, and the friendship stuck. Only now, Holly had a standing Tuesday night dinner date with his girlfriend, Toria. They each had full-time jobs at Melton County offices. Toria worked in records, and Holly was the supervisor of County Public Works. He and Toria took turns driving into work together.

Nice work if you can get it, thought Slim. Receiving his beer, he sucked the foam off the top. *Suck.* Everything sucked.

The bar had three big TV screens, two tuned to sports and one to the news. When all three showed the same advertisement, Slim took it as a sign to get home before he wasted himself for work in the morning.

He was sliding his lanky, six-foot, four-inch, frame off the stool when JJ Gilbert, a reporter at the *Melton Monitor*, came in alone and headed for the bar. He'd known JJ and her four older brothers all his life. She looked wrecked.

Curious, Slim checked his move to leave.

"Hey," he said. "Where's the rest of your news rat team?"

She managed a pale smile. "On my own tonight." She slid onto the stool next to his.

Slim cocked an eye at Loy as he asked, "What's your poison? My treat."

"Coffee. Black," she said, not looking at him. It wasn't until Loy had set the mug in front of her that she gave Slim another pale smile. "Thanks."

"Been chasing a story?"

"Not one I want to write."

The day JJ Gilbert didn't want to write a story was the day fleas gave up on dogs, but she was a word person, so Slim waited for the next words. Often impatient, there were times when he was good at waiting. This was one of those times.

Finally, she said, "A girl I know from Northwest Philadelphia, another writer, was mugged and killed. Police found her body dumped into the Wissahickon Creek." She paused and then added in a small voice. "She wasn't found right away."

Slim winced. He'd seen floaters. Never good.

"They found my phone number in her jacket pocket and they called me. I identified the body."

"Rough. You're just getting back from it?"

"Yes." She sipped more coffee, her hand unsteady. "I called one of my brothers."

"Hal?" Slim knew that Hal lived the closest.

"Yes, but I shouldn't have. It wasn't until I heard his voice that I got shaky. I was fine until then."

Slim nodded. He'd seen it before—keeping strong until a kind word turns a person to jelly.

"Hal's picking me up here and taking me to his house for the night. There's no reason for that."

"A brother's a brother. He's looking out for you,"

"I guess." Her small voice didn't sound like her.

Slim remembered playing basketball with the Gilbert boys in their driveway and how their kid sister, tomboy Joyce Jane, nicknamed JJ, kept shoving her way into the game. All gawky arms and legs, ponytail flying, she refused to be kept out. This meek manner wasn't like JJ at all.

Silent together, they waited until Hal came in with a caring face for his sister and a hello for Slim.

Slim told Hal he'd drive JJ's car home for her and have one of his men bring him back for his own car. Hal thanked him and got the key from JJ for Slim. She didn't make a fuss. Slim shook his head. Seeing that dead body had sure elbowed her off the court.

The next morning, feeling better than he'd expected, Slim checked on traffic running around road repairs on Main Street. He was returning to his chief's car when JJ Gilbert eased up and stepped from her vehicle. Her hair was pulled back as usual and looked wet like she'd just showered. She walked up to him.

"I wanted to say thanks for returning my car to my house. You could have left it at Teddy's."

Slim shrugged.

"What's the latest about the Pullen Farm break-in?" she said.

"Nothing to add to your two lines in the *Monitor*."

"That wasn't me. Somebody else's job is listing county police calls."

Slim thought she acted like she had something else on her mind. He waited and she said, "When I went to identify Carol's body—Carol Vetter was her name—the cops asked if I knew why she would have been at the Wissahickon Creek. She lived nearby so it didn't seem odd. I got the impression that the police weren't hearing what they wanted to hear."

"Like what?"

"Like there was something they hoped I knew that would help them, but they weren't going to explain if I didn't."

Slim understood. Cops wouldn't hand out information when they were trying to put the pieces together.

"You said she was a writer. On a newspaper like you?"

JJ shook her head. "Carol freelanced for fashion magazines. She had a book published about a society murder. The victim was a clothing designer, so it went along with her interests. She called a few days ago and said she was working on something new and could use my help." She glanced down at herself. "I was surprised. Fashion isn't my thing."

Slim nodded. She wore a jacket with her usual T-shirt and jeans.

"When Hal brought me home this morning, there was a message from a Philly cop, a Detective Antol. You know him?"

"I know some Philly cops, but not him."

"When I called him, he asked about Carol's computer equipment. I said she had a laptop, a home computer, and, of course, a phone. Then I asked Antol if the mugger got her keys to steal her electronics. He didn't like me asking questions. He wanted to know more about her work. I told him the same as I told you last night. He wanted to know more things that I didn't know. I was getting sick of it. By the time he asked if I knew where she kept her car, I let him know how I felt."

"What did you say?" Slim thought she looked stronger. Her narrow face had taken on that set-in-granite look he remembered from when she was a kid.

"I told him I didn't know anything more, but maybe he should ask the neighbors. I said I'd heard that was what cops did when they were really, really stumped."

Slim chuckled. "Guess he didn't like that either."

"I suppose not. By that time, I was using my brain. Muggers usually grab people's stuff and run. But if this guy took the time to drag her into the creek, it was different. I asked Antol if he thought she'd been selected for a reason. He thanked me for my time and that was that."

"But not for you," Slim said.

"I called a news guy who works for a Philly TV station. He agreed from what he'd seen of the report that it didn't look like a typical street mugging. Carol had been stabbed and then drowned."

"Yeah, not typical," Slim said.

"I started thinking. If Carol had my number handy, maybe she'd intended to call me and see if we could get together."

Slim nodded, thinking it was the things you'll never know that can nag the worst. He knew she was tough. Her brothers never pampered her, but they were protective. Hal had proved that the night before, but they would expect her to jump back into the saddle again, the same as any one of them.

She said, "You said you knew people on the Philly police force."

Slim grinned. "You want me to be your mole?"

That teased out a smile. "Whatever works," she said.

He had forgotten about the little gap between her front teeth. When she'd been young the gap had been huge, but now it was sort of cute. He said, "Can't do anything right away. Bugging them now would be acting like one of you news weasels, but later, when they might know more? We'll see."

They each knew that was as good as a promise.

Chapter 3

Alexander Fanshawe sat in his hole-in-the-wall New York City apartment mulling over his future, or rather, the lack of it. His doctoral thesis had been on the subject of the theater's influence on culture. The dramatists he'd chosen to make his point had done the job for him, but it hadn't gotten him where he wanted to go. He knew some people thought he was uppity, but why would having a Ph.D. at age twenty-four make him uppity? He considered himself a failure. He earned money with Internet advertising, miles from his goal of becoming a successful playwright. So far, every script he'd written had been rejected.

He also brooded because he dreaded the coming holidays and having to visit his hometown, JumpRope. He'd lied to his mother about Thanksgiving, saying he had other plans. Now she was issuing holiday invitations and he couldn't keep begging off. He hated his hometown because he'd never fitted in.

Aimlessly, he ran a finger over his computer tablet, pausing when he came to his home county newspaper, the *Melton Monitor*, with the headline, BLOOD-DRENCHED KITCHEN. Alexander was an expert with eye-catching headlines that meant nothing. He swiped on past the news and went to social media sites.

A notice caught his eyes and he paused on a query that had a picture of a pretty girl with the user name S^2 followed by a string of numbers.

He wondered if S^2 was pronounced "S-squared? She was seeking information about a David and Vivian Mather.

Alexander stroked the beard he'd grown to make him look older. He didn't know a David, but he'd heard that a Vivian Mather had moved into JumpRope. On impulse, he wrote to S^2 saying he knew of a Vivian Mather. He included his email address so she could reach him directly.

When S^2 hadn't answered by the next morning, Alexander was disappointed, but he told himself to shrug it off. He turned to a cheerful assignment. In no time, he had created and sent captions for a series of too-cute animal pictures to an ad company. He soon received an okay and confirmation that a check would go into his account. He was pleased, but at the same time, he wondered why he could deal so easily with people he had never met, but dealing with people in real life could be so hard.

His mother called and asked for his help with the latest issue of her newsletter, *The JumpRope Jive*. He told her he would, and thought, *there, that was easy*. But that was with his mother, so it didn't count. The only time he'd backed off from something she'd asked him to do was when she'd wanted him to create a flyer to encourage write-in votes to elect Jessi Spellman to the township committee. He told his mother that Jessi was the kind who would say something nice to a person's face and then laugh behind their back.

He later found out that Jessi had won. Okay, good for her. Maybe he didn't like her, but apparently, a lot of other people did.

Chapter 4

Mayor Holland Kingston Jr., known as Holly, sat at the table in his office, waiting for two township committee members, Hoyt McConnell and Max Osterhagen.

While waiting, Holly thought about his girlfriend, Toria. He was so in love with her, yet he hadn't proposed because in many ways she still seemed so shy. At least she'd stopped blushing ninety shades of pink every time he looked at her, and their relationship had progressed to some steamy kissing and cuddling. Toria was an old-fashioned, wait-for-marriage-girl, which Holly accepted because she was worth the wait, but he was thirty-seven to her thirty, and eager to start making future plans. Was Christmas the right time for an engagement ring?

Hoyt McConnell and Max Osterhagen came in, greeted Holly, and took seats so the special meeting could begin.

"As you know," Holly said, "Jessi Spellman will be sworn in at the January reorganization meeting. So far, she's shown no interest in any of our committee job positions. Do you two have any suggestions?"

Hoyt McConnell spoke up. Dressed in overalls and a flannel shirt, Hoyt was a straightforward young farmer. "Jessi didn't run to work, she ran to win." He turned to Max Osterhagen, who had been appointed to fill a vacancy when a committee member had died but he had lost the seat in the recent election. "You know Jessi only won over you because she got so many new people in the developments to write her name in. She ran a dirty campaign with the help of Pilar Fanshawe."

"Who made and distributed a bunch of flyers," Holly said.

"I know that's the rumor, but Pilar didn't," Max said. "She sent Jessi to an ad company that designed and distributed the flyers."

Holly was surprised, but he knew enough of Max to believe what he said, although he wondered how Max knew about it.

"Anyway, the damage was done," Hoyt said in a stubborn tone.

They all knew that the late committeeman, Reds Burke, hadn't been perfect, that was for sure, but to trash a dead man to get elected didn't set well with those who had sympathy with his family.

The flyers had been the kick-off for a campaign in which Jessi promised that if elected, she would repave all the roads, add a coffee bar to the municipal building, invite famous entertainers to perform for free at fundraisers, and have a stoplight placed at the corner of Main St. and Possum Smile Road where there had been an increase in accidents. She'd do it all, *and* lower taxes.

The stoplight was the only reasonable goal to anyone who knew anything.

"It's water over the dam," good-natured Max said. He was a long-distance trucker, a solid, middle-aged widower with pleasant features, a neat grey-brown mustache and a calm manner. His late wife's family had been involved in public service in North Jersey and Max had learned much of the ways and means of managing New Jersey municipalities. Although he'd only served on committee briefly, he was interested in the town and intended to remain so, whether he had a committee seat or not.

"Committee persons are each in charge of different departments," Holly said. "No matter where Jessi is appointed . . ."

"She'll twist it to her advantage," Hoyt finished. "Take the Law and Order Committee. She would use the position to try and rewrite ordinances to benefit her and her husband's rental properties and for that restaurant they're making out a couple of old buildings."

"How about Public Affairs?" Max said.

"That wouldn't work," Hoyt said. "Women's groups run the events. My wife says they have no use for Jessi and her tricks."

"Hate to say it, but everybody probably feels the same about her," Holly said. "That is, except for voters who aren't involved in the township. Jessi spread questionable information on social media, and her followers blindly accepted it."

"How about this?" Max said. "Add a new job and call it Township Liaison. That person would represent us at the state capital in Trenton. I think she'd view it as a plum position."

"Good deal!" Hoyt grinned. "Sic her and her schemes on our New Jersey career politicians. Might even work out for the town."

The three agreed to present their idea to the full committee. Holly didn't know how the plan for Jessi would work, but they had to do *something*.

Chapter 5

Two days later, Jessi Spellman was pacing in her bedroom, her mood down to zero. What was she supposed to do with herself?

She had just returned from visiting the property she owned with her husband, Arnie, and a realtor who went by the name Pastor—his clerical collar the courtesy of an online minister certificate. The three of them were partners in creating a restaurant from an antique gas station and an old barn. The project was filled with fantastic innovations due to Jessi's brilliance, but once she'd made her contributions, she was bored.

She should get away for the day, she thought. She studied a new silk dress that had an orange and yellow print that would fit her perfect little body to perfection. With her black hair and pretty face—her loving husband called her Kitten—she knew she looked adorable. In January, when she would be sworn in as a committee member, maybe she would wear this dress. She'd be the best-looking woman in the room.

Her grin faded as she thought about the township committee. Scheming to win had been exciting, but once she'd won, she didn't care about it. She never attended committee meetings. The meetings she did attend were for the land use board. Usually, because her enemy, property inspector, Darlene Gage, caught her rehabbing a house to flip for big bucks and doing unapproved work. That meant she had to go back to the board with a revised plan or get a citation to court. It wasn't fair.

Jessi's green eyes lit up. Once she was sworn into committee in January, she would be Darlene's boss, right? Old Boxtox Barbie. Jessi grinned. She had a lot of names for Darlene, most including the word "Botox" because Darlene's forehead didn't show frown lines.

Plus, as a committee member she'd have influence with the land use board, the police department, public works . . . there would be no end to her potential powers. Except it sounded like work. She'd now learned that the committee wanted her to accept some job assignment: Liaison to the State House in Trenton. It sounded important. It probably wasn't, but she'd agreed anyway.

If she wanted to have more influence, it should be in a bigger fishbowl than JumpRope. Thinking, she tapped her shiny white teeth with a polished fingernail. She'd met a State Senator Fergusson at a fancy funeral reception. He'd been up for reelection and was caging for votes, a guy with a pompadour and a big smile. He sure had smiled when he'd met her. Hey! Maybe this Liaison to the State House job could work in her favor.

Excited, she sorted through her clothes closet like Snow White's Queen picking the best apple for the job. Her fingertips paused at a sexy red suit. Yes!

She would drive to Trenton and somehow reconnect with Fergusson, who had also won his election. Two winners! No telling where it might lead.

Chapter 6

Alexander stared at his computer. After he had decided even his emails got rejected, there it was. An email from S^2 who apparently had no idea of capitalization.

S^2 wrote, "*i already got my answer. vivian and david are dead.*"

Her style of writing was irritating. He wrote back. "*By what authority do you claim that? The Vivian Mather I know of is alive.*"

"*where did your vivian come from?*"

"*Sorry, I don't know her life story.*" One thing about emails, he didn't have to phrase carefully like a playwright on the way to becoming famous.

She emailed back, "*find out.*"

Being deliberately obtuse, he wrote, "*You said she was dead, remember?*"

"*ask the LIVE ONE.*"

"*Maybe I will. But it's rude to SHOUT.*"

The wacky exchanges with S^2 had him thinking about JumpRope's annual December Jubilee. Why not show up for that? Finding out about the "live" Vivian would give the visit purpose besides pleasing his mother. Maybe this Vivian person would even be there herself.

Chapter 7

The busy affair of the annual Holiday Gift Jamboree began on the second Saturday of December. The Jamboree was an event in which the two friendly rivals, the Ladies Civic Group and the Ladies Joint Fire and Emergency Squad Auxiliary, worked together.

Francine Smithers, the Auxiliary President, her short, sturdy body garbed in the season's latest fashion, had finished making minuscule adjustments to items on a gift table when she saw Vivian Mather approaching with good-looking Nero Gibeau in tow.

"When you have a minute," Vivian said, "I'd like to speak with you."

"I'm heading for the food tent," Francine said. Moving on importantly, she called over her shoulder, "Follow me."

"We'll meet you there," Vivian said.

Francine had marched on several steps before Vivian's words sank in. Startled, she glanced back. Instead of being behind her, where they belonged, they were taking off on their own. This insult was soothed when others came up asking questions and needing her advice.

She finally arrived at the refreshment tent. American Legion members at one of the tables ate sauerkraut and bratwurst and drank root beer. Nothing hard was served on the Village Green. With them were Francine's husband, Bob, and Colonel McDuff. They were busy talking with that ridiculously bearded young Alexander Fanshawe. Vivian and Nero were sitting at a table talking with some other people.

Nero laughed at something, his teeth white in a face that always seemed to have a tan. Francine shook her head. The poor boy had problems adjusting after coming home from serving in Afghanistan. He lost his license because of drunk driving, and then Pilar Fanshawe took advantage of his misery. Imagine, a widow with a son almost the same age luring a troubled young veteran to her bed. A disgrace. Thank goodness it was over now.

The other people left and Francine moved to Vivian's and Nero's table. She slid onto the bench opposite them.

Vivian spoke across the table to Francine, "I need to ask you about something."

Well, thought Francine, the girl at least knew enough to know who knew things around town. Her dark brown, curly hair was in a neat braid instead of waving around her shoulders, and her coat concealed her figure. Francine recalled that Amy Newton had once quipped, "Her cups runneth over." Everybody chuckled except Darlene Gage, who dieted and exercised to the point of being too thin and didn't have much of a sense of humor anyway.

"I need to know how to add the name of my late father, a Vietnam veteran, to the monument at the JumpRope Memorial Park," Vivian said.

Francine didn't know of any Mathers in the town who had been in the military. She frowned. "Where did he live?"

"Not here, but the Mather family has had a long-standing town presence from years back, and there's no other acknowledgment of his service. I'll handle the expenses." Giving Nero a glance, Vivian added, "There are also no markers to honor those who served in later conflicts. I would like to have something established for them as well."

"I'll find out and get back to you," Francine said. "I'll need documents, of course. What was your father's name?"

Alexander, who had moved closer when the Colonel had identified Vivian, heard her say, "David. My father's name was David Mather."

*　*　*

When Alexander returned to his apartment, he still couldn't believe his good luck at the Jubilee. His mother had been delighted to see him, and first thing, he'd run into the Colonel and Bob Smithers, who always treated him like a regular guy. They were men settled in life: Bob, with his auto and towing place, Bob's Garage, and the Colonel, who had retired from the army, and now ran the town's historical society.

Most importantly, he had met Vivian Mather. She was gorgeous, and her father had been—drum roll—*David Mather*.

In his imagination, he could do anything, but he didn't think he could approach a woman like Vivian in real life if he hadn't been on a mission. Once he'd heard her say her father's name, he became an investigator, asking questions for the sake of S^2 rather than himself.

After Francine left, he talked with Vivian, learning that although her father had been from northeast New Jersey, he had died out west, where they'd lived after he'd left the service.

Alexander had then bummed a ride to the bus station after telling his mother he had plans for Christmas and New Year's Eve with his girlfriend, Ramona. He promised his mother that he would come back to visit her on the third of January, a date he picked at random.

In his apartment, he was about to compose an email to S^2, saying what he'd learned about David and Vivian Mather, but when he was about to send the email, he hesitated.

Suppose S^2 asked where out west, what state? He wouldn't know and would look stupid. He should find out more. Then again, with email to a stranger, he shouldn't worry how he presented himself, even if she was a girl.

Did he really know S^2 was a girl? She had her photo by her name. He didn't have a photo on his email because he didn't like himself in pictures. He thought he was average looking and tall enough, five-foot-ten. His mother said his late father had been six-foot. If he grew two inches that would help with the extra weight, none of which explained why people always read him as younger. At least he didn't get carded as much once he'd grown his beard. If S² was a girl, it would be a kick to act like a man about town.

Things never worked out with him and girls. At the university, he'd gotten into a fraternity. At parties, he'd met girls but when it went further he was always a fumbling failure. In despair, he decided to hold himself above carnal matters. But he couldn't say that. It made him sound like he was a monk. Imaginary Ramona came to his rescue. He'd said she was a dancer, out of the country on a ballet tour. *Artistic*, he thought, the right kind of woman for him. Then the guys asked if Ramona was always "moaning" for him. That made him not like the name so much anymore but he was stuck with it.

He didn't have to worry about that now because after graduating, he'd lost touch with them. And with this, he could be as fierce as Inspector Javert in *Les Miserables*, on the offensive, asking the questions.

He clicked *reply* on his last email from S² and demanded, "*Who told you Vivian and David Mather were dead? You can't trust it because somebody said it.*"

"*why lie?*"

"Naive."

"*HA-HA. real laugh if you knew me.*"

He wondered why he wasted time on an illiterate who only used capital letters when she was yelling.

"*I've met Vivian Mather, so there,*" he wrote

"*where did that happen?*"

"JumpRope Township, New Jersey."

"*that's where you are?*"

"No. Where are you?"

"*brooklyn.*"

That gave him pause. Brooklyn was just over the East River. He wrote, "*I'm in Manhattan. Where are you in Brooklyn?*"

"*wannabe stalker!*"

The accusation gave him a weird sensation. A stalker. Then he'd really be a loser. But he guessed that ran in the family. His mother was always hooking up with losers. Guys who had problems and needed her. She let them come to the house, get into her bed. Didn't she know how dangerous that was?

Why couldn't he have a normal mother?

He typed to S², "*You have it all wrong, babe. Around here, I'm the one who gets stalked.*" She didn't reply so he signed off, thinking, *babe*. He liked that. See some girl he hadn't met and say, *Hey, babe*.

He felt terrific, but his good mood was completely spoiled later when he was surfing the net and saw an advertisement that had the same image that S² used on her email. Alexander drew back. Her photo was a picture captured from an ad!

He didn't understand why he felt so insulted. He knew how bogus the Internet could be, but he instantly sent S² another email that said, "*Faker! Saw the picture you used for your email in an ad. Scared to show your real face?*"

He pressed *send*, wondering what answer he would get.

No answer came. He felt more disappointed than he thought he should be.

Chapter 8

*M*uch later that evening, the JumpRope Jubilee had finally closed down. Holly and Slim were at Sean's Pub, relaxing after a day when they both had been on duty—Slim on crowd control and Holly being handy for residents who wanted to talk informally.

"Next Saturday, Toria has off from volunteering at the town library," Holly said. "We're going to New York City to see the lights, a show and have dinner. Think you and Lana would like to come along?"

Slim sat back. "Lana and I haven't been seeing so much of each other lately."

Whoops, Holly thought. Slim and Lana had been on and off again, but at the end of the summer, they'd had wedding plans. He looked at Slim's expression and said, "You two break up?"

"Yeah." Slim wiped his mouth hard with his napkin, took a hefty swallow from his beer glass and wiped his mouth again. "It's the job. This is a quiet town. I go for weeks with hours as regular as a shoe clerk, then something comes up and I'm staying late, going in early and working weekends. That's not the life she wants."

Holly nodded. "And that wasn't going to change."

"I *do* put the job first," Slim said. "When there're accidents and sad messes, being in the right place at the right time and sticking with it keeps things from getting worse. Besides—" Another big swallow from his glass. "Besides nothing."

Holly recalled when Lana started making rules about small stuff, the snacks Slim ate, how much sugar he put in coffee . . . little things, trying to change him. She'd also impressed Holly as being a flirt. Maybe this was for the best. But he was keeping his mouth shut in case they patched things up.

They were silent for a while and then Slim said, "I'm doing JJ a favor, touching base with a guy I know on the force in Philadelphia."

"What about?" Holly said.

"A friend of hers, another writer, was killed in the Philly suburbs. JJ wants more information. The guy I called, Kroger, is a homicide detective where the dead girl lived. He said it first looked like a mugger found her by the creek, stabbed her, and shoved her into the water. Using her keys and the address in her purse, he cleaned out everything in her apartment, including her computer and other office equipment."

"Awful," Holly said.

"Yeah, but after they learned she was a writer, Kroger realized there should be documents in her files, but they had been cleaned out, too. One of her friends from a magazine they had both written for said that her interviews and notes for the magazine's spring issue would have been in her laptop bag, but it wasn't found."

Holly frowned. "Are you thinking she was killed because of something connected with her work?"

"Maybe," Slim said, "but she was a fashion writer, which doesn't seem it would interest criminals." He shook his head.

Later, when Slim was home in his apartment with the conversation still fresh in his mind, he called his Philly contact, Kroger.

The man answered, his voice raspy from when he'd been a rookie on foot patrol and got sliced in the throat by a would-be rapist he'd interrupted in an alley.

Slim said, "Anything new in the stabbing/drowning case?"

"The only new thing," Kroger said, "was finding the victim's car at an apartment complex in Glenside. Blood on the driver's seat."

"Hers?" Slim said.

"The report isn't back yet. The woman who identified the body, the one you're asking questions for . . . you hooked up with her or anything?"

Slim stared up at the ceiling in his apartment. "She's just a friend." As if a cop and a reporter could be friends.

"One of the guys who met her might be interested."

"Detective Antole?" Slim felt protective as if he was another big brother. She hadn't liked Antole.

"Not him. One of the younger guys who was at the morgue, following through because he'd found the body. He liked how she handled herself."

"Yeah." Slim could see JJ handling herself well.

"Hey," Kroger said. "You got plans for ringing in the New Year?"

Slim hadn't thought that far ahead. In the past, he and Kroger had only met casually at Phillies games and such but this conversation ended with him invited to Kroger's place, a condo in Northwest Philly.

As he hung up the phone Slim glanced at his wall clock. He was home not too much later than he should be. Just like it almost always was, except when it wasn't. Never good enough for Lana.

Her image rose in his mind: blonde, gorgeous and built like a centerfold. The kind of woman he'd always dreamed of. Damn, but it had been good when it was good. The best. It would be awhile before he'd feel like getting back into circulation.

Chapter 9

It was a week before Christmas. Jessi Spellman stretched luxuriously in one of the guest bedrooms in the swanky private home of State Senator Earl Smythe Fergusson. In bed next to her was her husband, Arnie, sleeping off the senator's terrific holiday party—catered, live music, everything smelling of money.

During the evening, Senator Earl had introduced her around to high-up elected officials. They weren't just from New Jersey, but also from Pennsylvania and New York City. He was telling them how he'd have the honor of swearing her in as committeewoman in her hometown.

The honor. She grinned. Her impulse to meet and greet at the state house had paid off big time. Wearing her red suit, she'd knocked the senator out of his socks. And it got her invited to this fancy party. Nothing like those drab JumpRope events. Plus, she'd learned about a high-toned New York fundraiser in January to support Earl's larger plans. She and Arnie were, of course, invited.

She never knew politics could be such fun.

* * *

The next day, she went to Pilar Fanshawe for advice about what to wear to the Fergusson's fundraiser. What Pilar told her made no sense.

"You've got to be kidding!" Jessi shrieked. "I need advice on what to wear to a Manhattan bash and you tell me to ask that walking barrel, Francine?"

"An extremely stylish walking barrel," Pilar said, gesturing to her own current outfit, a pinafore over a leopard print jumpsuit. Alice in Jungleland. "I'm not the one for fashion guidance."

"But you work for rich people, like Senator Earl's friends," argued Jessi. "Earl is quite taken with me. He's coming here to swear me in at our town reorganization meeting. It's called administering the oath."

"Umm," Pilar said, not sounding impressed.

Jessi bristled. Didn't Pilar realize how important that was? How important *she* was?

Pilar said, "My interior design work does put me in contact with people of wealth. However, I pay little regard to their talk of clothing and designers. My clothing style wins a pass because clients see me as—" she waved a hand in prelude to a word in French. "*excentrique.* The only person in JumpRope who can aid you, who understands fashion sensibilities, is Francine." She smiled languidly. "So, Jessi, my dear, get thee to Francine."

Chapter 10

*P*ilar made an urgent request for Alexander to come help her with the latest newsletter so she could have it finished before Christmas. He agreed only after he'd made sure he wouldn't be there when she would be "entertaining."

She often said holidays were hard on people who were suffering and sometimes she'd just take somebody in and he knew what that meant. A guy wasn't supposed to think about that part of his mother's life, or even worse, to know about it.

His mother used her computer for business and for the Internet, but she had no idea how to construct a newsletter for print or for the web. He arrived with his laptop and a flash drive to move material she'd already written from her computer to his.

He was surprised because this edition wouldn't have the *News and Noose* section which had amusing ditties and quips about local people, plus veiled hints about misbehavior that the offenders weren't pleased to see in the print. Others, of course, were delighted to try and figure out the culprits. He didn't know what caused his mother to make this change but he was glad. He didn't think it had been a nice feature.

He worked on the newsletter after lunch. His mother was off somewhere in her yellow Mazda, wearing a skirt trimmed with what she'd cut from an old fur coat, lined it with satin, and acted like it was an ordinary thing to wear. Embarrassing. Alexander hoped people would at least think it was fake fur.

The newsletter was only four pages long. When finished, he idly surfed the net. Remembering the product he saw with the picture S^2 used for her email, he found the ad with the girl's picture again. More messing around and he found the ad company.

He glanced at the time. It was only three in the afternoon, and he had an idea. Maybe he could find out about the real girl in the ad and email S^2 again. Show her he was a force to be reckoned with.

He would call the ad company and ask about the model. He was good at playing a role when he didn't have to perform in person. Maybe he couldn't sell his plays, but he could nail dialogue. And he had a deep voice that sounded older.

On the phone, his story to the ad guy was that he was looking for a model for a client who had seen her picture and thought she might be right.

"Oh, yeah," the ad guy said. "Had that ad plastered all over the place. I usually don't remember names, but hers was different. Solstice."

Alexander pursed his lips in a silent whistle. Great name.

"Solstice what?" he said.

"That's it, no last name," the ad guy said.

Having also learned the name of her agent, Alexander made a second call. The agent said Solstice wasn't his client anymore. He sounded as if he had drunk his lunch.

"It was too bad, Freddy," the agent said in a blurry voice. "She looks like nothing much in person, but cameras love her. I hated to lose out. She was catching on, you know?"

Alexander hadn't given the man his name. He must call everybody Freddy. Alexander didn't like being called by a nickname even when it wasn't for real. He felt the use of his full name was a standard that should be maintained.

He asked how to get in touch with her.

"I'll give you her email address," the agent said. "She goes with you, she'll need representation. If she doesn't have somebody else, don't cut me out, Freddy. I'm doing you a favor. Tell her I'm still here. Grab a paper and a pen. Here's how to reach her."

The agent spelled out the address, repeated, "Don't cut me out, Freddy," and hung up.

Alexander sat with the phone in one hand, his pen hand frozen over the paper. The girl's email address was S^2, followed by the familiar string of numbers. Alexander's stomach had gone cold. It was the same girl! The photo by her name was her *real* photo.

No wonder she'd ignored his last email.

My God! He knew how awful he felt when people made fun of him, laughed at him, or maybe even worse, ignored him.

How awful she must have felt to get his jeering insult.

He hastily brought up her last email, hit return and wrote, *"Mea culpa. The photo was you! I hang my head in abject shame. Please forgive me."* He hit *send* and then thrust his laptop away.

He didn't know what to do, but he couldn't just sit there. He'd go outside, walk around. Uncertain of when his mother would be home, he wrote her a note and left the house.

Outside, the weather seemed too mild for December. He wished it would snow. It had snowed in Manhattan a week ago, a dusting that disappeared quicker than a play closing on opening night.

His mother's house, the rancher he had grown up in, was out of town with no houses nearby. A long driveway led to the road. He started walking. He'd reached the end of the drive when Bob Smithers, coming back from somewhere in his tow truck, pulled up and stopped, motor idling.

"Give you a ride, Alexander?"

"Sure." Alexander kept eagerness from his tone. "Just hiking into town." He walked around the rear of the truck and climbed into the passenger seat,

Bob remarked about the warm weather. Alexander said yes, he'd been thinking the same thing. The cab of the truck looked clean but smelled like oil or grease. Man stuff. Alexander settled back.

Bob didn't ask about school, which is what ladies in town always thought they should talk about. *How are you doing in school, Alexander?* they would say. He'd made mistakes with questions like that. He would believe they wanted to know so he'd tell them, going into details so they would think well of them. Then he learned they thought he was bragging. But when he told them he was doing just fine, thank you, and left it at that, they thought he was aloof. He couldn't get it right no matter what. With men like Bob, it was different.

What Bob did was start talking about a motorcycle someone had brought into the shop to sell, mentioning make and model, as if taking for granted that Alexander knew about that particular machine.

"If you're ever in the market for a bike, let me know," Bob said when they reached his garage and pulled in. "I get one every once in a while. Good in a city. Cheaper than a car."

Alexander thought back to when he and Donny DeGarmo, who was now a cop, had fun with bikes a few times when they'd been in high school. Alexander had one when he started at the university before he got his now-defunct car. He'd kept up his license, but he'd been focused on a replacement car. Now he was thinking a motorcycle would be more practical. And if the weather was bad he could always ride the bus, which was what he'd been doing anyway.

He went with Bob to look at the machine, a bright red Yamaha. Bob showed him the features, describing them in a way that was explaining, but not making Alexander feel he was being talked down to. A customer came in. Bob shook hands with Alexander in parting and then went into the office with the customer.

Alexander stood in the garage yard, thinking about male camaraderie. At the Jubilee, the Colonel had seen him and stuck out his hand to shake. "Good to see you, Alexander," he'd said. Alexander thought the Colonel was old enough to be his grandfather. He didn't remember either of his grandfathers. He didn't even remember his father, who died when he was young. During the Jubilee, he'd walked around with the Colonel, feeling like one of the guys.

Then the Geezers started spoiling things. They were a group of ancient veterans who named themselves "Old Geezers." Summer or winter, they wore matching wool jackets with felt letters spelling out OLD GEEZER, each jacket with a different number. Nobody but them knew what the numbers represented. They entertained themselves by making mean jokes to each other about people who passed by.

With Alexander, they started talking about his beard.

"Think he's on the run?" Number 44 had said, talking about him as if he wasn't there but loud enough for him to hear.

"Bet so," said Number 15. "Shave it off if they've got one, grow it if they don't. That's what he probably did."

They'd laughed like maniacs and Alexander couldn't say anything because they would probably call him a bad sport and say he couldn't take a joke. But being ugly to people wasn't a joke.

Unbidden, his thoughts returned to S^2.

He'd been ugly to her. Had she opened his email yet? Seen his apology? Had she wondered how he found out the photo was really her?

He was positive she'd feel compelled to answer.

He tasted the name, *Solstice*. Magical.

Better than Ramona, that was for sure.

He took a second look at the bike and imagined how cool it would be to ride one again. Ready to leave, he turned and there was Nero Gibeau. He wore work clothes and a jacket with BOB'S GARAGE stitched on the pocket. Alexander hadn't known Nero worked at the garage.

"Hey," Nero said. "Interested in the bike?"

"Maybe," Alexander mumbled, turning back to the motorcycle. He felt all sweaty inside his jacket.

He remembered when he'd caught on to the fact that Nero was a man his mother was "entertaining." She mentioned something she'd read about veterans with problems and she mentioned Nero. Alexander vaguely knew who Nero was because he'd been ahead of him in school, but something in her voice made him glance up.

He saw her expression, and darn it, he *knew!* Nero was his

mother's latest "wounded bird." And it wouldn't have been Nero pursuing her. She would have connected with him when he was down and brokenhearted. She'd charge in, the warrior healer, picking up the pieces, like in some drama from ancient Greece.

Some of the older guys she'd taken in he could sort of understand. Like the one from Melton whose daughter had died in a fire, and the one from down the shore who had tried to kill himself after some awful thing. He'd heard that something had happened to Nero in the service that twisted him up and drove him to drink, but it didn't seem right that his mother would swoop in on him.

He'd only given Nero a quick look before he'd turned, but the guy looked fine now. Maybe his mother hadn't gotten together with him like he'd thought. Not in bed. He started feeling better. Considering his mother's age, would a young guy really want to, well . . . *do* her?

Whatever it had been, it was over. At the Jubilee, he'd seen Nero with Vivian Mather. Alexander felt relief rush through him. Vivian was young and beautiful. He could stop thinking about that other stuff. Besides, he'd just thought of something he wanted to know. Something important.

Turning toward Nero, he said, "The Colonel told me Vivian's father lived out west. Do you know where?"

"He moved around," Nero said with an easy shrug of his broad shoulders. "Vivian was a kid when she was with her dad. I know they were in Colorado when he died."

"Hey, thanks." If S^2 ever answered, he'd know more than before.

Feeling bold, Alexander stuck out his hand, his grip firm as Nero returned the gesture. Men of the world, both of them. All that other stuff erased itself from his mind. Like it never happened—if it ever had.

After leaving Bob's Garage, he hurried home to his mother's house to email S^2 that the Vivian Mather he knew had a father, David, who had died in Colorado.

No reply.

* * *

He thought he would never hear from her again, but then, the day after Christmas, a day when he'd played computer games and eaten alone on ordered-in Chinese food, S^2 emailed. It was an answer to his last email about Vivian's father dying in Colorado.

"*sez who?*"

Somehow, her stupid words charged him up.

"<u>Says</u> me," he wrote back, underlining the correct spelling.

"*can't be. they're dead.*"

Putting on his most elevated hat, he wrote, "*Who is this individual whose words you hold more authentic than mine? Why do you doubt my veracity?*"

"*la de da.*"

"*Excuse me. I forgot you're barely literate. Do you personally know who told you about them? As in, did you ever meet him or her? Could this stranger show proof that they're dead?*"

"*don't know YOU either!*"

Unable to think of anything brilliant to say, he wrote, "*So why, S^2, are we bothering with this conversation?*"

He waited.

Nothing.

Chapter 11

With an alarmed cry, Nero Gibeau suddenly sat up in his sleep, awakening Vivian who lay by his side. She knew what was happening. He was caught in a nightmare from his experience from the war. She had learned from his grandmother, Yvette, the details of the incident that eventually left him the only survivor.

He and four others had been on a road in Afghanistan when a mine exploded. One of them, Yancy, was literally blown apart. Sam, one of Nero's close friends, his lower body destroyed, had died in Nero's arms. There had been three survivors, Nero, Quint and Greg, all who somehow suffered only cuts and bruises. They wondered why they lived when two companions had died so horribly. A week later, Greg, the most troubled, acting bravely but recklessly, died in battle. Nero's grandmother had said, "It's called, suicide by enemy fire."

Nero and Quint had come home safely, but Quint was unable to adjust. Then there seemed to be a positive change. He invited Nero to his farm in Pennsylvania. He appeared to be in such good spirits that Nero came home believing Quint was finding his way back to normal life. What Quint really intended was a final goodbye. He took his own life that night.

When Nero learned what Quint had done, he had turned to alcohol. He had since conquered drinking, but his mental anguish remained.

Vivian had once asked him what he and Quint had talked about.

"About what happened?" He'd sounded annoyed. "There was no point to that. We were *there*. Talking wouldn't have changed anything."

When Vivian had researched Post Traumatic Stress Disorder, she had found the term, "avoidance," which meant trying to avoid thinking or talking about the traumatic event. She saw that's what Nero did.

Now, he had awakened in a panic, thrashing, fighting shadows, shaking, sweating and crying out. Gradually, the sound of her voice and her touch calmed him, and then, the closer touch, the joining together that erased everything except the moment and the proof of being alive.

She knew he hadn't been sleeping well since the Jubilee. It had been a lovely day for her, talking with people and especially being with Nero among those who'd always known him. That evening, they had wandered away from the crowd and entered Main Street, clasping hands as they strolled through the chill evening. Windows on both sides of the street had sparkled with lights. There had been a feeling of snow in the air.

As they moved on, they each realized that their mutual destination was the memorial park. Vivian had visited there before, thinking that her father's name should be added to the Vietnam marker. And markers to honor men like Nero, who served in later conflicts—thoughts she had put into motion that day with Francine.

They reached their destination. The park was illuminated by a tall light in the center. They walked among the memorials, moving slowly. The First World War memorial was polished granite with carved names. They moved to the WWII monument, a huge stone with names on a brass plaque. Nero touched a name. "My grandfather," he'd said softly to her. Vivian touched his hand as he fingered the chill metal as if it could connect her to a man dear to him that she had never known.

The names of the Korean and Vietnam veterans were also on brass, and on both sides of the same rough granite monument. Vivian saw names she knew on the Vietnam side: Holland Kingston Sr., the Mayor's father; Robert Smithers, Francine's husband; and other names she had become familiar with. The Colonel's name was on both the Korean and Vietnam sides.

Nero had run his finger over a star that signified someone who had not come home. "Bob's brother," he'd said.

As they'd left the park, Vivian noticed that Nero was quiet in a way that told her he was troubled. The memorials meant memories of courage, causalities and loss.

And now, this nightmare.

At some point when they were quiet together again, she whispered, "Do you think you should talk to someone with experience with these sorts of problems, the one I told you about?"

"The head-shrinker with a clergy collar? "

Vivian had found someone experienced with veterans suffering from post-traumatic stress. He was also a man of the cloth, known simply as Father Tom. She had told Nero about him but he wasn't interested. Then, or now.

"Come on, Vivi," he said, using his pet name for her. "No priest can change what's in my head."

After a silence, he said, "I should visit their families."

"Quint's family?"

"All of them. I've been thinking about it."

Vivian had noticed the times recently when he had gone quiet. She knew now what he'd been thinking about. It troubled her. The other part of the PTSD avoidance she'd read about, was avoiding people who reminded the sufferer of the traumatic event. Now, it seemed he wanted to go directly into that situation.

"Won't the family members want to talk about what happened?"

He looked at her, his expression surprised. "No, that's not what this is about. It's, well . . ." He stumbled around, and then said in a rough voice, "It's the last thing I can do for them. To see if everything is all right."

Vivian looked into his eyes. "You want to see if there's anything their families need. Things that they would do if they were still here."

"That's it," he said, quietly. "That's it."

Vivian leaned toward him and rested her head against his shoulder. He embraced her. "You understand," he said.

"Yes," she said, and she did. As the only survivor, he felt a responsibility to do what none of them could now do—but at what cost to himself? If memories from a memorial site could bring back his nightmares, what harm might come from visiting his dead companions' loved ones? But she knew how he was. When he decided something, his stand was firm. She could only support him.

"All right," she said. "We have holiday plans to visit your mother's family over Christmas and my Aunt Elizabeth before and after her New Year's Eve party. You've already said you'd renew your prescription so you'll be more comfortable with a bunch of people around. Then, when the holidays are over, we'll visit the homes of the men you knew."

"That's good," he said.

"Yes," she said. She could only hope he was right.

Chapter 12

Holly had enjoyed Christmas Day, especially Toria's gift to him. She had geared out his painting room in the attic of his apartment with oil paints, canvases, and everything else that an amateur artist could desire. When he opened the boxes, she said, "Didn't I tell you this is what I'd buy when you had your starving artist's garret?"

For his gift to her, Holly had found out that she would like a special set of dishes for when she entertained members of her club. She was as delighted with his gift to her as he was with her gift to him.

A loving success all around, although sad thoughts kept sneaking into his mind. Slim was still brokenhearted over his breakup with Lana, and JJ, whom Holly had known all her life, was down in the dumps over the death of her writer friend. And there was the unsettling question of the blood in a vacant JumpRope house. Whose blood was it, and what had happened? No solutions for any of it.

But now, on a Saturday the day after Christmas, Holly had no sad thoughts as he prepared to pick up Toria and shop for a birthday gift for his stepmother, Peggy.

Holly had lived long enough to appreciate that he was in one of life's sweet spots. Although his father was getting older, he still had his health and his interests. Holly's grief over his mother's death was years past, and as far as his stepmother, his Dad couldn't have chosen anyone better than Peggy. Holly had enough money and work that he felt he was good at. Best of all, he now had Toria.

He thought that just when a person has something all set, something happens to turn it all around. At least, that's what he hoped would happen in this case. If Toria accepted his proposal of marriage, his apartment, which now was perfect for him, would probably be too small for the two of them. It was the same with her house. It was tiny, built in the late forties, with no basement, a crawl-space attic, and Toria used one of the two small bedrooms as her office.

Maybe they would soon be house hunting.

Or maybe he was getting ahead of himself.

First, was getting a ring on Toria's finger.

"Off to the mall," he said after he'd picked her up. They'd each taken off from work early.

"Not going to Penguin's here in town?" she said.

Penguin's was really Gwinn's Fine Jewelry. It had a logo of a pair of penguins on top of a wedding cake, the female with a sparkly tiara, the male with a top hat and a gold watch and chain across the white part of his middle. The establishment was owned by a man of Welsh descent named Penn Gwinn. It was no surprise people called it "Penguin's."

"If we buy Peggy's gift here," Holly said, "word will get around and she'll know ahead of time."

Toria agreed, but what Holly was really thinking was that if Toria said *yes* to his proposal, she would want to tell people herself. If she said *no*, that might get around, embarrassing them both. Yes, they would look at rings out of town.

With Peggy's gift chosen, wrapped and paid for—Holly felt guilty at not spending his money in town and now he was going to compound it—he steered Toria to the engagement ring section.

She started to say something and then she stared at him, then she glanced back at the display of engagement rings.

She grabbed his hand and pulled him from the store.

Heart sinking, Holly figured he'd gotten his answer. She wasn't one for confrontation or public displays, but her answer had clearly been *no*.

Outside the store, she said, "Give me the truck keys."

Numb, he handed them over. With her in the driver's seat and him the passenger, he realized she wasn't angry. When she was, she got all tight and constrained. Maybe pulling him from the store hadn't been an outright rejection. Had she jumped into one of her rare in-charge moods?

In the summer they'd been driving to Sunshine Shores, a New Jersey beach community along the Atlantic where several JumpRope residents owned vacation homes. She had unexpectedly started telling him to make different turns. They ended up at a beach where they had never been before. Her reason had been the bikini she'd worn under her sun dress. The bikini was a first for her, and she didn't want to feel self-conscious if she ran into anyone they knew. *Volunteer town librarian goes wild.*

Holly believed that anything Toria did was darned near perfect, but he was still bowled over by how terrific she looked in a bikini. She was tall and slender and had lovely curves.

And now she was off on some other bent, and he didn't have a clue. She was always surprising him. He decided to keep calm and see what happened.

They left Melton and entered the road to the county park. Toria stopped the truck, got out and silently beckoned him to follow. The mild weather and lingering sunshine made their light jackets almost unnecessary as they moved on trails marked by placards created by the JRope High Nature Club.

They crossed a little bridge over a stream. Past the bridge was a plot of winter-brown grass with a bench and a man-made pond with another sign that read TRIBUTE TO WALDEN POND. In a large field in the distance, a woman threw a stick for a dog, but no one was close by.

Toria stopped by the bench, turned around, and faced Holly.

"I'm going to feel stupid if I'm wrong," she said in a shaky voice.

"Wrong about what?"

Aflame with blotches like she'd had when they first started getting to know one another, she said, "Wrong about what I thought you might want to say in that mall jewelry store. There's a tradition I've dreamed of. If you want to say what I thought you might say, I wanted the setting to be pretty and romantic because I want to remember it forever. If I'm right, that is."

That's when he caught it. *She hadn't been rejecting him at all!*

He took a step, lifted her gently, and lowered her to sit on the bench. He then knelt before her on one knee.

Keeping his eyes on hers he said the words that he had only imagined himself saying out loud: "Toria Dahlgaard, I love you with all my heart. Will you marry me?"

The blushes on Toria's face all seemed to blend together until she was like a red hibiscus. Her arms went around him and somehow—he couldn't later figure it out because he didn't remember moving at all—he was sitting on the bench and she was on his lap and they had their arms wrapped around each other.

"I've loved you forever," she said against his neck. Then she drew back enough to look into his eyes. "I liked you and wanted to get to know you, and when I did, I started to love you, only I couldn't tell you, because—"

"Because?"

"Because I didn't know if you could love me back."

"I do."

"I do?" She giggled. "Aren't we getting ahead of ourselves with that line?"

"Wait a minute," he said. "We're not getting a chance to say 'I do' until you answer 'yes.' "

"Goodness!" Flustered, she tried and failed to smooth hair that seemed as flustered as she was. "Yes, of course, I'll marry you. Yes!"

They sat for a while, just holding one another.

Earlier in their relationship—and he had started it—*having breakfast* had meant breakfast after a night together, which they'd never had. Now he said, "I don't know how long it will be until we have our wedding, but whenever it is, we'll have the most wonderful breakfast anyone on this earth ever had."

She gave him a searching look, then smiled and said, "June. We'll have a June wedding. That's less than six months away."

A long six months, he thought.

Then she said, "The ring! Weren't we going to look at rings?"

"We were shopping for Peggy's gift. Then you shanghaied my truck keys and . . ."

"Ha!" she said. "We're going to Penguin's."

"That will be like sending up smoke signals. I figured you'd want to tell people yourself."

"And you're the JumpRope Mayor? Don't you know? Buying rings at Penguin's is how a JumpRope couple announces their engagement."

He laughed. "I guess you're right. Say, since tradition means something, aren't I supposed to ask your father's permission for your hand in marriage? And I should talk with your mother, too."

"I don't think so," she said. For an instant, it seemed there was something different in her tone, but then, after a hesitation, she grabbed his hands and said, "Off to Penguin's."

"Right," he said, but he was thinking, *Someday, Toria Dahlgaard, you're going to tell me more about your parents.*

Chapter 13

On the Tuesday after Christmas, Holly was back in town hall.

He had always thought that the few days between Christmas and New Year made routine work seem frivolous. This year it was different, with people buzzing over his and Toria's engagement, including Slim's laconic, "About time, bud," and the town hall floating secretary, Iris, said excitedly, "I just had a feeling something special had happened."

Yes, it had been special, Holly thought, smiling. On Saturday, when he and Toria had returned to Penguin's, they selected a ring with a one-carat stone in white gold with additional diamonds in a halo setting. After the ring was sized, they returned to the park for Toria's romantic memory, take two. He proposed all over again and Toria accepted and he slid the ring on her finger. By the time they returned to town to share their news, Holly's father and stepmother had already guessed because someone had seen them through Penguin's shop window.

Now, it seemed everybody knew.

From his office, Holly texted Toria at the county records building and found her morning was also filled with excitement and best wishes. But it was still a workday for them both, in Holly's case, reviewing plans for the town reorganization meeting, to be held on the first Friday of the New Year, with public notices appearing according to the Open Meeting Act.

The reorganization meeting meant resolutions for fiscal matters and the appointment of professionals. Also the swearing-in of two committee members.

Holly would swear in reelected Azalea Roundtree, with her sister, Iris, holding the Bible. Newly elected Jessi Spellman, whose husband, Arnie, would hold the Bible, would be sworn in by State Senator Earl Smythe Fergusson. His appearance was a surprise.

Holly consulted Suzanna, the municipal clerk.

"What do you know about Fergusson?"

"Only what's in the news." She had a tawny-brown complexion, and as she tilted her head, the beads in her hair extensions caught the light. "You can expect his people and photographers and TV to show up. He apparently has an active publicity person."

Holly nodded. "I've read that he's lining up backers for a serious run for a congressional seat but I don't see why he's blessing JumpRope with his presence. There's none of the moneyed people here that he chases. Fergusson knows that because he didn't even bother to give a 'hey, hello and how are you' when he campaigned last year. Now he's fawning all over Jessi Spellman."

"Jessi talks a good talk and she looks adorable," Susanna said. Her dark eyes sparkled with amusement. "Fergusson can't know what she's really like. Maybe he finds her delightful. We'll see how he behaves with her at the community get-together at Teddy's restaurant after the meeting."

Chapter 14

Near the end of the week after Christmas, Alexander's email played its soft *bing-bong* doorbell sound. There was a message from S².

She ignored his apology for his error about her photo, and wrote, *"don't know you, you don't know me. want to meet?"*

Boldly he wrote, *"Sure."*

Just when he thought she had shut him out again, she wrote, *"buy me lunch. today at 1:30 or nothing."* She added a midtown address.

Buy her lunch? As if it was a condition? Today? She gave him stage fright. Not only was she a girl, she was a strange, bossy girl.

He wrote back. *"What if I can't make it? I have a life, you know."*

He waited.

Nothing.

At eleven he started getting ready, mad at himself for fussing over his appearance, combing his thick dark hair and trimming his beard and mustache so that there was not a strand out of line. He made sure he took his glasses. Looking older was important. Trouble was, they were for reading and made the world look blurry if he didn't peer over them. But that gesture made him look older, too, didn't it?

All too soon, or so it seemed, he stood on a corner across the street from their assigned meeting place. He peered over his glasses through the passing traffic at a collection of shops on the ground floors of tall buildings with business offices above. The foot traffic was busy. He decided not to cross the street until he saw her waiting. He was early. He wanted a look at her first.

He saw a girl dressed in a grey coat and a bright green scarf, with a backpack dangling from one arm. It was too early for her to be there, wasn't it?

There was something a little off in her movements. He couldn't figure out what it was.

Solstice had arrived early and positioned herself so she could see him from whatever direction he came. If he came, that is. In their emails, she'd felt free to say whatever she wanted, to be brave in a way she'd never dared before. She'd cut him off and then when she contacted him again, he was there. She thought he would show up, if only because he was curious.

His email name was AFanshawe and he'd said he was from JumpRope Township in New Jersey. That gave her what she needed to search for him on the Internet. His first name was Alexander and he was twenty-four years old and had his doctorate. So, he was smart—or thought he was. His photo in his high school yearbook, also on the Internet, showed a dark-haired young man with a roundish face. He was broad-shouldered and chunky. He wore an uncomfortable smile as if he hadn't liked having his picture taken. He looked sort of geeky like he'd come across in his emails. Trying to show off and then apologizing for his mistake with her picture. In Latin of all things: *mea culpa*.

That had made her laugh and she didn't laugh often. At work, she kept to herself and shied away from others. The office was mostly women. A bonus. She'd had enough of men.

Except she'd invited this one, Alexander Fanshawe, to meet her. He could take her to the Vivian Mather he knew, who was maybe the right one. When she'd gotten the email that Vivian was dead, she'd believed it, but when Alexander said she wasn't, she'd tried to look up Vivian's name in the town he'd mentioned. The address was in the country, at a farm, not like on a street where numbers could be followed. She had no transportation of her own and even if she got to the town, she'd be stuck asking questions of strangers, which made her uncomfortable. Alexander seemed her safest bet.

A sturdy figure appeared across the street and she thought, *there he is*. He was dark-haired and had grown a mustache and beard since his high school photo. He was having trouble with glasses that kept sliding down his nose. Again, he made her laugh.

She'd been trying to think how she would act when they met and all at once, she knew. She would be the same girl she'd been in the emails, the take-charge person she would like to be. The one who said whatever she wanted, whenever she wanted, and let the chips fall. And maybe that was really her—if she ever got herself straightened out.

Another encouraging thought came. Although she hadn't yet gotten a close-up look, he didn't remind her of anyone she'd ever been afraid of.

Alexander lost sight of her as he crossed the street, but as he reached the opposite sidewalk, he saw her reflection in a window. He'd seen enough to be convinced she was the girl in the email and the ad. Stricken with hesitancy about what he should say when they met, he veered away.

After a half dozen steps he paused to pretend interest in a window display. Behind plate glass was an array of medical items, trusses and splints, bottles of pills and cures, plus shampoos and hair dyes. He was about to chance turning to see where she might be when he felt a poke in his back.

Startled, he wheeled.

It was Solstice. She was no more than five-foot-two. One shoulder was higher than the other. It made her look like she was ready to start going somewhere when she was standing still. She had a pale complexion, a snub nose, a tiny chin, enormous brown eyes and freckles.

There was a flash of silence in the busy street where people were pushing past them on both sides. Solstice seemed to be studying him.

He looked at her and that little face suddenly reminded him of the sketch of Cosette, the Paris street waif from the *Les Misérables* posters. She was all huge eyes and uncertainty.

Any impression of uncertainty vanished when she opened her mouth.

"Hey, Alex," she said with a cheeky grin. "Decided to go through with it, huh?"

"Alexander," he corrected stiffly.

"Prissy prig."

He glared into her freckled face. "You look like a little kid."

"It was a money-maker in my old job. I'm hungry. Let's eat."

"I had lunch," he said. Not true, but lunch was her idea and he had never actually agreed to it.

She gave him a grin. "Come on, Dumbo. We'll work on your social skills while I eat."

He stiffened. "Dumbo?"

She raised her eyebrows. "Oh, I'm sorry. Is that another nickname for Alexander?"

He didn't know what to say so he trudged along behind her as if pulled on a string. She led him into a fast food place with tiny tables, tall stools, and a ledge against the window. The ledge stools were the only ones vacant. She sat and shrugged off her scarf and coat and let them drag down over the stool. She dropped her backpack to the floor between her feet.

Her uneven shoulders were skinny and her hair, collarbone length, was straight and thin and plain brown. Her upper lip was a cupid's bow and the lower one was a pouting curve. No lipstick, just soft-looking lips.

Her palm up, she beckoned for money. "Lunch isn't free."

He handed over several bills, not even looking at them. Let her think he was wealthy.

She came back with grilled cheese, a milkshake and fries, and plunked the register slip, a twenty, a five, and loose change on the table. Was it the correct change? Did she expect him to add it up? He shoved it all into his pocket without looking. The smell of food made him hungry but he tried to ignore it. The stool was too small for his backside. He wriggled around.

"What's the matter, Chunky?" she said. "Butt won't fit?"

He clenched his teeth. "Eat your lunch."

"Sure, I can always eat. My parents were into weird food, lots of plain rice. That diet maybe did things to my spine, stunted it or something. My baby teeth fell out early and my second teeth came in late. I didn't get my period until I was seventeen."

He goggled. This was the girl stingy with electronic words? And she was telling him when she started her *period*? What could he say to that? He finally drew himself tall and said in a superior tone, "I tracked down your picture from that ad and talked to your agent. That's how I know your name is Solstice. He said you're not modeling anymore."

She rolled her eyes. "Internet spy."

"That's me. So how come you stopped modeling?" She was interesting looking, he thought, but not styled up as in the ad photo.

"I was tired of being the object."

"Of what?"

"Being looked at." She bit into her sandwich, closing her eyes blissfully as warm cheese filled her mouth.

Back to email style talk, he thought. She reached for the fries. He should have told her to get a double order. How could she stay so skinny?

"What do you do?" he said.

"I'm at a trade publication. I'm a proofreader."

"*What?*"

"What, *what?*"

He didn't believe her. He bet she didn't know anything. "What magazine? A lowercase e. e. cummings copycat?"

Eating, she didn't look at him. "I said a trade publication, not a poetry journal."

He frowned. He hadn't expected her to know that Cummings was a poet.

She said, "I spent years saying, 'Yes, Mister,' 'No, Mister,' 'You want me to jump, Mister, just tell me how high.' Now I don't follow rules. After all day correcting printed nonsense I take a vacation."

Her words came out fast, like bullets from a machine gun. Blinking, he was still trying to make sense of it, when she spoke again.

"I'm having dessert. You should have some, too." She looked him up and down, noting his broad chest, the muscle padded with plumpness that Alexander hated. "You're a big eater, no question. Watching me chow down, I bet it's slaying you and you regret being so—" she paused for effect, "—obdurate." She giggled and picked up her milkshake.

Smarty, he thought, but was afraid to say it. Who knew what she might come up with next? He felt homesick for imaginary Ramona. *She* never acted wise. And he hadn't come here for Solstice to gorge herself, he had questions. Summoning an aggressive tone, he said, "So who told you David and Vivian Mather were dead?"

"Somebody who emailed, like you did. They said David died in the 1980s and Vivian married and died in an accident. I knew David was old. He was a Vietnam War guy and you told me he went to Colorado. So, is your Vivian, the *right* Vivian? I want to make sure. How old is she?"

"Maybe three or four years older than me."

"So, you're what, twenty-four?" She said it with a smirk as if she already knew.

He scowled. "Yes, you?"

"Twenty-two." She reached into a purse she had strapped around her waist and pulled out a cell phone. "I need to meet her. Call her for me."

He straightened. "I will not. In the first place, I don't have her number. In the second place, I don't know if she would want to talk with you. In the third place, if I did have her number and used your phone to call her and she didn't want to talk with you, you still would have her number on your cell."

"Hey, smarter than you look." She stood up. "I'll get two apple pies. A la mode for you, too, Lochinvar?"

Lochinvar? The brave young knight of Sir Walter Scott's poem? Who was she kidding? Okay, she knew more than he'd thought. He wasn't going to give her the satisfaction of acknowledging it.

He said, "I'm allowed a dessert option?"

"Sure. I'm an equal opportunity chow-hound."

"And you think I'm made of money?"

For the first time, he saw what looked like genuine emotion cross her face. "Hey, I'm sorry I never thought." She touched her purse. "I've got money."

"It's all right." He pulled out the now crumpled twenty. "Of course, I can pay." As if anything he did would impress her. Why was he even trying?

When she came back with his change and two servings of dessert, she plowed into hers and ate like there was no stopping her. He didn't touch his own even though it looked really good. When she was about finished he slid his over to her.

Solstice gave him a look, then polished off her plate and started in on his.

He was thinking that if anybody watched them it would appear they were a couple sharing lunch. He's never been a part of a couple. Fooling people was kind of fun. Maybe.

"Thanks," she said when she was done. "I want to meet Vivian. Can you make that happen? Is where she is far away?"

"Maybe forty minutes away by car, which I don't have, and a couple of hours by bus."

"I can go tomorrow," she said. "I've worked a lot of extra days, so I've got time off. I have to make sure it's the right Vivian. We'll just go. I'll pay the fare both ways. What time do we leave?"

Everything was happening too fast. His head whirled. "Just go and come right back again?"

"Sure. How long would it take? See her and make sure, talk with her, that's all. Why not?"

Alexander frowned. He had told his mother he couldn't come until after the New Year because of his social life and the next day was the thirtieth of December. That meant he couldn't possibly show up in town for this crazy reason, but he heard himself say, "I have assignments to finish and send in. I won't be ready until three o'clock."

"Great," she said. "I'll meet you at the Port Authority tomorrow at three." She told him exactly where to meet her, like giving him his marching orders. Then, quick as a flash, she had her coat whipped up around her skinny little body with the scarf twisted around her head, revealing only her eyes and the freckles across the bridge of her nose. She grabbed her backpack from the floor and slung it around to one shoulder, the high one, and off she went.

He went home feeling like he'd gotten caught in a stage curtain rolling up. He was lost in the dark. Who was Solstice, really? He guessed the only way to find out was to go along.

She emailed that evening to ask about their trip details.

He told her the time they would take the bus out of the city then switch to another one and then they would be picked up and driven to their destination.

She reminded him that she'd pay the fare for the trip. She didn't want him to feel he'd been "roped" into something.

Ha! He was roped and tied.

Chapter 15

Alexander arrived early at the bus terminal. Solstice was waiting, holding their tickets. They nodded at one another without exchanging words. Good. He had nothing to say to her. It wasn't as if they really knew one another.

They passed a snack display on their way to the escalator that would take them to the bus loading area.

"I'm hungry." She took out her money. "You want anything?"

"I do not," he said.

As she made her selection, he decided to try for the upper hand. Looking skyward, he said, "This is like traveling with a four-year-old."

She turned, candy bar in hand. "Kids always want the bathroom. Thanks for the reminder." Shoving her backpack at him, she took off.

He stood there like a dunce, holding her backpack. So much for the upper hand, he thought glumly. He had a pack too, with his laptop. Even with his handy cell, he hated being without his laptop.

Her pack was light. He wondered what was in it. To think he'd once felt bad because he thought he'd bruised her tender feelings. Her skin might look soft, but she was as tough as nails.

She returned so quickly he figured she hadn't needed the bathroom at all, she'd just been acting ornery, but he didn't say anything. Suppose she'd really had a purpose and his question inspired details? He shuddered. He couldn't be certain with her.

With her nibbling on the candy bar as delicately as a mouse but making it disappear awfully fast, they continued to the escalator and then on to the gate where their bus would load.

Neither of them noticed the man in an overcoat who took photos with the cell phone he pretended to be speaking on. Minutes later, after seeing which bus they waited for, he disappeared.

Later, when the bus left the terminal, the man, now driving a tan car, followed as the bus made its way through the city traffic then passed through the Lincoln Tunnel and to the New Jersey Turnpike, where lengthy traffic jams kept holding up progress.

When the bus finally pulled off the turnpike to where passengers could transfer, the man in the tan car pulled off too. He parked and went on foot to where he saw which bus the girl he was following and the beefy guy with her, were boarding.

Pulling his coat close against a temperature drop, the man returned to his vehicle. He was soon on a highway behind them and saw when they pulled into a shopping center transportation stop. He watched the girl and the guy get out. Motor idling, not sure what was happening next, he waited until a black limo pulled up and the girl and guy got inside.

Alexander had arranged to call Chuck Newton when they arrived at the highway shopping area bus stop so he could take them to town. Chuck soon arrived. He was caretaker of the Sycamore Shade Cemetery and he made extra money using the funeral parlor car as a taxi when it wasn't otherwise in use. It was a long black limousine with tinted windows. Alexander hoped Solstice would be impressed.

Chuck was six or seven years older than Alexander. He was in an amateur theater group in Melton, so Alexander felt a kinship with him. He'd asked Chuck to keep mum about his arrival in town but hadn't explained why. Men don't need to explain to one another. Private reasons were respected.

He told Chuck to drive them to the Gibeau farm, which he remembered from when he was a kid. The slow turnpike traffic had made them later than Alexander had expected. They traveled through the already darkening countryside, which would have looked even darker without the snow flurries that had whitened the ground.

When they arrived at the farmhouse, a yard light came on. Alexander didn't know what kind of reception they would get. He wished he knew why seeing Vivian was so important, but Solstice had refused to explain, and he wouldn't embarrass himself by asking again.

As soon as they stopped, Solstice was out her door. Alexander was about to follow when Chuck halted him. Leaning across the back of the front seat, Chuck said, "Just a warning, pal. She looks like jailbait to me."

Alexander blinked. Did Chuck think he had something going on with Solstice? Flattering, but not fair to her. "It's not what you think." Embellishing the truth, he added, "She's a friend of Vivian's."

Chuck snorted. "Not enough of a friend to know Vivian's not here. People in town know stuff. I brought you here because that's what you said, but the hired man, Stanley, is keeping an eye on things while Vivian and Nero visit family over the holidays."

As this was said, Solstice was trudging back to the car, her little lopsided shoulders hunched. Seeing how dejected she looked, Alexander decided that maybe she wasn't as tough as he'd thought. He left the car and met her in the yard. The flurries had stopped, but it seemed to be getting colder by the minute. Was her coat warm enough? At least she had her scarf to cover her ears. His own ears were freezing.

She said to him, "A man came to the door and told me Vivian Mather will be home the day after New Year's Day. I can't go right back like we planned." The yard light showed the pale shape of her face.

"Drop me someplace where I can stay until Vivian comes home. The man gave me her number so I can call. You go back to the city."

Alexander started to say there was no place to stay in town but then remembered that Juan Buenaventura rented rooms above his café. Solstice could stay there. He figured a café would make Solstice happy because there would be food.

He told her about it, and she agreed.

As they returned to Chuck's car, Alexander decided it wouldn't be right to leave Solstice alone in a strange town. He would rent a room, too. The thought grabbed him, made him feel bold. At last, he'd be taking charge with this strange girl.

Making no explanation, he told Chuck to take them to Bob's Auto Body and Towing, which wasn't far from Juan's.

On Main Street, the stores still had Christmas lights. There were lights inside of Daisy's bakery, but no one on the street. Bob's Garage had a pole light in the yard and a lighted wreath, but the shop was dark.

Chuck pulled to a stop along the street at Bob's. "Okay?" he said.

"It's good," Alexander said. As Solstice got out, he leaned forward and paid Chuck the predetermined trip amount. He felt smart because Solstice hadn't remembered to pay. He stepped out and joined her on the curb next to the car.

"Which way do I go?" she said, looking around, her arms hugged against her body as if to keep from shivering. "You don't have to show me, just tell me. I'll pay the driver and set it up with him to take me to the farm once I know I can see Vivian. You go on back to the city."

There was the sound of the motor revving. The limo pulled away.

"Hey!" Solstice whirled around, staring after the retreating tail lights. She spun back to face Alexander. "What's going on?"

"I not leaving you stranded in an unfamiliar town." Saying it, he felt like a hero. "The place we're going is right down the street. I'm staying there, too."

She backed from him, her fierce expression showing in the light coming from the garage yard. "I'm not leaving you breathing if you think you're trying something."

He saw that she'd jammed one hand deep inside her coat pocket. Did she have a weapon?

"No, no!" Alexander put his hands up. "It didn't seem right to just drop you off. I'm getting my own room. We'll each have our own room."

She studied him for what seemed a long time. Slowly, she relaxed. "Your own room?"

"Sure. The place, Juan's Hacienda . . . I don't know much about it." Taking charge wasn't working out as he'd planned. "I thought maybe it wouldn't be safe for you to be alone."

She surprised him by laughing. "You were worried about me?" She shook her head and spread her empty hands. "Wow, if you knew some of the places I've been."

"Alexander!" A cheerful bellow came from across the street.

Colonel McDuff came from the rear of Daisy's Doughnuts and Cakes, crossed the street and came up to them. "Alexander, good to see you again." Shifting the bakery box he carried to his left arm, he stuck out his right hand.

Alexander was warmed by the greeting but dismayed at being seen. Numbly, he stuck out his hand to shake.

The Colonel asked, "And who is this young lady?"

Alexander stumbled through introductions, realizing he didn't know Solstice's last name and hoping that Colonel McDuff didn't notice the omission.

She immediately spoke. "We came to see Vivian Mather. Due to a mix-up, we arrived at the wrong time."

"That's a shame," the Colonel said. "She and Nero are away visiting their families. If you haven't eaten, why not come to Iris's house with me? She's going out to a meeting, but there're leftovers from Christmas to use up."

Solstice looked at Alexander and said, "That sounds splendid, doesn't it?"

"Sure," he said. Who was this normal acting, polite, well-spoken person? *Splendid?*

"Why not just pile in with me?" the Colonel said. "I can drop you back to your car, later."

Alexander was about to say that they didn't have a car, but Solstice giggled and said, "I'm not going to say it—I bet you've heard it a million times."

The Colonel's laugh was hearty. "You mean, 'Lead on McDuff?' So I have, but come along." He gestured to the parking area behind the bakery. "I'm parked right over there."

Chapter 16

"Guests! What a lovely surprise!" Iris beamed as the Colonel brought them through the front door of her neat bungalow. Her round face became rounder as she smiled.

Alexander had seen Iris around town since he'd been a kid. She wasn't like so many of the older ladies who always asked about school. She was just cheerful and nice.

After welcoming them into the dining room where the table was set for one, Iris said something about needing two more place settings. Alexander noticed Solstice's suddenly hesitant manner, her poise gone. He was thinking that she wanted to help but wasn't sure what to do. It tickled him for a moment to see her at a loss, but then, looking at her, she reminded him once again of Cosette, all big eyes and fearful.

He went to her rescue, saying to Iris, "Show us where you keep the dishes and we'll do the table."

"Thank you, Alexander, that's so helpful." Iris pointed. "Dishes are in that china cabinet and silverware and napkins in the drawer underneath. And no place setting for me. I'm going out later."

He and Solstice set the table together. When they were done, she gave him a little smile instead of being a smart aleck, which made him feel good.

After Iris brought out the food and they started eating, she sat at her empty place and said to Solstice, "It's too bad Vivian's away and you didn't know. Are you returning to the city this late?"

"No, I'll wait until she's back. I'll stay at a place with a Spanish name and he . . ." She looked at Alexander. "He should return to the city."

"Oh, dear," Iris said, "I've heard the place isn't very clean. You can stay here. I have a spare room. And hon?" She looked at the Colonel. "Alexander doesn't want to travel all the way back to the city or disturb his mother. Could you put him up?"

"Certainly." The Colonel looked up from his food with a baffled expression. "No difficulty. But why wouldn't he—"

"You know Pilar," Iris said pointedly. "If she isn't expecting him, she might have other plans."

"Oh . . . yes, I see," the Colonel said.

Alexander flushed. Did everybody know about his mother's *entertaining*?

The phone rang. Iris jumped up to answer. She looked flustered when she returned. "Francine called to see if I was all right. With such delightful company, I lost track of the time. She knows I never miss our Voodoo Club meeting."

"Voodoo?" Alexander said.

"A harmless ladies group," the Colonel said with an indulgent chuckle. "They have sessions with a fortune-teller who works at the restaurant. I called it voodoo and they took the name for their group." His tone made it clear he thought the whole thing was nonsense.

Iris laughed, taking no insult. "Mar-see-ah is a medium, not a fortune-teller."

"But you enjoy it," the Colonel said.

Iris cast an apologetic glance around the table. "It's a dinner meeting and I'll arrive late." Her eyes landed on Solstice. "Since you're staying the night, why not finish eating and come with me? We'll clean up here and arrive in time for dessert."

"Dessert?" Solstice was clearly interested in that.

"Run along," the Colonel said. "If two men can't clean a few dishes, what's the world coming to?"

Alexander wondered if his mother planned to write about this club with its unusual name. It sure would give readers something to talk about. That's when it dawned on him that Solstice showing up at this ladies club meeting made it certain his mother would hear he was in town. That also meant he would have no excuse to avoid her New Year's Eve party.

With a girl.

A sudden thrill of anticipation shivered through him. He slid a sideways glance at Solstice as she stood with Iris, preparing to slip into her coat. She wore a cream-colored sweater and a long brown skirt with patch pockets. She didn't look much like her picture in the ad. He liked the freckles and was glad she didn't try to hide them.

The tedious party would surely be more interesting with her along. Did she have anything special to wear? Women cared about that. He'd have to ask the Colonel to tell Iris. If Solstice wanted to get a dress, maybe Iris could take her. He smiled to himself. It should work out. Unless Solstice did a thumbs down on the party.

She was always so bossy, except for when the limo left and she'd been afraid of him. He didn't like that at all.

The man in the overcoat and tan car who had followed Solstice and Alexander to Iris's house had watched from a hidden location and then left. All this traveling to get to this godforsaken burg. He was hungry and tired. He figured the girl and the guy were set for the night. He drove around looking for a motel, but only found a place with rooms to rent.

In the rented room, which was as dreary as he'd expected, he called and made his report.

The person he reported to said, "I've received your email with the photos and now know for certain she's the one. You figure out how to do it, but it's time for her to have an accident."

Chapter 17

The next morning at the Colonel's house, the last day of the old year, Alexander learned from the Colonel that Iris was indeed taking Solstice shopping. He wondered if she would buy something that didn't look all outsized and droopy on her small frame. Too late, he wondered if she had enough money. He wondered again, assuming that Vivian Mather was the correct Vivian, why it was so important for Solstice to meet her? And, darn it, why did Vivian have to be away when it would have worked out so well if she had been home? Solstice could have learned whatever she was after and he could be home in his apartment and everything could be back to normal. Only now, it wasn't.

The Colonel went off on historical society business. He'd invited Alexander to come along, but Alexander said he had work to do.

His work was website articles to write to pay his rent, like "Canceled TV Shows that Should Come Back," with descriptions about the shows—most of which he'd never seen—along with invented reasons for their resurrection. He also created a series of catty comments to match photos of actors from a Hollywood fashion event. Why readers ate up trash about people they didn't know and would probably never meet was a puzzle to him. At least his mother's *News and Noose* feature used people that readers were personally acquainted with. That was probably worse but at least it made sense. Except she had given it up. Had there been a particular reason?

His phone rang. It was his mother.

Cringing, he answered. Making his voice sound calmer than he felt, he said, "I was just thinking about you."

"As well you might," she said. "I learned you were here from the town network."

"Oh," he said.

"Yes. When Chuck Newton reached home after dropping you and your young lady off at Bob's, he told his wife, Amy, who was dressing for dinner with the Voodoo Club—she's a member. Later, when Amy called Shirley DeGarmo about helping clean her house, she mentioned that Iris had brought a girl, a stranger, to the club meeting. Shirley told her son, Donny, that you had shown up in town with a young woman nobody had ever seen before. Donny told his pregnant wife, Bethany, who works at Daisy's Doughnuts and Cakes. Bethany told Daisy, and when I went in to order more pastries for my New Year's Eve Party, Daisy told me."

Alexander couldn't tell whether his mother was annoyed with him or not. He took a breath, then, doing his best to sound lofty and in command, he said, "Fortunately, Mother, I've had a change in plans. I'm now able to accept your New Year's Eve invitation. Also, I'll be bringing a guest."

As he disconnected, he imagined a phantom playwright ferociously scribbling behind the scenes, setting the stage. For what, he didn't know.

Chapter 18

On New Year's Eve, Slim Parkerson crossed the Delaware River from New Jersey to his destination in Philadelphia and found parking along the street near Steve Kroger's condo.

Last night of a rotten year, he thought, but he was determined to put it behind him and kick back with pals and booze. Carrying a case of beer, he walked in on music, a rerun of an Eagles game, and a bunch of guys of all colors, all sizes, but mostly big and most with hair buzzed short, laughing and talking loudly. It was like a locker room of a winning team at half-time. Slim felt right at home.

"Yo!" yelled Kroger, who was holding a beer in one hand and, with the other hand, illustrating some point in a story he was telling.

"Yo!" Slim called back, guessing his way into the brightly lit kitchen and swinging the beer up to an empty spot on the counter.

There were women there, cops' wives and girlfriends, he figured. *Observant,* he chuckled to himself. It's why they made him Chief of Police.

One of the women, a brunette with her back to him, was broad across the beam and wearing a black dress that looked too short. She turned, and she was pretty with black eyes that snapped.

Seeing him, she grinned and called, "Hey, you Steve's pal all the way over from Jersey?"

Slim grinned back at her. "Guess that's me." Wife or girlfriend, she looked like she'd be a blast to hang around with. The skirt still looked too short, but how could a skirt on a good-looking female be too short?

The women were doing things with food. When he returned to the living room, he spotted a table loaded with crock pots and good smelling stuff waiting until it was time to grab a fancy paper plate and load up. If it had just been guys, it would have been booze and salty snacks—just tear open the bags and dive in.

For an instant, he remembered a previous New Year's Eve bash with Lana before they had one of their breakups. He thought he didn't want to remember how good it had been, but now he wondered—had it really been so good? Her telling him what to eat, what not to eat. "Go easy on that cake, sweetie. Got to keep a watch on those calories."

Hell, he was six-four, and the only time he weighed more than one-seventy-five was when he had to wear a plaster cast. That had been when a kid hopped up on a witches brew from his grandma's medicine cabinet went rampaging through the JumpRope Sports and Hobby Shop. Slim had tried to stop him. The kid swung a tennis racket hard enough to shatter a bone in Slim's left forearm and ran for the street. Not feeling the pain, Slim chased after him. Weaving around an Old Geezer hobbling by, Slim mowed the kid down on the sidewalk. Kid was in college now, studying to be a pharmacist, go figure. Slim was left with a titanium pin mark on his arm that wouldn't tan.

"Hey," said Kroger, coming up. "Grab a drink and meet people."

There were at least fifteen guys there, all cops except the brother of one of them who was in the Navy, and another who was a prosecutor for the City. A woman came out to add something to a buffet table, the black-eyed brunette Slim had noticed before.

Kroger pointed and said, "That's my doll over there. Married three years, two kids already." She caught her husband's eye and gave him a big smile. "Ain't she something?" Kroger glowed. "Knockout in the looks department and a knockout personality."

"You're a lucky man," Slim said, meaning it.

He thought of what he would have been doing if he hadn't accepted Kroger's invitation. He'd either be home alone or stuck alone at a party in JumpRope with Holly and a bunch of other people all feeling sorry for him.

He and Kroger threw themselves down on a pair of couches with some other guys trading insults about opposing favorite teams. Slim lounged back and took a long draw on his beer.

The door to the hall opened as more people piled in. Slim paid no attention until he noticed one of the cops helping a newcomer off with her coat like she was helpless, smoothing her hair in an unnecessary gesture, an excuse to touch. She turned a bit sideways, and Slim saw a sharp-featured but pretty face, softened because of her fluffed hair and makeup.

Startled, he said to Kroger, "That's JJ Gilbert!"

Kroger looked up. "Yeah, like I told you, one of the guys took a shine to her, admired her standup style when she identified her dead friend." Expression questioning, Kroger made a back and forth gesture between Slim and JJ, who hadn't noticed them. "You said Dan wouldn't be poaching, right?"

"Right," Slim said. "She's the kid sister of guys I went to school with. Four brothers. Guess they made a man out of her."

"Looks all girl from this distance," Kroger said. "Hey, don't like to talk the job at a party, but since you're here . . . you know anything about a toy manufacturer or a toy shop in your area?"

"There's a sports and hobby place in town," Slim said, thinking it was funny because he'd just recalled the incident with the kid and his arm. "There's another toy shop at the Melton Mall. Why?"

"That dead girl—one of her magazine friends we interviewed said she'd talked about going to a toy place in Jersey."

Slim shook his head. "Means nothing."

One of the women, a brassy blonde, turned down the music and yelled, "Feeding time! Mix some food with that booze or fights'll break out. Us ladies'll have to call the cops. Ha-ha. And don't ask for anything more—we're done with you and having our own party just for us."

There was laughter and whoops and shouts as the guys hauled themselves to their feet.

It was around eleven o'clock when Slim noticed JJ near the door, putting on her coat, managing the task all by herself. He guessed that Dan character had faded or left because he was on call. JJ and another woman, also wearing a coat, were clearly preparing to leave.

Standing, Slim realized he hadn't said a word to her and decided it was about time.

"JJ," he said, as he reached her. "Looking good."

She lifted her brow. "I clean up on occasion."

That wasn't what he'd meant, but he guessed it didn't make a difference.

"Heading to another party?" he said.

"Yeah, then bunking in. You know the old saying, Philly's even better overnight."

She introduced her companion, a TV film editor, and they went off.

It wasn't until after the door closed that he thought he should have asked if she remembered her friend Carol ever showing an interest in some toy manufacturer or a store.

For several ticks of the clock he stood staring at the door after it had closed, and then he moved back into the room grabbed another beer and cruised by the food table a second time to load up another plate.

An hour before midnight in JumpRope, Pilar's rancher was ablaze with lights. Both sides of the drive were packed with vehicles, some at reckless angles. Alexander played it safe and parked the borrowed Colonel's SUV along the road. He didn't want to risk somebody scraping the paint.

The Colonel and Iris had gone to the American Legion New Year's Eve celebration in Iris's car. The thought of those rotten Old Geezer veterans at the Legion made Alexander feel even better about his mother's party.

Solstice wore her long coat with a winter scarf looped around her neck. He wore the jeans he'd come in, but he had a clean shirt, underwear and socks from his backpack. He always carried extras.

He learned that Solstice did too, but she had to go into detail. She told him she never went anywhere without extra underpants and—she had bracketed her fingers in the air and said in a squeaky voice that he guessed stood for italics—*"feminine products."* He knew she was trying to freak him out. And succeeding. She was somebody he could easily hate.

As they emerged from the SUV, he moved to take Solstice's arm but she shrugged him off. *Independent woman*, he thought. Okay with him.

Inside the house, she slipped off her coat. Alexander thought she looked pretty good in what must be the new dress she had shopped for with Iris. It was green, with a longish skirt and she wore it with a flashy necklace. Her hair was tied up high and topped with a sparkly green barrette. Her eyes looked bigger than ever and her mouth was painted pink. In addition to the freckles across her nose, there were freckles across the tops of her skinny, lopsided shoulders.

He took his outer clothes and her coat and scarf and threw them on a couch in the TV room on top of other coats. There was a guy in there with three little boys, busy playing a board game.

When he came out, his mother appeared. She wore a slinky gold silk dress that could have been a relic from the Roaring Twenties. Her earrings were like real chandeliers, only miniature, with tiny crystal dangles. He knew she could be touchy-feely, but after giving him a hug, she merely smiled at Solstice.

To his surprise, Miss Sass Mouth turned charming and raved over the decorations. His mother beamed. She had found a stash of vintage paper party hats, the New Year dates in dye-cut metallic numbers, and had hung them around the rooms from the picture rails. Guests were hunting for hats marked with significant years and exclaiming things like, "Look! The year my mother was born!"

Pilar told Alexander to show Solstice around and then she was off greeting other new arrivals. Figuring food was a sure-fire winner with Solstice, Alexander ushered her to the big spread on his mother's dining room table. Spread? *Take the word literally*, he thought. The table cover was an embroidered bedspread with blue-stitched designs.

He filled his own plate and looked around the expansive living-dining room, pleased to see nobody who made him super uncomfortable, like Francine Smithers, who was probably at the Firehouse hoopla, or nasty Jessi Spellman.

A committeeman that had been pointed out to Alexander at the Jamboree, Max Osterhagen, the one Jessi had whipped in the election, was manning the bar. Alexander saw him and his mother talking, and he wondered if Osterhagen was her latest wounded bird. He acted like he was all in one piece, but you couldn't tell just by looking. Alexander edged closer and heard him mention Jessi's name. Sounding amused rather than resentful, Osterhagen said, "She's been visiting the State House as a JumpRope Committeewoman-elect and has wrapped some state senator around her finger."

A bit later, Pilar came over and took Alexander's arm. Her dark hair was pulled away from her fine-featured face and as always, she wore too much makeup. Alexander didn't know why she did that. He could see her beauty even though she was his mother, but he also saw she looked troubled in that special way she had.

What now, he thought.

"Be careful," she said.

Alexander mentally rolled his eyes. His mother was always getting notions, acting like a soothsayer whispering, "Beware the Ides of March." Maybe she belonged in Iris's Voodoo group. The weird thing was, his mother often got her lines right. She was smart and probably noticed things other people missed.

"Careful because of what?" he said.

"Because of Solstice," she said. "She seems so alone. Take good care of her."

* * *

It was forty-five minutes before midnight at the spacious Weehawken,

New Jersey house that belonged to Vivian's Aunt Elizabeth. The room vibrated cheerfully with live music and the guests who had gathered for the New Year, including Nero and Vivian.

As planned, she and Nero spent Christmas Eve and Christmas Day with Nero's late mother's family in Melton. Vivian was already thinking that next year, she and Nero would switch things around—Christmas with her family and New Years' with his. How startling, she thought, how easily and wonderfully it was that she was now thinking of a future with this man she had come to love.

Smiling, she turned back into the special entertainment for the evening, four young acrobats who performed in a generous space at one end of what had been a ballroom when the house was built in the late eighteen-hundreds. Elizabeth had learned of the acrobats who performed for fun and donations in New York City's Central Park. Now, thanks to her sponsorship, they attended a privately endowed performing arts school for inner-city teens.

She knew that Elizabeth had also sponsored Acer Wolfgang, having found him as a teenage orphan on the streets of New York. Something about him had caught her interest. She had taken him into her home and seen to his education. Vivian was thirteen when she came to live with her aunt after the death of her father. By that time, Acer was a financial success with properties of his own. He was nevertheless a frequent visitor.

Despite the difference in their ages Vivian and Acer formed a relationship that was like a sister and an older brother. He was someone she could always talk to, a person she could trust and depend upon. She saw him even more often now that he was planning a development in the town where she lived with Nero, and she was delighted to see him again for this weekend with her aunt.

Aunt Elizabeth was a grand old lady and lots of fun. The day before when Vivian and Nero had first arrived, Elizabeth told Nero that if she painted portraits instead of landscapes, he would be her subject. Closing her eyes, she had touched the planes of his face as if she were a blind person.

"So strong and beautiful," she'd said. "If only I were a sculptor." Opening her eyes, she said with teasing smile, "Or sixty years younger."

"I never felt so silly," Nero told Vivian later in the bedroom when they were unpacking their luggage.

"You handled it very well," Vivian said, and then she started giggling and couldn't stop.

"Oh, you like to laugh, do you?" He'd started tickling her.

He was ticklish too, which made it quite entertaining. Weak with laughter, the session had turned into something even more entertaining.

At the luncheon table, it had elated Vivian to watch Acer and Nero hit it off. Although Nero had no formal training in engineering, he'd been an Army mechanic and worked with road equipment and engineers, gaining practical knowledge on assorted and difficult terrains. Acer, who had built his empire after achieving several degrees, including engineering, had been delighted to talk with him.

Now, at the party, the music and dancing began.

Acer, who had come to the party alone, stood talking with the senior director of Elizabeth's art league and her husband. Since Acer was so often accompanied by someone both beautiful and celebrated. Vivian asked him later why he hadn't brought along someone to help him ring in the New Year.

He gave her a quiet smile. "Not even I could compete with the charm of a grandbaby."

Vivian narrowed her eyes. "The grandchild of the town property inspector, Darlene Gage, who lives to find fault with you?"

Acer's sea-blue eyes twinkled. "She's softening," he said.

"I'm sure," Vivian said. She had never before known Acer to be besotted with a woman he couldn't have . . . correction, she had never known of a woman impervious to his appeal. No wonder the steely Darlene Gage had captured him in her barbed wire snare.

As Vivian and Nero returned to dancing, the high ceilinged room was filled with music, talk, laughter and people—so many people. Vivian was thankful that Nero had given in and taken the medication that had once been prescribed for his post-traumatic stress, which could be unexpectedly triggered. The result had been good. Throughout their time with his family and now hers, he had not only been mostly in control, he'd enjoyed himself.

Now, as Vivian swayed against him to the dance music, she murmured, "Do I have to wait until the clock strikes twelve to kiss you?"

He arched a single eyebrow in question, his hands toying with her dark, glossy hair, which hung in waves down her back. She tried and failed to arch a single eyebrow in return. Would she ever learn that trick? He was always saying she needed more practice.

In a teasing tone, he said, "I'm reading your mind, and a certain word comes to me: *practice*. "Maybe you need practice in kissing, too."

She lifted her face to his, thinking, *Oh, how I love this man*. That was a thought she'd never put into words because it wasn't necessary. She loved him more than words could ever say.

In Pilar's house in JumpRope, it was a quarter to midnight almost before Alexander knew it. He had dismissed his mother's concerned words about Solstice, who had been circulating, eating and behaving herself as far as he could see, but then, she abruptly came up to him.

"I want to talk with you. She showed a tight, anxious expression and her eyes seemed bigger than ever. "I need to go outside."

What was up with her now? "Okay," he said, "I'll get our coats." He should have known she couldn't keep hiding her quirkiness. Maybe she smoked. He hadn't seen her do it, but if she did, it probably wouldn't be regular cigarettes.

When he returned wearing his jacket and carrying her coat, she snatched her coat from him and backed off so she could shrug into it herself. He led her to the back door. She flung on her scarf and shoved out the door ahead of him. Outside, it was cold and very still. It had started to snow, big fat flakes floating down.

"Okay?" he said. Feeling the cold, he wished he'd thought to grab his cap and gloves.

"Yes," she said, "and this is why. At midnight, there's all that hugging and kissing. I don't want any part of it. You can go back inside if you want, but I'm staying here until the fuss is over."

He stared at her, feeling stuck. He wouldn't go back inside the house and leave her, but he didn't want to freeze, either. There was enough light from a window to see that snowflakes had joined the sparkles on her hair barrette, winking like twinkle lights. They were also landing on his glasses, melting in streaks, and soon, he knew, snow would melt on his neck and run under his collar.

"You don't have to worry about me crawling all over you." What a laugh, him crawling all over some girl. He hadn't even thought about midnight and kissing. He had no interest in kissing her. He wasn't even going to look at her lips, a thought which contrarily made him look at them. They looked even softer through his blurry glasses.

"It's not just you," she snapped. "I told you, it's everybody, pawing each other, even strangers, hugging and kissing. I'm not having it."

He stamped his cold feet. "If we're going to stay outside, at least let's move around a little." He would have liked to take her arm. It would have warmed up at least one of his hands, but considering her apparent aversion to contact, he didn't dare. He took off his glasses and fumbled for the pouch in his shirt pocket under his jacket. He finally got his glasses tucked away. His chilled fingers worked too stiffly to get his jacked zipped. So he would freeze faster, who cared?

He started walking and she followed him around to the front of the house where he could make out cars parked all the way down the long lane. Snow was starting to accumulate. The man he'd seen with the kids was now outside with them, huddled near the far side of the house, hiding from the light cast through a window, acting sneaky. Alexander bet they were setting up fireworks to go off at midnight. He steered Solstice to a shelter by foundation plantings.

"So why are you so weird about this?" There. He had said it out loud, called her *weird*.

"I'm celibate," she said.

"What?"

"Too big a word for you?"

"No." He was shocked. "I just never heard anybody say it. Are you like, religious?"

"Yeah, sure. I'm a born-again virgin."

"What's that?"

"It means I've done it and don't want to do it ever again. Okay?"

He thought about it. "And nobody is supposed to touch you? Not even to take your arm when we're walking?"

She made a jeering sound. "Why, Snuggle Bunny? Wanna take my arm?"

"Yes, darn it. My hands are freezing."

"Oh, I'm sorry—I never thought." It was the second time he had heard her actually sound sincere. "Here, take my scarf."

He accepted it and put it around his neck, but the fringed ends tangled with the glasses pouch in his shirt pocket, revealed because his jacket was open. Right then and there he decided to give up his act with the glasses. He only needed them for reading, so who was he trying to impress. *Her?*

"Here," she said, clucking like some fat hen when she was more like a scrawny pullet. "Put your head down."

She started fussing with the scarf, drawing the sides up to cover his ears then smoothing the ends. She tapped his chest. It was a light touch but it made him suck in his breath as if he'd been punched. "Hold your hands out a little," she said. Like an automaton, he complied. She wrapped the scarf ends, muff-like, around his hands and then shoved his glasses pouch firmly in his pocket, and zipped his jacket up.

"There," she said, sounding satisfied.

He stood with his hands clasped to his chest, all ready for a lily and the funeral parlor hearse, except that his flesh tingled warmly from the brushing of her fingers.

"So, it's okay for you to touch me?" He tried to sound insulted by her inconsistency.

"That's different," she said.

Off by the side of the house, the kids were whispering and giggling. Solstice stared. "What are they up to?"

He told her what he thought, and then added, "Maybe even Roman candles and cherry bombs. Some towns have a big public fireworks display. Here, when the fire whistle blows at midnight, people shoot off rockets and fire guns."

"Guns?"

"Into the sky. Shotguns. There're woods around here and people go hunting."

"I don't like killing stuff."

He snorted. "I've seen you eat. You're no vegetarian."

She snorted back. "Excellent deduction. But my parents were."

"Vegetarians?"

"They gathered plants and we ate them."

"Gathered?" he questioned. It sounded strange. He waited for her to say more, but she didn't.

It had to be nearly midnight and then they could go inside again.

Melting snow was running down the back of his neck despite her scarf and he couldn't see his watch.

He wriggled his hands and found his watch, only it was too dark to read and he needed his other hand to push the illumination button. He moved into the light cast from one of the dining room windows and she moved with him.

He read his watch. Less than a minute to go.

"It's almost time," he said. "Any second now . . ."

And then they could go inside and he could get warm.

The fire whistle blew and explosions and wild lights came from the side of the house where the kids screeched and yelled in triumph. Somebody threw open the front door of the house and guests streamed out blowing party horns and screaming, "Happy New Year!"

Midnight!

From several different directions on the horizon, fireworks blossomed into the sky and spread wider and wider like huge colored webs of light, followed by the cacophony of whistles, screamers, booms and bangs. All of a sudden, Solstice's barrette exploded into a million pieces and went flying, stinging Alexander's forehead.

A fraction of a second to think, then he yelled, "Somebody's shooting at us!"

He jerked his hands free of the scarf and lunged, wrapping his arms around Solstice and throwing them both to the ground. The second bullet zinged against the side of the house where they'd been standing. Brick chips landed on the back of Alexander's neck and on the exposed flesh of one hand, stinging like red sleet.

The tan car that had been parked by the road at the end of the long line of cars in the lane eased away as fireworks all over the county made magic in the sky and people in the front yard of the Fanshawe house were still cheering and shouting, "Happy New Year!"

Chapter 19

Alexander kept Solstice pressed to the ground with his body to protect her, but she was screaming at him

"What in hell are you doing?" She sounded terrified.

Oh my gosh, he thought, did she think he was attacking her? Did she think that was his style? "Happy New Year, babe!" Leap. Land. Sproong! As if she wasn't wrapped in the protection of a full-length, buttoned-up winter coat.

He scrambled to his feet and yanked her to a standing position and hustled her around the corner before any of the loopy party crowd carousing on the lawn could look over and see them.

Now that he'd had a minute to calm down, he knew that no one could have actually been aiming for them. That made no sense. Someone had fired shots in the air and they'd come down where they were. Just as lethal if they'd been hit, but nothing deliberate. And now it was over.

"We're going inside," he said and took her along with him.

Back in the house, he saw his mother and that Max character putting out more food so the party could continue. Alexander only wanted to get into the Colonel's vehicle and leave. Solstice hadn't said a word after she'd screamed at him. Still wearing her coat, she had hunkered down in a big chair, her face pale and her hair messed up because of the destroyed barrette. She had her hands clasped together as if to keep them from shaking.

Alexander stared at her. She looked in a state of shock, which made sense if she'd believed him about shots fired at them, but she clearly thought he'd made it up as an excuse.

His mother stepped to them. "What happened? Is she all right?"

"Some fireworks scared her," he said, which gave him the cue for his next line. "We're leaving."

"How long are you staying in town? You told me you'll be at the Colonel's, and Solstice will be at Iris's."

"Right. We're staying until the day after New Year's Day. That's when Vivian Mather is supposed to be home. Solstice wants to meet her."

"I've heard that," Pilar said, "but what for?"

"She won't tell me until she knows if it's the 'right' Vivian."

"Right Vivian for what?"

"I don't know." He shrugged and then said. "The Colonel has been super but I don't want to ask him for another favor when it's time to leave." He looked at his mother. "When we're ready to go, could you take us to the shopping center to catch our bus?"

"Of course," she said, sounding pleased.

When they reached Iris's house, she and the Colonel were just getting out of Iris's car. Iris took Solstice into her house for the night. The Colonel took the wheel of his SUV and Alexander slid into the passenger seat. They were soon at the Colonel's. Yawning, the man showed Alexander to the guest room, and bid him good night.

Alexander got ready for bed, thinking about the gun shots. He figured they had come from a rifle because the bullets had to have traveled a distance. They kept going until their downward arcs reached the Fanshawe house with enough force left to plow into the brick facing. An accident like Solstice thought, only they weren't fireworks. He was positive they had been bullets. But hadn't he been quick in removing her from danger? She hadn't appreciated it, but right or wrong, his reaction had been lightning fast.

He remembered her panicky response, which in retrospect was comical. The way she had squirmed under him, hissing into his ear, one of her arms trapped full length along his body and ending in sort of a sensitive spot. Even though he had told himself he was above common carnal impulses, he went to sleep with a smile on his face.

Solstice, in bed in Iris's house, couldn't settle. She punched her pillow and rolled over, thinking that Alexander Fanshawe liked to make a fuss over nothing. A real gun going off? Ridiculous. Nothing but fireworks.

From the start, she could tell how proper he was. Stuffy prig. Despite that, he was well-meaning and scandalously easy to push around. And his voice sounded rich and deep and, well, soothing. She enjoyed listening to him even though he spouted nonsense, which was most of the time. He had turned out to be even more fun in person than he'd been in emails.

But she couldn't shake her remembered panic when she'd been trapped beneath his weight. It made her feel sick to her stomach. Put her on the scales and she was ninety-six pounds. He had to be twice that and more. She'd been powerless. Yet, that ninny imagined he was protecting her. With a harsh sob, she punched her pillow again. During those few horrid moments, she was once again a prisoner of those early years when she'd been caught in the worst possible traps. And then, yet another trap.

When she'd finally escaped, she'd managed to take Toodles, the little dog she'd loved, with her. Stroking his soft, curly coat had been her only comfort back then. Toodles had since died, but his blanket in her apartment had a frayed binding with loose threads that reminded her of his coat. The binding on the blanket she had in Iris's guest room was disappointingly perfect.

When she and Iris had gone shopping, the woman hadn't known why it had taken her so long to choose a party dress. That's because she needed one with pockets, like all her skirts. But fancy dresses weren't made that way. She'd settled on a green dress with a full skirt. Later, she opened a seam and fashioned the pocket-like slit she had needed.

Although she'd felt safe in this tiny town with this stuffy bearded innocent, she knew to keep on guard. Not to keep safe from outside dangers because that was over—she had to believe that—but to ward off the paralyzing threat of her own emotions. To do that, she needed the constant reminder that she could protect herself.

She fell asleep with her hand on the clever and versatile razor-sharp blade in its Velcro holder that was safely secured to her thigh.

Chapter 20

Darlene Gage had been awakened from her solitary bed by bells and whistles, hooting and hollering and the clamor of fireworks. Her window showed colored lights streaking into the sky. Explosive and aerial fireworks required permits that were only granted to experts in the field. What she saw were coming from all directions and they surely weren't all permitted.

Where were the police? All drunk, she supposed.

Returning to sleep was hopeless. She couldn't stop her thoughts. She had told a lie and felt disgusted and ashamed. When Acer Wolfgang had invited her to a New Year's Eve party, she had panicked. Instead of telling him she wasn't interested, she'd told him she would be in Pennsylvania with her daughter's family and, of course, her darling grandbaby, MacKenzie.

The truth was, she *had* expected to babysit on New Year's Eve, but then her daughter, Marie, said she and her husband, Joe, were going out and had hired a sitter. Darlene suspected that the couple had thrown their own New Year's party and didn't want her around. She didn't blame them—they were young, but it had disappointed her. They had lied to her, and she had lied to Acer.

Darlene clenched her fists so hard the fingernails dug into her palms. She liked to think of herself as strong, but with Acer Wolfgang she was nothing but a coward.

With a rare curse, she propelled herself from bed.

She'd had no New Year's Eve plans, but now she did.

It didn't matter that it was only minutes into the New Year and as dark as pitch outside now that the flare of rockets had faded. She wasn't a cop, but she had authority of her own. She knew she had the nickname, the "Empress," for her inflexibility with the rules of her department but if there were rules, then someone had to see that they were followed. That someone was her.

She dressed hastily. Pausing by the downstairs door, she shrugged into her coat and hat and jammed her stockinged feet into her boots. Clipboard in hand and wearing her ID tag, she got behind the wheel of her car. She smiled at the sound of her tires crunching on the snow as the car invaded the dark street.

She drove while her eyes scanned the sides of the streets, left and right. People thought she was always out to "get somebody," and maybe she was, but the point was making a better town and rewarding good residents who maintained their properties by correcting their scofflaw neighbors. Rules and regulations served a purpose. Little things ignored gradually destroyed a property, then the street, and if ignored too long, an entire community.

Darlene had seen in her long-ago brief marriage how ignoring little signs and signals eventually destroyed everything. Evasions, off remarks, words she hadn't wanted to question, then became afraid to question. She had once been a wide-eyed bride: naïve, trusting, stupid. She couldn't regret it because it had given her Marie, and now her little granddaughter, MacKenzie, but her despicable ex-husband, had made her what she was now. Flinty, guarded and giving not an inch. Always expecting the worst and rarely disappointed.

She drove toward the old Mather house that Acer Wolfgang was converting into a showroom and office for his housing development. She remembered he'd asked her to accompany him when he'd come into town to view an adjacent property that Jessi Spellman had been eager to unload. The sale had tanked because, as Acer indicated later, he didn't trust Jessi. Darlene figured it took one shyster to know another one. The confusing thing was that he'd brought two little children along. He'd said they lived in the city, meaning New York somewhere, and he was treating them to a country outing. Darlene loved children, and couldn't help being charmed by them, but really, why had he brought them?

Nothing about Acer Wolfgang made sense to her.

She made the turn leading to the Mather house. There were no lights on the dead-end street but a sliver of moonlight reflected off the snow that was gathering on the ground and coating the tree branches. She stared at the house. Because of the snow, she couldn't be sure, but the roof line now looked square instead of dipping like a swayback donkey. Had it actually been rebuilt and reroofed? The porch also appeared rebuilt. Wolfgang's work crew had gotten the permits but she never expected them to follow through so quickly—if at all.

As Darlene continued her after-midnight tour, she avoided areas where there were signs of ongoing parties. She hung door-knocker reminders on houses that had either set refuse and recycling out too early or who had neglected to store empty containers inside fences or around to the rear, leaving them in forbidden public view.

She noted addresses on her clipboard so she could do follow-ups and snapped pictures with her digital camera, proven to take fairly decent photos in dim light. She understood that on holidays, residents were distracted and busy with guests. That didn't mean she would be lax, but she would be fair. That meant letters to write. Letters were work, but work was her job. She didn't issue citations until property owners had received official warnings and ample time to correct failings yet hadn't done so.

After several hours of dogged touring, she took a side turn to Juan's Hacienda. Juan's ROOMS TO RENT sign was in the window despite the many times he'd been ordered to cease and desist renting rooms. The building was dark. A streetlight showed a car pulled far back in the lane. She moved closer on foot. The vehicle bore New York plates. No doubt it belonged to someone who had rented a room—perhaps a partygoer who'd over imbibed and realized it was unwise to drive home. If so, Juan Buenaventura had kept a drunk off the road. However, there were rules. There was no other public lodging in town, but if Juan wanted to continue offering rooms, he was required to seek planning board approval for a hotel in a residential neighborhood.

By the fierce glare of her headlights, Darlene jotted down the plate number and snapped a photo of the tan car.

Chapter 21

The heavy snow that had kept coming on New Year's Eve, ceased by morning. The view from the Colonel's breakfast bar showed tree branches resembling lace against the backdrop of a clear and brilliant blue.

Alexander's mood was lazy despite the excitement of the night before. Gunfire? It seemed pointless, yet he still needed to prove he'd been right. Surely he could find where the bullets had struck.

The Colonel had invited him to go with him to the historical museum to show him around. Alexander had agreed. He thought about asking the Colonel to detour by his mother's house so he could look for evidence but then he would have to explain. If he didn't find anything, he would look like a dunce. Better to find a way to do it by himself.

Still feeling lazy, he thought about how he and Colonel would go to Iris's for a New Year's Day dinner with her and Solstice. He imagined Solstice snacking the whole time during preparations in the kitchen and then sitting her scrawny self at the table and end up with the equivalent of two full meals. The image made him smile.

His smile faded as he considered, not for the first time, what an odd girl she was. Her secrets, her quirks, and the weird things she came out with. Like being a born-again virgin.

Before they left for the museum, Alexander's cell sounded.

It was Solstice, who said, "At that Voodoo dinner, I met a lady called Francine. I told her and the others I was in town because I wanted to meet Vivian Mather. This Francine just went ahead and set up a meeting for me with Vivian tomorrow at that farm house."

"Sounds like Francine. Pushy." Alexander made his tone sound all-knowing. "But it's good we know what we're doing." Only he didn't know. Tomorrow would be the second day of the New Year, and he still had no clue why Solstice was so intent on meeting Vivian Mather.

"See you at dinner, Chunky-Wunky," Solstice said with a giggle.

Scowling, he put away his phone. Okay, maybe he should lose a few pounds, but she was the one who chowed down like a starving squirrel.

Alexander was impressed with the museum and the work that had been done to preserve historical records. Later, while the Colonel filed yellowed clippings, Alexander used his computer to send articles to their respective editors and he checked his bank and credit card accounts. Good. He wouldn't starve during the coming month. He smirked, remembering his behavior when he'd first met Solstice, thinking how stupid he'd been, showing off like he had money. He didn't even *like* her!

With the Colonel still busy, Alexander surfed random websites, gathering article ideas. Maybe he should devise a joke name for Solstice. She made up names for him, didn't she? He'd find one for her. Fingers moving on the keys without him having to think, he searched Disney character girls—they always looked small and frail. *Tinkerbell?* Too nice. *Stinkerbell?* Too mean. She didn't smell funny—just clean, with maybe a scent from shampoo. He decided to take her web user name, S^2, and spell it phonetically. *Esstwo*. Create a name from that.

Fingers working as he thought, a name appeared in the web search field. *Esstu.* Shocked, he stared, hardly able to believe it. There was her picture. Solstice, her big eyes made up to tilt at the corners. Her name wasn't how he'd spelled it, but it was Solstice for sure.

In the photo, she wore a timid smile. Timid? *Her?* Her blouse had a round collar and her plaid skirt had matching suspenders. It looked like a photo from a church elementary school.

He clicked on the picture and it took him to the site that had generated it and he almost fell off his chair.

Big letters, blazing font:

LEGAL BUT DON'T LOOK IT.
LITTLE GIRLS! DADDY'S GIRLS!

Then in a smaller font: *Gentleman's Escort Service.*

He gasped aloud.

Solstice was a *hooker*!

He sat stunned, as inert as a stage prop.

Solstice, who freaked out if she was touched. The celibate.

She'd been having him on like the gullible moron he was. She claimed she was a magazine proofreader, but she was really making money from men in exchange for her body.

But did that line up with how she acted? Was she that good of an actress? Maybe he just didn't want to believe he was so stupid, but he couldn't reconcile her behavior with the website. She'd been so fierce about avoiding physical contact. When he'd piled on top of her to keep her safe from the gunfire, she'd reacted with panic. It had seemed genuine.

Seemed. The operative word.

Alexander felt demolished.

Was he really such a fool?

He didn't know what to think. He stared aimlessly around the museum at the collection of old papers, sepia-toned photos with faded edges, all memorabilia from times long gone, what people imagined was a more innocent age. Only there was no innocent age.

Alexander's eyes lost focus as he turned his thoughts inward and he did what he always did when he was hurt and confused: he sought refuge in his extensive knowledge. He thought about the Victorians and their prudish society and their repressive standards for women of high birth. Brides weren't supposed to know what happened in the marriage bed until their experienced husbands taught them. And how did the husbands gain their experience? From randying about with lowbred women. Poverty-stricken women whose only coin was their flesh. And not only women. Young children of either sex were sold to providers of sexual filth, in some cases sold by desperate parents who had too many mouths to feed.

Alexander shook his head. So much for an innocent age. He shook his head again as one of his thoughts repeated . . . *young children.*

He refocused on the screen. There was Solstice with freckles across her nose and the uneven shoulder line, but she was much younger than she was now. In the picture her chest was flat, but it wasn't flat now. In her green dress . . . well, he had noticed. He realized what he looked at was a photo from when she was practically a child, a photo now destined to run forever on the Internet.

He moved the cursor and saw photos of other girls who also looked young. He clicked back to Solstice. She wore a smile that, now that he was thinking more on it, appeared more fearful than timid.

What kind of man would be attracted to a scared-looking little kid? That was easy. A weird guy attracted to children.

Alexander clicked on the contact line under her photo and saw an email address. He clicked on other young girls' photos and got the same address. All the same operation.

A stable of kids, working for an outfit.

Sex trade.

The remarks Solstice had said came back with new meaning. That she wasn't naïve; that looking young had been an advantage in her work; that her last job had been, "Yes Mister, No Mister. You want me to jump, Mister, just tell me how high."

That all *had* to be about her experience in the sex trade.

No wonder she acted so strange. She must have been either desperate or forced into that sort of life. Forced would explain it best. Maybe she now acted smart-mouthed and bossy because there had been a time when she wasn't the boss of anything, not even herself. As for avoiding being touched, it now made perfect sense. He knew what it was to be pushed around, although he had never been subjected to anything vile.

The last thing Solstice would want was his pity, but he had never felt so sorry for anyone in his life.

He backed out of the site with enough haste to sting his fingers and shut down the laptop and then sat staring at nothing. It wasn't until the Colonel called his name for at least the second time that he looked up. The Colonel was ready to leave and he wanted to know if Alexander needed to return to the house for anything, or should they drive straight to Iris's place for the New Year's dinner.

Alexander knew he couldn't face Solstice. Not after what he'd just learned. She would be able to tell something was wrong. She would read it in his eyes. He might be a failed playwright who ironically possessed an actor's gift, but he couldn't pull *that* off.

But he did know how to get out of dinner.

Without further hesitation, he looked over at the Colonel and dredged up an uncharacteristically weak voice as he said, "I don't feel so good. Too much celebrating last night, I guess." Although he had only had two glasses of punch, he now blotted his face and neck with a tissue as if breaking into a sweat. "I couldn't eat," he said. "You'd better take me back to the house."

At the Colonel's look of concern, Alexander figured he'd better ease up on the seasick act. "My stomach's actually better," he said. "But my head is pounding." He touched his forehead. "I'm sorry about this. Once I'm in the house I'll take a pain pill and crawl into bed."

Chapter 22

On top of Slim's list on the second day of the New Year was asking JJ about her dead friend seeking a toy shop in New Jersey. He left her a message to call him.

When his phone rang later, it wasn't JJ, it was Kroger.

After a back and forth about the New Year's bash—which Slim figured had saved his sanity—Kroger said, "You wanted to know if anything new happened about that dead woman your friend identified?"

"Did and still do," Slim said.

"The blood in her vehicle was hers," Kroger said in his raspy voice. "And on the day before the date the ME gave as her death, an Easy Pass record shows her vehicle crossed the Turnpike Bridge from Pennsylvania to Jersey in the late afternoon, then back here to Pennsylvania a couple of hours after dark. If she was the driver, she was on your side of the river before she drove back here."

Encouraged, Slim said, "You never found the location where she was stabbed, right?"

"Right."

"Kroger, you told me her death date. The day after, we found a vacant house broken into and with blood on the floor. Never found answers. Suppose she was attacked here?"

"So how's the blood get in the car?"

"There looked like a lot of blood in the house, but it wasn't judged to be a fatal amount. She may have gotten away from whoever stabbed her and headed for home. Her attacker could have followed."

Kroger said, "You don't know it's her blood in the house."

"The county will send you a sample."

"Proving something would be good," Kroger said.

"Her purse or her phone, papers, or anything ever show up?"

"Negative," Kroger said.

"The first time we talked about the case, you said you found her vehicle in Glenside, not where she lived. Learn why it was there?"

"That's a story and a half." Kroger laughed. "This fourteen-year-old finds it parked a few blocks from the dead woman's apartment—before her body was found. Keys left in the unlocked vehicle. Kid doesn't see the blood smeared on the seat. He takes the car to Glenside to persuade a pal to joyride. The friend's dad overhears. The next thing, the kid's being taught a lesson, dragged by his own dad to the nearest station. It gets worse for him when it's discovered the owner of the car is missing and her apartment looks ransacked. The fourteen-year-old spends a few rough hours, but his dad gets a lawyer and there's no proof the kid did more than boost a vehicle. Plus, there's verification from a resident who saw the ride on the street where the kid said he found it. So he's off the hook. And get this. When the body's found and makes the news, the kid has the nerve to call and ask for a reward for finding the car."

Slim chuckled. "Sounds like he's got a career ahead of him."

"Politics, probably," Kroger said.

"Got that right," Slim said, thinking of devious committeewoman, Jessi Spellman. After he disconnected, he left a message for the prosecutor's office to send a blood sample to be sent to Kroger.

Chapter 23

"You didn't come to New Year's Day dinner yesterday," Solstice said, her eyes narrowed. She and Alexander were in the back seat of the Colonel's car, heading for the Gibeau farm. "The Colonel said you were sick." She said it like she knew it was a lie.

It *had* been a lie and it made Alexander feel bad, especially his reason for it. Summoning his nerve, he said, "Did you miss me?"

"You wish," she said. "I want to talk with Vivian alone, so don't try butting in. I think she's the right one, but I won't be able to tell just by looking. It was a long time ago."

"How long ago?"

"Long enough." She wrapped her coat around herself tightly and curled into her corner.

How long is long enough, Esstu? he thought. But saying that wouldn't be fair. Her past was her secret. He remembered her saying she'd had sex and didn't want to do it ever again. It had been an awful part of her life. It made him angry, and he didn't know what to do about it.

He gazed out his window as snowy fields, woodlands and occasional houses rolled by. He'd grown up here, but it didn't seem familiar. He had wanted to forget it and realized he'd done a good job. He felt it would be the same looking out a bus window at city streets, nothing personal. Probably because he never felt he fit in anywhere, neither at home nor anyplace else. The only place he felt truly comfortable was when he was busy working inside his own head. Only now, with this business about Solstice, he was in the world and it wasn't pretty.

At the Gibeau farm. Nero and Vivian and the grandmother welcomed the foursome into the kitchen of the house. Greetings, female air kisses and hugs, male handshakes.

Solstice hung back, keeping her coat on, her hands jammed in the pockets, her eyes twin lasers on Vivian, except for a glaring shot at Nero, like she hated him. Alexander figured she'd never met him before, so why the attitude? He thought that if he were casting romantic leads, he'd choose Vivian and Nero in a heartbeat.

"Still thinking about that bike?" Nero said.

"The red Yamaha, yes," Alexander said, thinking that after Solstice went off with Vivian, maybe he and Nero could talk.

But when Solstice went with Vivian, Nero went too. They closed the door and disappeared. The grandmother invited Alexander, the Colonel and Iris to sit at the table. There were matching cups and saucers on a tablecloth with a pink and green flowered border.

"Tea or coffee?" she said. "And lemon for tea if anyone wants it."

Like a stage set, Alexander thought as he sat across from the Colonel, the wrinkled grandmother to his left and Iris to his right. If it had been a performance, the lights would have darkened on the kitchen scene, and the lights where Solstice, Vivian and Nero had moved would have lifted. They'd now be in another "room." They would speak their lines. The audience would hear every syllable, while those in the "kitchen," only a few feet away, were supposed to be as deaf as umbrella stands.

Only this was real life with a closed door instead of an illusion wall. Alexander had good ears, but he didn't stand a chance. Three players had exited to a place that could have been as far off as Pluto, leaving the four in the kitchen to work up their own dialogue.

He wondered what the script would be between Solstice and Vivian.

Death Spins an Indigo Web

* * *

Vivian led Solstice through a dining room and into the small space Nero used as an office. She closed that door and pulled out a chair to sit opposite the desk chair, where she positioned herself. Nero sat on a small couch away from them. Solstice, her coat still on, her hands still in her pockets, took the indicated chair opposite Vivian. She sat hunched and wary.

Vivian thought that Solstice looked frightened and almost dangerously alert. She had known her identity as soon as Francine had said the distinctive name, *Solstice*. The girl had been a child when she had last seen her, but she was still skinny and had those big brown eyes and freckles, and that fragile shoulder. Solstice's parents had her with them when they joined the ragtag group that gathered around Vivian's father, David Mather.

What did Solstice want with her? Seeing the girl biting her lip and holding her silence, Vivian took the lead. "I'm glad to see you again," she said. "I never knew what had happened to you. I understand you've been looking for me and my father, David."

When the girl offered no response, Vivian forged on, disliking how formal she sounded. "I'm sorry to tell you that my father died a number of years ago."

Still no reaction. She strove for an icebreaker. "I remember your parents. You were named after your mother, and became Solstice Two, only with the numeral two superscripted."

"And my brother's name?" Solstice said, her eyes slitted as if she suspected she'd been lured into a con game instead of being the one who had wanted the meeting. She flicked a glance at Nero and snapped it back to Vivian.

"Your brother was Equinox Two. He was named after your father, also with the numeral superscripted." Even back then, Vivian knew enough to realize the names were strange.

Solstice nodded, knowing this the *right* Vivian, with the right answers. And she looked right, with shiny, dark brown hair that had curly waves.

She wondered why some stranger had emailed that David and Vivian were dead, but that must been other people, and it no longer mattered.

She shifted in the chair, her right hand pushed through the hole in her coat lining and then through the slit in her skirt pocket so she could touch the weapon secured to her thigh. The finger blade was fashioned so the backside of the blade was harmless against her palm, but if she extended her hand and index finger, she could flick out the blade with her thumb and it became a miniature scimitar.

Although her eyes were on Vivian, she was all too aware of Nero. She and the other trapped girls had learned to steer clear of handsome men, the men they called the *pretty ones*.

Keeping a wary eye on Nero, Solstice said to Vivian, "My brother was a baby. You changed his pants and stuff. You seemed so grown up."

Vivian smiled. "I wasn't very old, but I'd learned to manage things. After your brother was born, he was sick and your mother couldn't care for him. His food went right through him. I tried to keep him clean."

"My brother died," Solstice said.

Vivian nodded. "He became sicker and wasted away. I'm sorry."

Solstice hunched further into her coat. "What happened to my brother's body?"

"I never knew. We were always moving. He was probably buried in the desert. Were you hoping to learn where he was buried?"

Solstice gave another glance at Nero. He didn't look threatening. He looked concerned for Vivian as if the conversation was dredging up bad memories of the past for her as well. Maybe. She assured herself of the blade's position.

When she'd been twelve and looked more like eight, the old woman who watched the girls gave her a warning. "*The old men are mostly harmless, wanting to imagine they're schooling an innocent. Play them right and you'll be a money-maker. It's the pretty ones to watch out for. They could have anybody, so if they're coming after a young-looking one like you, something's twisted.*"

Solstice had learned the hard way that the old woman was right.

Remembering, Solstice felt her insides tremble. "Send him away," she pleaded. She looked at Vivian—she didn't dare look at Nero. She fought to sound demanding but she only sounded scared. She feared she was going to cry. She gave a cringing glance at Nero, and then back to Vivian. "Please . . ."

She tucked her head down as if her request might lead to punishment. She recalled too well the danger of speaking her mind. She didn't hear any words spoken, but she heard the man, Nero, get up and walk toward Vivian. Solstice sneaked a glance and saw him rest a hand lightly on Vivian's shoulder. Vivian reached to place her hand on his, like a comforting gesture shared.

Solstice watched as he left, and saw the door close behind him. "You wanted him here," she said in a whispery voice to Vivian.

"His presence upset you," Vivian said. "He must remind you of someone."

Solstice didn't answer.

Vivian said, "I was asking if you wanted to find out more about your brother. I don't know where we were when he died. I doubt your parents made an official record of it."

"Why didn't your father save him? People said that your father, that David Mather, could have saved my baby brother."

Vivian looked surprised. "That's a misunderstanding. My father wasn't with us when your brother died. Your brother needed a doctor, but we were in the wilds, and the only vehicle didn't work. My father was a mechanic. If he had been there, he would have fixed the van and gotten your brother to the hospital. That's what people meant."

Feeling desperate, Solstice said, "You were really there? It's really you, Vivian Mather? You knew my mother and father? You really saw them?"

"Yes." Vivian said, "And I knew you, too."

Vivian wondered what was going through the girl's mind. Did she feel that her life back then barely existed? She stretched her brain to try to remember something about that time besides the girl's kooky parents.

"There was a book you liked," Vivian said. "It was called The Little Fur Family."

"It was about furry animals." Solstice's voice was hardly louder than a breath. "They were all nice."

Vivian nodded. "I read it to you." *Many times*, she thought. The little girl had loved the book, probably because the little fur family was such an improvement over her real family.

"Do . . . do you remember anything else?"

Vivian wasn't sure what to say or do, but then she decided. "Let's sit on the couch," she said, getting up. "It's more comfortable." She reached for the girl's hand. Solstice drew away, but not forcefully. Together, they moved to the couch.

"I'll try to remember things," Vivian said as they seated themselves. "I was older. I may recall things you were too little to notice." Vivian wasn't sure what she would say, but once she started, it wasn't hard. She wouldn't lie, but she would only talk about the good things, not the bad things.

"Your father liked to sing," Vivian said. "He had a good voice. Your mother was very beautiful." It was like telling a bedtime story, with all happy endings. "Your father had a guitar. People would gather around." An exaggeration, but it could have happened like that if he hadn't distrusted so many people. "I'll tell you some of the songs I heard him sing."

"Tell me everything," Solstice said in a tone of desperate need. "Tell me everything."

"I will," Vivian said. Solstice curled very close.

"And then," Vivian said, after she'd talked awhile, "when it was time for you to go to bed, I would read the book to you. Your favorite part of your favorite book was when the little fur child picked up the littlest fur animal in the entire world and kissed the little fur animal right on his little fur nose."

For Alexander in the kitchen, time ticked as slowly as grease paint running up hill. The grandmother, Yvette, and Iris and the Colonel seemed to find much to talk about, but there was nothing for him. Nero had come out, but then he'd gone back, apparently to check on what was happening between the two women.

When he came out again, he said to Alexander, "You've never been here, have you? Come outside. I'll show you around."

Alexander leaped at the chance.

Outside, the day was bright and sunny—even more so because of the glare of melting snow. They walked together and talked about the bike. Nero showed him chickens and cows and farm equipment, including an old tractor from two generations back that still ran just fine.

When they came inside again, Alexander felt like a million bucks. He and Nero had gone rambling around, talking the whole time. It had been great. They stamped their chilled feet on the door mat and entered the warm kitchen to find the Colonel and Iris and Solstice standing by the table chatting with Vivian, obviously ready to leave. Solstice still had her coat on. Alexander wondered if she had kept it on the whole time. He looked across the table at her.

"The right Vivian?" he asked.

"Yes." She smiled. That was the third time Alexander felt he saw a totally natural expression on her face.

Nero and Vivian stood looking through the kitchen window at the Colonel's disappearing car, Vivian leaning back against Nero's strong body, his arms about her waist. His grandmother had told them there were leftovers in the refrigerator for lunch if they wanted, but she was going for a "lie down."

Inclining his head, Nero said softly, "I hope it wasn't too tough, reliving unhappy times."

"I think it was good for me to realize how much in the past those days actually were," she said.

"Solstice asked you a lot of questions when I was there."

"I don't think it was those answers she cared about."

"I peeked in once. What was that about the fur nose?"

Vivian smiled. "That was from a story book I once read to her. She needed memories of when she was a young and innocent child. Things were hard for her, but she didn't know anything different. I remember one morning when she and her family were suddenly gone."

"What? The entire family just disappeared?"

"Yes. When my father looked in their tent, there was nothing left except the weird foods they ate, foods that left them sick and skinny. Solstice's parents were strange and paranoid—maybe they thought someone in camp was poisoning them."

"Did you call the police?"

"It would have been the sheriff, but no. Some of my father's friends had an aversion to law enforcement. They had nothing to do with the run-off family. Why endure a bunch of meaningless questions?"

"And nobody cared where Solstice was?"

"She was with her parents."

"But they didn't give her good care."

"Life there was different. Yes, she was always hungry. I used to sneak food to her, knowing her parents would be angry if they found out. Solstice was told that evil people were after them, that they sent general delivery packages to trick them into answering so they could be tracked down. I don't think anybody in camp saw any sense in their fears and they considered it none of their business."

"I'm trying to imagine people thinking that way," Nero said. "Here, everybody's business is everybody else's business."

Vivian smiled, seeing his face reflected in the window glass as she answered. "Our camp was the only town I knew. There, the rule was, if people wanted to be private, let them be private."

"Not so easy to disappear."

"It was a big county out west. It wasn't like it is now, with cell phones everywhere, or GPS tracking and traffic cameras."

"And that was the last you knew of Solstice until now?"

"Yes. Today I learned she thought that her mother must have died in a hospital and then her father gave her to other people. She never saw him again."

"He just gave her away? That's incredible!"

"Actually, I suspect he sold her. These people took control of her in a way that was very wrong." Vivian's voice choked momentarily. "It took her a long while to tell me and I don't think she would want me to tell you more. But . . ." She turned, pivoting within the circle of Nero's arms to face him, her body never losing contact with his.

She looked up into his clear gray eyes. "Remember how I told you Aunt Elizabeth sent money to my father? Solstice's parents might have had family who did the same, only they had rejected everything from their past, including their real names. There was a small stove in their tent they fueled with collected sticks. They were always brewing awful tea that probably scrambled their brains. One time I came in and stinky stuff bubbled on the stove. The fire was burning and they were adding fuel from a cardboard box. It looked like real money, but they told me it was fake money from a game."

"You didn't think so?"

"I accepted it at the time. But I know we stopped at a post office that day and there was a package for them. Thinking back, I believe their family was sending money to help them. It wasn't fake money—it was real. They were a starving family, yet there they were, feeding the fire and laughing as they watched real money go up in smoke."

Chapter 24

Alexander was struck dumb by the great thing his mother had done. She had bought him the red Yamaha! And two helmets so he could have a passenger.

The Colonel and Iris had dropped Solstice and Alexander off at his mother's house after being at the Gibeau farm. Alexander expected his mother to immediately drive him and Solstice to the bus stop. Instead, there was this wonderful surprise.

Solstice, who'd been quiet after meeting with Vivian, stared at the second helmet, but didn't say anything.

"Bob Smithers told me you were interested," Pilar said. "It seems smart since your car broke down. You used ride a bike and you've said you still have your license. Bob told me that once a person knows how to ride, it's not forgotten." She frowned. "The problem is the weather. You should take the bus back to the city today and pick the bike up later, when it's warmer."

"No!" Alexander caressed the bike handles. He couldn't bear leaving it behind.

Pilar smiled. "I shouldn't have given it to you without expecting you to feel that way. Bob said that the roads are clear despite snow on the ground. The problem is the cold. I learned from him what gear you both need to keep from freezing. The helmet visors are special to keep them from fogging. There are ski masks to keep your faces from freezing, and gloves and socks and boots."

She looked at Solstice. "I guessed at your size, but probably too big is better than too small."

"For me, too?" Solstice's eyes were wide.

"You came here together, so I assumed you would return together. I bought warmers for you both to tuck inside your boots and gloves. And also, leather jackets with thick linings."

"Such wonderful gifts!" Alexander said. "For me and Solstice, too."

While Solstice was in the bathroom changing into her new warm underclothing, Pilar said, "Of course I made purchases for her too. I'm pleased that you finally have a real girlfriend."

Alexander's face went hot, like cooking under a spotlight. "You knew Ramona wasn't real?"

"I suspected you made up a girlfriend so I wouldn't worry about you being alone on holidays." Her smile became all-knowing. "Also, she was an excuse when you didn't want to visit."

Alexander tried to work up a scowl. His mother always knew *everything*. Then he laughed. "Okay, you got me."

His mother gave him a hug. "Now you can use Solstice as an excuse."

"Maybe," he said, and laughed again.

The reason he was happy was because his mother really didn't know *everything,* like how he messed up with girls. He'd be in bed with a girl and in the second act, first scene, his traitorously eager body would jump ahead to the third act, final scene. The curtain would drop and it would all be over. He'd be so ashamed he would want to dissolve through the mattress and commune with the springs. Claiming he had a girlfriend had kept him safe from embarrassment. But he wasn't going to explain *that* to his mother, God, no!

Alexander and Solstice were soon rolling down his mother's driveway.

Her long coat and their other clothing and items were in a case behind the seat. His mother had thought of everything.

He drove past the snowy bushes against the house, leaving behind his questions about the gunshots. He was too excited about the bike to worry about bullet clues. They could wait.

He played with the steering, tried different speeds, tested the balance, then took a few side roads, being cautious, getting used to the machine, but Bob had been right—once you knew how you didn't forget.

Solstice was pressed against his back with both arms tight around his middle. He felt he was in a cozy cocoon. Luckily, she didn't mind touching *him*.

He thought about the escort website. He was sure she didn't know about it and would hate that he'd found it. She was so secretive. He still had no way to reach her except email, and no idea where in Brooklyn she lived. She had called him from Iris's phone, so he didn't even have her cell number. He doubted that anything could be done about that skanky website. The people who controlled it were the only ones who could fix it. They wouldn't want to, and he didn't want anything to do with them.

He realized like a light dawning how perfect he and Solstice were for one another. She didn't want anybody to touch her, while he, well—could a guy be a born-again virgin, too? The thought made him laugh and the vibration made him aware anew of the arms clasped around him. It went through his head that if her hands got cold, she could tuck them inside his jacket. He thought about that one a little bit more and then decided he had better concentrate on his driving.

His route would have been shorter going directly to the new highway connecting Melton to the New Jersey Turnpike, but he went toward the old highway because it took him through town. He wanted the thrill of riding up Main Street, and then through Rancine, or Rancidville, as JRope kids called it. Rancine was only a few minutes away from JumpRope, but the kids went to a different high school and were sports rivals. He'd once played in a football game against them. *Zoom through Rancine and let them eat my dust.* Alexander grinned behind the mask that kept his nose from freezing into an icy stump.

He reached the turn onto the old highway with surprising quickness and was soon approaching the newly reconstructed bridge that went over the Three Sisters River. A car moved alongside on his left and it seemed to be keeping pace. From the corner of his eye, Alexander saw it was a tan-colored sedan.

The road was two lanes in either direction. A car could still pass, if that's what the driver wanted to do, but ahead were double white no passing lines on the steep incline leading to the bridge.

When the car continued matching Alexander's speed, he accelerated. The car did, too, and then started edging toward him. He tried to see the driver, but with the helmet, he couldn't see without turning his head, and he needed to keep his attention on the road. Solstice's arms had tightened and she started yelling. He didn't try to understand her. He was too busy keeping on the road with this nut crowding him. What did the guy think he was doing? Any second, the tan-colored fender would sideswipe the bike.

Alexander saw the bridge guard rail coming up ahead. Another few seconds and his bike would be caught between the car and the rail.

Worst place to be! Alexander steered to his right and slammed on the brakes. His tires skidded in gravel and snowy weeds along the verge.

The bike spun off the road. It happened in an instant. He was sailing free and tumbling. He landed hard, the thin snow cover on the grass incline doing little to cushion his fall.

The bike slid sideways down the slope toward the river and stopped.

With the wind knocked out of him, Alexander didn't know which way was up. The sounds of tearing metal came from somewhere to his left and above. Still lying on the ground, he looked up and saw the tan car ripping along the edge of a bridge guard rail. With a horrid screeching, the car flipped like a circus acrobat over the torn railing.

In free fall it turned once in what seemed an impossible suspension of time and then smashed upside down alongside the bridge approach. It spun and then skidded in the snow as the bike had done only it was heavier and didn't stop until reaching the slushy edge of the river.

The sounds seemed to echo and re-echo. Then all was silent except for Alexander's gasping attempts to draw air into his lungs.

He stumbled to his feet and frantically looked for Solstice. In relief, he saw her standing, clutching her helmet in both hands. She stared at the car.

"Are you okay?" he said, helmet in his hand and tearing off his mask. He hurried toward her as fast as possible on the snow-slicked ground.

"The motorcycle landed," she said, her voice strained. "The car flew."

"But you're not hurt?"

Not answering, but looking okay, she continued staring at the car.

Alexander struggled off his gloves and fumbled his phone out from beneath his bundled clothing and dialed 911.

Chapter 25

Holly heard about Alexander's bike accident the day it happened. The driver was dead, but Alexander and his girlfriend were unhurt. They had even been able to drive the bike back to New York. As to the cause of the accident, the only thing Holly knew was that the driver was a stranger. It was Friday, and the final plans for the evening's reorganization meeting had Holly too busy to think more about the accident.

When Slim called him down to his office, Holly feared it meant trouble connected with the coming evening.

Walking to the police department end of the building, Holly fingered his necktie, a pattern of row upon row of gray knots: bowline, clove hitch, anchor bend and more, on a dark gray background. A clever design. Know Holly's necktie, know his mood. Holly was all knotted up.

He wasn't comfortable with State Senator Fergusson coming to swear in Jessi Spellman. Holly knew nothing bad about the man, except that he had ignored JumpRope for years. Yet now he was coming and making a fuss over Jessi. Fergusson even had a security team—an outfit that employed former military men for events. They'd come to check the building. It all smelled like a publicity stunt.

Holly found Slim slouched in his office chair, the heels of his boots propped on an open desk drawer. A half-empty bag of cheese snacks rested in one of his long-fingered hands. The small office had a single window, too high to show anything except the sky. Bright blue, cloudless, untroubled.

Holly took a seat. "Don't tell me there's bad news about Fergusson."

"Nah. He'll arrive with his security guys and a raft of news people. I called to tell you good news because of a problem that's been delayed. I heard from Isaac over at the county. The blood in the vacant house is a match to the woman the Philly force found dead over there, JJ's friend."

Holly frowned. "How is that good news?"

"It's the delay that's good," Slim said. "The prosecutor's office won't release their findings until tomorrow. There will be nothing on the news tonight to compete with the reorganization."

"You're right, that is good," Holly said. "I can imagine the headline: *Knifed in JumpRope, Dead in Philadelphia*. Sounds like a sad song."

"For Carol Vetter it was. What made her a victim, and who used the knife? Hate to say the words, but it's a mystery. I'll be telling JJ the little we know later tonight."

"After reorganization," Holly said.

"Yeah, she can wrap up an article about tonight before she turns to writing about Carol."

"It will be a shock for her to learn her friend was attacked here."

"Maybe not so much." Slim took up a handful of snacks. "Remember I got word that Carol had talked to magazine co-workers about coming to a toy store in Jersey? They remembered it wrong. I found out from JJ that Carol joked that JumpRope sounded like the name of a toy town in a kids' book."

"So she came here for an article?"

"Don't know. Her writing career was fashion-related. Nobody like that around here."

Holly grinned. "Did you forget about our fashionable Francine?"

Slim grimaced. "Stylish and her nose into everything." He finished the snacks, crumpled the bag and wiped crumbs from his mouth.

"Here's something else. The name on the dead man's license was Neil Bannister, which hasn't yet made the news. Alexander and his friend, a big-eyed girl named Solstice, say they never heard of him, but somebody here must have."

"Why? He was a stranger passing through, wasn't he? That's what I heard."

"Don't think so. In the wee hours after midnight on New Year's Eve, Darlene Gage spotted a car at Juan's Café. She figured Juan was up to old his tricks, renting out rooms. She recorded the New York State tag number and turned it over to the department to run it. It was the same car that flew off the bridge."

Holly frowned. "He must have attended a New Year's Eve party here and drank too much to drive. Juan probably had his room-to-rent sign up. When Bannister's name is printed, somebody will say something."

"Maybe. I sent a couple of men over to Juan's place. Juan swears he felt sorry because the man was lost, so he gave him a room out of the goodness of his heart. You know how much we believe that. But Bannister stayed two nights. He was here for a reason."

Holly couldn't help smiling. "And Darlene missed the car being here a second night? I've heard that Juan calls her the code enforcement dragon."

"Yeah, but she wasn't here the second night. She went to her daughter's for a New Year's Day dinner, stayed over, and wasn't back until after the accident. We notified the department in Bannister's area. Haven't heard from them yet."

Slim put his feet down to the floor and turned in his chair. "There was a rifle in Bannister's car. Used but not cleaned."

"A surprise, but what's it mean?" Holly said.

"Hate to repeat myself," Slim said, "but that's a mystery, too."

Chapter 26

The JumpRope Township Reorganization meeting that night enjoyed a packed house.

Francine Smithers was steamed. She was dressed in her finest and carrying her new Valentino purse and then had to sit and listen to State Senator Earl Smythe Fergusson blather about how the town was so lucky to have a fine public servant like Jessi Spellman on committee. Anybody with a brain knew Jessi was a skunk. What did they feed those idiots in Trenton? Hallucination pills?

Bad enough to have seen Jessi's little paw on the Bible. If Jessi Spellman touching Holy Scripture wasn't a sacrilege, Francine didn't know what was.

Posed photos of Jessi and Fergusson were taken after the oath had been completed. Francine winced from the glare of the senator's used car salesman's smile, showing every tooth he owned. His smile was like one of those . . . Francine drew a blank at the word she wanted, but it was some sort of musical instrument. Pilar would know.

By the time the meeting had concluded, everyone was ready for the celebration at the Teddy Bear Bar and Grill Restaurant. The dining tables in one of the medium-sized sections had been exchanged for tall round tables without chairs, allowing more people to occupy the space. The chairs were lined up against a long wall. Pilar sat in one of them with a plate of refreshments on her lap. Her blonde-streaked dark hair was pulled back to reveal vintage rhinestone clip-on earrings.

"So how's Alexander doing?" Francine asked, plunking down in the chair next to Pilar. "Bob checked out the bike. It's was in good shape despite the punishment Alexander gave it."

Pilar failed to react to the wrongheaded notion that the accident was Alexander's fault. "Bob was very helpful," she said. "Alexander wasn't hurt, and fortunately Solstice wasn't injured either."

"I guess not. They rode the bike to New York City later, didn't they?"

"Solstice insisted." Pilar smiled. "She said that if he was scared to climb on it again, I could drive him back in the car and she would meet him there with the bike."

Francine showed surprised. "She's a wisp, with freckles and something wrong with her shoulders. Nancy Lou said the girl has an S-curve in her spine—scoliosis." As she spoke, she tucked her chin in and sat even more soldier-like, as if to make an example of proper spinal alignment. "I'm surprised she knows how to drive a motorcycle."

"I doubt she does." Pilar took a bite of a miniature éclair. "She told me she said it to get Dimples off his duff."

"Dimples?"

"They play a game with names. At least she does."

Francine cocked her head. "I suppose Alexander did have dimples. Hard to remember he used to be good-looking. With that beard, who can tell?" She waved a hand. "The real reason I came over was to ask the name of that musical instrument that's like a little accordion, a squeeze-box thing. We saw a framed picture of one when we shopped. A silly picture to have hanging in a person's house."

"A concertina," Pilar said, ignoring Francine's bull in a china shop style of conversation.

"Concertina," Francine repeated with a nod. "That's what our state senator's smile reminds me of. The more he stretches it out, the more teeth you see. Holly doesn't know why the man was so set on swearing-in Jessi. Toria said politicians keep lists of people to tap for funds, and there's no one here to tap."

"If the senator thinks of politics in terms of money, he probably assumes that if Jessi won, she has wealthy friends," Pilar said.

"It doesn't take big money to win in JumpRope," Francine said.

"See it from Fergusson's viewpoint," Pilar said. "His experience had taught him the necessity of generous financial supporters."

"I suppose. And who knows what Jessi told him to make herself sound important. You should never have directed her to that ad company that produced that flyer she sent out."

"I accept blame for that," Pilar said. "I never guessed she would say things that would bring a dead man's family additional pain."

"You should have known she'd use anything," Francine said, but she knew it was true. Jessi had crossed a line with Pilar when she demeaned a dead man. Pilar had been a widow for over twenty years, and she still went into seclusion on the anniversary of her husband's death.

Leaving Pilar behind, Francine made her way through the crowd and to the group standing around Fergusson. He was holding court with Jessi and Jessi's husband, Arnie. The mayor was there too, along with Toria, her new engagement ring gleaming in the pleasantly subdued light. Iris, the Colonel and several other residents were also there. Standing with pad and pen was reporter, JJ Gilbert.

Nancy Lou, Darlene, and Amy stood further back, near one of the teddy bear village murals that decorated the restaurant walls. One of Fergusson's security men stood next to the entrance, perhaps imagining he was in a bodyguard film.

"Fergusson didn't only snub the Auxiliary," Darlene said quietly to her friends, her ash blonde hair falling so straight it looked starched and ironed. "His office kissed off the Ladies Civic Club with a form letter when we invited him to our Memorial Day observance. We weren't impressive enough."

In contrast with Darlene, Nancy Lou wore her black hair in a flaring style that made the most of her natural curls. "A news magazine showed him attending a New York benefit auction with a crowd of moneyed people," she said. "He likes being with movers and shakers."

"So why is he here?" Amy said. "None of us have struck oil."

The three of them joined Toria, Iris, and Francine, to stand near Fergusson, who remained the center of attention as he expounded on the delights of JumpRope. JJ took notes as Fergusson raved about his enjoyable day, mentioning by name several local business locations he had visited. All six members of the Voodoo Club—Amy, Toria, Darlene, Nancy Lou, Iris and Francine—listened in stoic silence as he launched into a rhapsody of how he was looking forward to returning when Jessi and her husband opened their new restaurant.

"Such brilliant plans! Committeewoman Spellman explained them all. And such a marvelous location, on a main highway and next to what promises to be a master housing development. Now, what was the developer's name?" He snapped his fingers as if in the attempt to aid his memory as he looked at Jessi. "I know you mentioned it to me, said what a good friend he's been to you. I thought he would be here."

"Acer Wolfgang," JJ said, getting her words out before Jessi could speak.

"Oh, yes, I suppose that's right." Fergusson's manner was vague as if he had never heard of Acer Wolfgang, Manhattan wheeler and dealer extraordinaire and the wealthiest individual to set foot in JumpRope in all recent memory.

The members of the Voodoo Club, positioned as they were, received the flipper bounce of Fergusson's professed ignorance of Wolfgang's name, realization striking them each like the chrome steel ball in a pinball machine. The six of them lit up with a sudden but silent understanding of Fergusson's true interest in the community.

Darlene's mind lit up with: *Acer's his target!*

Francine's brain *binged* with the thought: *Can't tell me Fergusson doesn't know about a man who wears a forty thousand dollar watch.*

And Toria said to herself: *I see who he's chasing.*

And Nancy Lou and Amy simultaneously thought: *Bingo! Acer Wolfgang.*

And Iris, always the last to catch on to things, looked at Fergusson in puzzlement. And then, as Iris glanced at her friends, she suddenly lit up with: *Now I see! Senator Fergusson hopes Jessi will get Acer Wolfgang to give him money!*

Chapter 27

Two articles to write, thought JJ Gilbert
One was about her murdered friend, Carol Vetter.
The other was about the town reorganization meeting and the following social gathering.

Experience had taught her to tackle the tough job first. That was the one about Carol. She looked at her notes from Slim when he'd told her it was Carol's blood in the empty Pullen Farm house.

Her article wouldn't reveal her personal emotions, and someone on the *Monitor* staff would supply the headline, probably something shocking to grab attention. Her story would tell readers of the unexplained and tragic death of a talented writer who had made her mark with award-winning magazine features and a successful book, a woman who surely would have had many more accomplishments had her life not been cut short.

As she wrote, she remembered that shortly before her death, Carol had wanted to get in touch. Had it been a story that had brought her to JumpRope? JJ felt despair. Would she ever learn the truth? Putting that question aside, she reviewed the Philadelphia news report about Carol's body being found. Her article would contain some of that as background, plus information from Slim.

Tall, rangy Allen "Slim" Parkinson, with his easy manner and rumpled, sun-streaked light brown hair. *Someday*, she thought, *I'll have to buy him a thank you drink.*

She finished the article, sent it electronically and tried to clear it from her mind as she turned to the reorganization meeting. Straight reporting. A good thing, because her opinion of Fergusson wasn't flattering. She considered him a scheming politician, looking to fill his war chest for a race to a national office even though he'd barely started his second term at the state level. His attention to Jessi? He thought she would win him friends. He had no idea what the people who really cared about the town thought about her.

For intensive interviews, JJ used the recorder on her phone, but for brief comments from a politician in a noisy room, her written notes would be enough to give readers the flavor of the evening. Besides, there was nothing Fergusson had said that was any different than what he said wherever he went: he loved his job, he loved the state of New Jersey and he would do everything possible to answer the needs of the people, and so on. The only interesting thing was his pretense that he didn't know the name of Acer Wolfgang.

She sat back in her chair, wondering. Had Fergusson already tapped Wolfgang for funds or had he hoped they'd meet for the first time at the reorganization meeting? What was going on, if anything, between the two of them? She wanted to pursue the question and thought of a way to achieve her goal.

The finished piece included photos of reelected Azalea Roundtree and Jessi Spellman, with brief notes about each. A photo of State Senator Fergusson would show a neat, moderately handsome man, his hairstyle adding an extra inch to his average height and a smile bright enough to be battery-powered. The article closed with Fergusson's mention of the coming housing development on the former Mather farm and included a reference directing readers to learn more about the development and Wolfgang by turning to the newspaper's business section.

Anyone who jumped there would find another one of her articles. It wasn't much, but she would use it to justify calling both Fergusson and Wolfgang with additional questions.

Taking a break from a San Francisco conference, Acer Wolfgang's electronic tablet gave him news from JumpRope via the *Melton Monitor*. He took a moment to consult his Breitling—a pocket timepiece on a matching chain. The old-fashioned embellishments satisfied some quirkiness within him to feel somewhat Victorian.

His thoughts went to the fascinating Darlene Gage. Did she have quirky moments? So much he didn't know, so much he was determined to learn.

Returning attention to the *Monitor*, Acer narrowed his eyes at the photo of the newly sworn-in Jessi Spellman. Was anything more certain than death, taxes, or the idiosyncrasies of the voting public? He studied the photo of the man who had officiated at the ceremony, Senator Earl Smythe Fergusson. Acer was familiar with the name, but not in connection with the township of JumpRope. He noted the reporter's byline: JJ Gilbert. Acer had spoken with her when he sought information about the town before acquiring the Mather property. He swiped the screen to the referenced business section and found the piece about himself.

Nice writing, nothing new, and quickly researched. Still, the fact that it had appeared at all intrigued him. He felt he saw JJ's quick and clever mind behind it.

He knew she would soon call for an update about the development's progress, and also would call the senator to discuss his new-found interest in the community. Would she create veiled questions about their possible association?

Another story, also with JJ's byline, had a different tone. It was about a murdered Philadelphia fashion writer, stabbed in an empty JumpRope house. There was also a report of a fatality when a man drove his car off a bridge.

Acer shook his head. So much tragedy for the quiet country community.

Another online subscriber to the *Melton Monitor* was also reading the report of the bridge accident and was exceedingly displeased. So difficult to find good help! Little surprise that a town with such a silly name had been the site of two bungled assignments.

The magazine writer had been finished off, but the newly resurfaced Solstice creature had escaped the obituary page. Neil Bannister had proved beyond useless. The gathering of materials from the writer's apartment had been well done, but the murder itself had been sloppy. The magazine writer had known entirely too much, but attacking her in New Jersey and not finishing her off until she reached Philadelphia and then drowning her? Suppose she'd gotten away? Why not a simple fatal mugging on her city street? No one would have blinked twice at that. Bannister had been a screw-up—good that he was dead.

Eyes flicked over another story, caught and held attention. It was an entirely different story, and yet . . .

Was there a way to spin it so it could all weave together?

Chapter 28

At the end of the week after the holidays, Vivian and Nero had made sure that the farm and his grandmother would be cared for during their absence. Early in the morning, they set forth on Nero's mission, Vivian with her fingers crossed.

The families of two of the men who had been in his company were in nearby states, Pennsylvania and Delaware. Another was in Virginia. The most distant was in Tennessee. Vivian found her experience as a traveling concierge helpful. When she'd first come to JumpRope, she had intended only a short break from her job. Back then, she'd led an independent life. And now? She only knew she was content at the Gibeau farm with Nero and prayed she could help him with what he suffered.

His driver's license restored, he was at the wheel. Over the holidays, the pills prescribed for him had worked well, but he'd refused to renew the prescription, He stuck to his conviction that visiting the families would settle his mind. He normally paid scant attention to town events, yet now, that's what he wanted to talk about.

Vivian's suspected that it was another example of avoidance. He didn't want to discuss what might lie ahead. Instead, he spoke about what they were leaving behind.

He said how good it was that Solstice had found Vivian after so many years, and also what Bob had told him about State Senator Fergusson and the anger the members of Francine's club felt toward him.

Vivian decided she might as well go along with his mood and the topic. "I met the Colonel in the food market. He said Iris told him their club was investigating Fergusson because he'd ignored the town until he thought Jessi was a way to interest Acer in his political plans."

"Investigating?" Nero said.

"That's apparently what Iris told him. The Colonel said Iris and her Voodoo friends are probably making a Fergusson doll to jab with pins."

Nero chuckled. The miles spun away. They left the New Jersey Turnpike, then crossed the Delaware River and were on the Pennsylvania Turnpike.

"Acer is no friend of Jessi, so that will hardly play into Fergusson's scheme," Vivian said.

"Come on," Nero said. "Fergusson thinks he can persuade Acer to be a backer with the promise of rewarding his engineering firm when he's in a power seat."

"Won't work," Vivian said. "Acer is his own man."

"I like Acer," Nero said with a grin. "Even if I didn't, it's too fine a day to argue."

Their first stop was at a farm in Pennsylvania where Quint's wife, who had remarried, greeted them warmly. She and Nero embraced and she cried a bit. She said that Quint had been a good man when she married him and was a good man to the end. Unfortunately, they had eventually lived apart for the sake of their son. Quint could become confused and violent and that put the child in danger.

"Even though we were apart, we still loved one another," she said. "I would never have made the final break from him, and he knew it. He felt he couldn't continue as things were. He made his decision so his pain would be ended and his son and I could eventually move on."

Nero and Vivian didn't stay long. There was nothing more to say. The woman who had been Quint's wife embraced Nero again as they parted.

As they drove away, Nero said. "We'll never see her again."

"Is that okay?" Vivian said.

"She'll never forget Quint because of their son, and she can be happy because she's moved on. That's what Quint wanted for her. There was nothing she needs now, nothing I could do for her. Quint would be content."

"Yes," Vivian said and she could see that Nero's mind had been settled. *One down and three more to go*, she thought, still not trusting that this was a good thing.

Yancy's destruction had left no remains to be sent home for burial, but his parents in Delaware had managed to accept it. His father said, "From the beginning of time there have been men who never returned to their families. Many parents never knew what fate had overtaken their sons. With Yancy, we knew," he said proudly. "He died doing his duty and in the company of his friends."

Nero and Vivian left. "That's good,'" he said.

"It's wonderful that they feel proud instead of being filled with questions," Vivian said.

"It was," Nero said. "It was good to touch base with them. To hear what they had to say."

Two more to go, Vivian thought, *maybe Nero was right about this journey.*

They reached Greg's family in Virginia on their second day. That visit took an entirely different direction from the one with Yancy's family.

Greg's parents were bitter against the war and resentful of their son's death. They insisted, as if it were a shared badge of honor, that they would never recover.

Greg hadn't been married, but his sister came to the house when she learned of Nero's and Vivian's visit. She privately told them, "My parents' marriage was in trouble before Greg went into the service. Their resentment of what happened to him is what's keeping them together now. They will never give it up because without it they would have nothing."

Vivian and Nero held hands as they drove away, not speaking of Greg's family and a tragedy that went far deeper than his death.

Vivian thought she'd never heard a story so senseless and sad. She was worried all over again about what it did to Nero. That night, however, he was willing to talk about it.

"Greg wouldn't have been happy with how his family has reacted to his death, but there's nothing I can do to change things."

"The sister made that clear," Vivian said, not sure that was the right thing to say.

"If they decide to pull out of it, they'll have her," Nero said. "She'll do what she can."

Vivian decided he sounded resigned to the situation, and that night he slept well, but she knew visiting Sam's family would be the hardest, not only because he and Nero had become close friends, but because Nero had held Sam as the man drew his final breath.

Chapter 29

They reached Tennessee the afternoon of the next day.

Sam's wife, Helen, greeted them warmly. As she reached up to embrace Nero, she said, "My goodness! I've seen your photo, but you're even better looking in real life." Leaving him red-faced, she turned to Vivian. "And you! What a splendid couple you two make."

Neither of them knew what to say. Vivian was glad when Helen turned and led them into a neat living room with country-style furnishings. Vivian thought that no matter how often Nero's good looks were mentioned, it made him feel awkward. He simply didn't believe it—he was just him.

Their coats off, Vivian and Nero sat on a plaid couch. Helen sat opposite on a matching chair. Between them was a low round maple table. Helen set out coffee, cream and sugar, and a plate of cookies.

When they were settled, coffee mugs in hand, Helen said, "Our son, Sam's and mine, is on a play date with a friend, and will be back soon. I want you to meet him. Ethan was born after Sam died. Ethan was Sam's late father's name."

Helen rambled on about Ethan. It seemed to Vivian that there was something Helen wanted to say but was having trouble with it. Looking at Nero, Helen finally said: "When it happened at the last . . . did Sam say anything?"

"He wanted to," Nero said. "He tried, but he couldn't get the words out. I can tell you this: from everything I knew about him, his words would have been about you and the coming baby."

Tears in her eyes, Helen turned to speak to Vivian. "Several months before Sam's death, he had a leave. We met in Italy for what we called our second honeymoon. After that, we communicated over the Internet."

"You told him about the baby on Skype," Nero said. "He was so happy. You'd had testing and he knew it would be a boy. He kept saying, 'I can't wait to kiss his little face.'"

Helen's eyes widened. "Those exact words? I know he was thrilled but I never heard him say it in quite that way."

"Those exact words," Nero said. "He said them to me a couple of times. Not at the end, but I know he was thinking of you and the child."

Helen nodded and then said, "I'm sorry, there's something I have to do." She stood and moved around the coffee table and toward him. Even seated, Nero was tall. Still standing, Helen didn't have to bend far to peer directly into his face. She stared into Nero's clear grey eyes for what seemed a long time before she stepped away.

Vivian thought Nero looked shaken by Helen's actions and relieved when she resumed her seat.

"I'm sorry," Helen said. "I needed to look into your eyes, the last eyes Sam looked into before he died. I thought that somehow. . ." She broke off, ducking her head and clasping her arms about herself.

After a long moment, she lifted her head. "Sam and I talked about what we would do if anything happened to either of us. We said that the survivor should feel free to marry again. He joked and said that if it was him who went first, he'd give me a sign. I've met this man, Jerry. He's a good man, and he would be a good father for Ethan. But I've been waiting for a sign." She looked at Nero. "It's so silly of me.

Looking into your eyes . . . as if I'd find a message from him." She began to cry. "So silly."

A knock on the front door broke the moment. The door burst open and a little boy dashed into the room. A woman stuck her head in and called to Helen, "Ethan had a great time. Got to run!"

The door closed.

On her feet, and looking steady again. Helen went to the youngster who had halted, startled to see strangers. Helen introduced Nero and Vivian.

Ethan had trouble with Nero's name and his mother enunciated, *"Near-row."*

"Row?" he echoed, and then he giggled. "'Row, row your boat!'"

"He knows the nursery rhyme," his mother explained.

Nero laughed. "Ro is what my grandmother calls me."

The child, who was plump and blond like his mother, turned to Vivian. "Mayree?"

Vivian, thinking he was calling her Mary, repeated her name, but Helen shook her head. "It's still the rhyme. Mayree is how he says merrily."

"I get it." Vivian smiled and recited, "'Row, row, row your boat,' and then the other part, 'Merrily, merrily, merrily, merrily.'"

"'Wife is but a dream!'" Ethan chortled.

"'Life is but a dream,'" his mother corrected with a smile, then said to Nero and Vivian, "He has trouble pronouncing the letter L."

Helen brought a cup of juice for Ethan. He gulped it and ran off. He returned with toy vehicles, a blue pickup and a silver Jeep. He took them to Nero, who moved to sit on the floor. It soon became clear that Ethan's game was to scoot the trucks across the floor toward one another and make them crash. Each time they connected, Ethan laughed and clapped his hands.

"He's all boy," Helen said. Her voice faltered. "He needs a father."

Vivian smiled and nodded, not know what else to do.

"He's excited to have someone to play with," Helen said, "but he usually has a nap around this time. All at once, he'll collapse, like a switch has turned off." She turned to Vivian. "I don't see rings on either of you. You two aren't married yet?"

Vivian shook her head, feeling uncomfortable.

Helen's attention went to her son and Nero. "He'll make a good father," she said.

It went through Vivian's mind that Nero's grandmother once told her she had good hips for bearing children. Back then, she hadn't thought of having children and would have vowed she never would. Now, well—her gaze went to Nero—she was no longer the same person.

Ethan, his eyelids becoming heavy, curled on the floor by Nero's knees, pushing the toy truck with one hand and starting to suck his thumb.

"I think he's had it," Helen said with a fond laugh.

Aware of his mother's intention as she started to move toward him, Ethan crawled forward and launched himself into Nero's arms.

"Tired, Buddy?" Nero asked. "Maybe we should get up off the floor." Holding the boy, Nero stood and moved back to the couch beside Vivian, the child cradled against his chest. "How's this?" Nero said. Ethan gave Nero a sleepy smile.

Helen, who had been ready to take the child, paused as Ethan, peering up at Nero, made a sudden movement. Shifting, he reached to place his chubby hands on either side of Nero's face, pulling his head down so he could peer into Nero's eyes.

Vivian held her breath not knowing why. The child was intent as if something was happening although no one was moving at all.

Ethan said something so softly that Vivian couldn't make out the words. The toddler took one hand from Nero's face and placed it on his own cheek, his expression expectant. Vivian saw the emotion in Nero's face as he bent forward and kissed Ethan's cheek. The child laughed in delight and gave Nero a wet, smacking kiss in return. Smiling in contentment, the child rested his head against Nero's chest and closed his eyes. His body sagged softly.

Helen, who still had not moved, said to Nero, "Ethan stared at you and said something. And then . . . well, it seemed odd. What did he say?"

"He said . . ." Nero's voice broke. Still holding the boy cradled against him, he regained control and struggled to lighten the moment as he looked at Helen and said, "You told us Ethan has trouble with his Ls. He said 'widdle' instead of little." Nero's voice broke again. "I don't know what he thought he saw, but he looked into my eyes and said, 'Kiss my little face.'"

Chapter 30

Vivian and Nero were silent as they left Helen's house. There was no doubt in Vivian's mind that Helen was convinced that her dead husband's spirit, working through Nero and Ethan, had given her the sign she'd been looking for. With joyful tears, she had taken the child from Nero's arms and repeatedly thanked him.

"Her parting words were that she would call us," Vivian said. "I don't know what to think about what happened, but if Helen does call, I'm sure it will be about her and Jerry."

Nero made no reply. Vivian looked at him. His expression seemed inward as if he wasn't fully aware of his surroundings. He'd paused at the car, which was parked with the passenger side facing them. Nero stared at the keys in his hand, as if uncertain of what they were.

"He was warm against my chest," he said. Vivian thought he spoke of the child, but then he said, "I was holding him . . . he was warm against me . . . he was trying to speak . . ."

Vivian tensed in distress. Was Nero slipping into the past? He had seemed fine in the house, still shaken because the experience with Ethan had been so strange, but he had seemed himself.

He leaned against the passenger door and closed his eyes. "He looked at me as if I were someone else, someone he didn't know but was glad to see . . . he was trying to tell me something."

Nero opened his eyes and Vivian saw he was trying to pull himself together. "What Helen thought . . ." He stopped as if unable to go on.

"What matters is what it meant to her," Vivian said. She took the car keys from his hand and opened the front passenger door. He slid in and sat as if on automatic pilot. Vivian closed the door and went around to the driver's side.

She started the car. "Seat belt," she said.

Robot-like, Nero pulled out the belt and fastened it.

Vivian drove to the nearby motel where she'd made reservations. She hadn't known how long they would stay with Sam's family, but she'd planned nearby lodging.

Once there, Nero stretched out on the bed, coat off but otherwise fully dressed and staring at nothing. He said he didn't want anything to eat. The motel didn't have a restaurant but there was an adjacent take-out place. Vivian got herself a burger and hot chocolate and for Nero, a large iced tea. Winter or summer, he liked iced tea, but that evening she had to coax him to drink it, then had to coax him to get undressed. He seemed confused and she ended up helping him.

Sometimes in the night, he jerked awake, crying out warnings to figures only he could see. He was clearly reliving something horrible. Vivian managed to calm him to where he came back into himself enough to gasp, "Have to walk. Have to get up. Have to move . . ."

Vivian got up and pulled on her clothing. Although he seemed awake, she knew he was lost in a world that held only pain. He had been mistaken about the trip. The past few days, especially today, had been too much. Instead of bringing healing, the process of seeing and hearing the families had thrown him backward.

He mumbled in despair as she struggled to get him redressed. When they had checked into the motel, it had been bitterly cold outside. Her watch showed it was three o'clock in the morning. She could only guess that the temperature had dropped even further as the night had worn on.

Socks, boots, gloves, coat . . . and all the while he was shaking and groaning, repeating that he had to get outside, had to walk, had to move.

She threw on her jacket and was almost outside when she went back for her purse. But no, she didn't want a purse swinging on her arm, she just needed her wallet. She shoved the room key card and her wallet into her coat pocket and guided Nero outside while closing the door behind them.

They started walking.

The motel was on the highway but Nero's steps were too erratic for them to be close to traffic. He seemed to move with no purpose except determination as if he could outpace the past. She steered him down a side street and then to a street parallel to the highway. Although she had a reasonably good sense of direction, she knew they could easily become lost if he became stubborn and wouldn't follow her lead. In the country where his farm was, they could walk whichever way and still be safe. Here, she had no idea. She only knew that if she kept the highway to her right she would have some concept of where they were in relation to their motel.

She'd learned that before she had come into his life he would sometimes walk until he collapsed and simply curl up someplace outside and fall into an exhausted sleep. Then there were other times when he said he couldn't stand himself, when his thoughts were so dangerously dark he knew he couldn't dare be alone. If there was someone he could go to, he would go there. Pilar had been that person for him. She would welcome him, enfold him and take him to her bed. Pilar, thank God, had saved him from self-destruction. Vivian could only think of Pilar with gratitude.

They crossed another street.

Dark buildings rose on either side of them. How far had they walked? She had no idea. It was cold and dark—no one else was out on foot. The wind stiffened, blowing through the tunnel made by buildings on either side. A few cars passed by, their headlamps boring straight ahead through the darkness until only their taillights glimmered and faded. Vivian was grateful that no one slowed. That no one seemed to see them. If they were in a bad section . . . she stopped the fearsome thought and plodded on.

She knew they were still oriented to the highway because at cross streets she heard traffic, heavy trucks, roaring off to her right. They were now far from their motel. She felt frozen. The act of breathing pinched her nose with the cold. Shivering within her coat, she kept talking to Nero as they walked, hoping that the sound of her voice would serve as a line from whatever labyrinth he had fallen into and guide his safe return to the present.

Gradually, she felt the change in him.

His steps seemed less random, less frantic.

"I'm okay," he finally said, but he kept stolidly putting one foot in front of the other.

She didn't think he was okay at all, but it encouraged her to take a turn on the next street toward the highway. And there, blessedly, was another motel.

"Come on," she said through chattering teeth. "We need shelter."

She helped him into the motel lobby, which was no more than an alcove off the desk area. She had to hold the door because Nero didn't seem to know what he was supposed to do. She got him seated on a bench. She had seen him like this before. Once the horror of the nightmare faded, he was disoriented, caught between one time and another.

She blew her nose, which was running from coming into the warmth, then went to the desk. It looked deserted. Then a door opened and a yawning clerk appeared. Vivian took out her wallet.

"We need a room on the first floor." She didn't think she could get Nero safely up a flight of steps.

The sleepy-eyed clerk, who looked like he had seen everything and couldn't care less, had her sign the register and then pointed to a blank space. "Vehicle license?"

"We broke down and had to walk." Not as much of a lie as it could have been.

The room rate was advertised on the desk card. The clerk gave her a key, not a key card, but a key on a wooden tag, after she paid. He told her the location of the room, which meant they had to go back outside to find it. It was a struggle to get Nero on his feet again and out the door, but they made it.

Finally, they were in the room. Not as nice as the one they'd left behind but it was safe and warm.

Shivering, she wrestled Nero out of clothing that was not only cold but damp with sweat. She stripped him to his underwear. He helped as if he wasn't quite sure what they were doing, but still trying to cooperate. She pulled the covers back and got him into bed. Under her coat, she wore a knit top and jeans. She hadn't bothered with a bra. Kicking off her shoes and socks she yanked off her jeans. Wearing her knit top and underpants, she crawled into bed beside him and under the covers.

His skin was warmer than hers. His body heat stopped her shivering. Soon, she was warm. And exhausted. Only now could she appreciate how uneasy she had felt on the streets with him, virtually helpless. And to think she had once insisted she wanted a life in which she had no one she needed to care for.

She dozed off and awakened to feel him cuddling her.

"Hey," she said, lifting to one elbow. It went through her mind that she had earlier thought of her love for him. Loving him seemed the most natural thing, but she hadn't put it into words to speak to him. Was it the same way for him? Knowing, but not saying the words?

The room was dim, but the curtain fasteners at the top of the window were broken. The fabric hung in scallops, showing colored neon from outside. She saw the outlines of Nero's face and touched his cheek, smoothed her fingers through his hair, and said, "Do you know where we are, who I am?"

"I'm in bed and you're Vivi." His voice was groggy but she could see his faint smile.

"Right." She snuggled down.

After a while, he stirred again. "Did we change rooms?"

"We changed motels. We went for a really long walk and ended up here. It was too far to walk back tonight. We can get the car in the morning."

His hands moved, pulling her closer. "Vivi?"

"Yes."

"We must have walked a long way in a strange place at night. We must have walked through strange streets."

"Yes, but now we're safe," she said. "We're both all right."

"Anything could have happened to you," he said. "You must have been scared. I would have been no help."

"But nothing bad happened. We're okay."

He was quiet for a long time and she thought he had fallen asleep. But then he said, "What happened today with Helen and Ethan was good. How I was afterward was bad. I'm glad we came. But you're right. When we're home again, I think I could use some help. I want to see that counselor, that priest that you talked about."

Chapter 31

Alexander was out of the shower and dressed when he saw his phone message light blinking. He was excited to see that the caller had been Donny DeGarmo.

He and Donny had reconnected when Donny was one of the arriving officers when the car forced him and Solstice off the road at the bridge. In the commotion afterward, including the discovery that the man in the tan car was dead, plus the questioning and getting Alexander's Yamaha back on the road, he and Donny had discussed their old bike riding experiences.

Donny had respectable employment with the police department, a man among men kind of job. He even knew how to deal with a dead body! And he had a wife with a baby on the way. Donny was making good.

Alexander returned the call. Donny said he and his wife, Bethany, would be in New York on a theater jaunt, his mother's Christmas gift to them. They had tickets for two plays and a gift credit card for dinner and other New York City trip expenses.

"Since you and Solstice both live in the city," Donny said, "why don't we meet on one of those nights for dinner and see a play together?"

Sounds great," Alexander said, delighted that Donny took for granted that he and Solstice were a couple. He had told Solstice about Ramona, his absentee ballet dancer/lover still away on her endless tour. At twenty-four, he couldn't appear to be a monk, and he figured it proved to Solstice he wouldn't make moves on her. And she could hardly pry about his invisible soulmate when she was so secretive about herself. However, she *finally* had told him she had needed to see Vivian because she was the only one alive who had some connection to her past. But she still refused to give him her address or phone number.

"I'll have to check with Solstice, of course," Alexander told Donny, putting easy confidence into his voice, but who knew how Solstice would react? He was also thinking of his money. "What are the two plays?"

"The first night is *Hamilton*, the second isn't on Broadway. It's called *The Fantasticks*."

The way Donny said the names told Alexander he wasn't familiar with either play. Alexander knew that the cheapest *Hamilton* ticket was over two hundred dollars. *The Fantasticks,* the longest-running musical in the world, had tickets he could afford.

"To be safe, we'll see the *Fantasticks,*" Alexander said. "Solstice may have seen *Hamilton*." Maybe not a lie, because maybe she *had* seen it, but he doubted it.

"Good," Donny said. "We can meet at the restaurant before the show. The place is called the Glass House Tavern."

"I'll call Solstice and get back to you," Alexander said, but with no other way to get in touch, he had to email about Donny's invitation. He was prepared for her to have no interest.

She surprised him by emailing back, "*sure.*"

Alexander called Donny, who said he would make reservations for four at the restaurant. Alexander emailed Solstice the meeting time and then looked at the restaurant online. It had a prix fixe theater special. Drinks would be extra. That meant peanut butter crackers for the rest of the month, but that was fine. It hadn't been since the university that he'd gone on a double date. And this time, he didn't have to worry what the girl might expect from him at the close of the evening.

With Solstice, it would be N-O-T-H-I-N-G.

His email beeped. It was Solstice. She would meet him at the Glass House.

He wrote, "*Don't you want me to pick you up?*" Since it was already costing him a bundle, he decided they could travel by taxi.

She didn't answer.

He knew the reason. Her Brooklyn address. Big secret. Who cared?

On theater night, Alexander took a bus and then walked the last few blocks through the cold, clear evening. It had snowed again, but the streets and sidewalks were passable. When he reached the restaurant, he saw Solstice standing outside in the cold. Donny and Bethany arrived a moment later. They went inside together and were shown to their table.

Bethany was a chatterbox and Solstice surprisingly responded. Soon it was as if they were friends. Solstice wore the same green dress as on New Year's Eve. No barrette this time. Her hair, wispy and straight, hung halfway down her neck.

They were seated at a white-covered table with menus at each place. After they ordered, Bethany, who had retained a menu, embarrassed Donny by insisting he show off a trick. She asked Alexander to select any item by its position on the menu, right side, left side, and how far down.

Not sure what was going on, Alexander said, "The fourth one on the right bottom."

Red-haired Donny's face bloomed bright pink as he described the entrée in detail.

Bethany flourished the menu and Donny was absolutely right.

"You have a photographic memory!" Alexander was impressed.

"I trained myself and now it's automatic," Donny said, at ease now that his ability had been well received. "It's good for remembering a plate number when I can't write it down right away." He laughed. "Remember Mrs. Smithers for math? I couldn't catch on to the way she explained things. I must have memorized the whole math book just to get through."

"She was a horror," Alexander agreed, thinking that Francine hadn't changed.

"Mrs. Smithers preferred the girls in class, but she still wasn't my favorite," Bethany said. She looked at Solstice. "Did you have a favorite teacher?"

Solstice nodded vigorously. "Yes, someone wonderful."

A few times, Bethany, whose pregnancy was showing, would give a startled jolt and put a hand to her belly. Once she took Donny's hand and placed it there. They looked into one another's eyes and smiled.

The interaction between Donny and Bethany made Alexander feel strange, but then again, he was always feeling strange about stuff. He figured it was because of his mother. When he was little, she would have depressed moods and people felt sorry for her. Now, they were critical because of the tales about her and men. They also had mixed feeling about her *News and Noose* items. He was glad she wasn't doing them anymore.

After the main meal, Bethany and Solstice went to the ladies' room. Donny, dessert menu in hand, said, "You two sure you didn't know that guy who ran you off the road? Neil Bannister? He rented a room at Juan's. We figure he knew somebody in town."

"Wasn't us," Alexander said, aware of a narrow escape. If it hadn't been for the Colonel, he and Solstice would have been at Juan's. That would have convinced Donny they'd known the Bannister guy.

"He was a crazy driver," Alexander said. "I kept trying to get out of his way, but he kept crowding closer."

Donny nodded. "The medical examiner says he had a heart attack. His heart was torn-up by a busted rib, but his arteries were clogged."

It seemed to Alexander that Donny was about to say something more, but instead, he said, "Always something. We had a mess with a bunch of rambunctious teenagers on the river. The sign saying the ice was unsafe was posted. One kid thought he knew better. He broke through and was lucky enough to be rescued."

The remark about teenagers made Alexander remember his theory about kids firing guns on New Year's Eve. He told Donny about it.

Donny looked shocked. "Bullets actually hit your mother's house?"

"Two of them, but I can't prove it. Don't say anything to Solstice, it would only scare her. It shattered her hair ornament, but she wants to believe was it was stray stuff from kids with fireworks in the yard."

After a hesitation, Donny said, "I can look if you want."

"That would be good," Alexander said, but again he had a feeling that Donny had been about to say something else, but that's when Solstice and Bethany rejoined them and he thought no more about it.

Solstice didn't want dessert because it might make them late for the theater. Alexander didn't understand her obsession about always being early. Donny and Bethany choose the warm chocolate cake with berries and ice cream and assured Solstice that they had time. Alexander also ordered the cake. Solstice, who had put away every scrap of her meal, claimed she wasn't hungry. Alexander figured she was still fussing about being late. He spooned berries and ice cream into his coffee saucer and pushed them over to her.

"Cream in a saucer, meow," she said, but she ate it, which made him feel ridiculously satisfied.

When the bill came, she got out her credit card.

Alexander protested, but she narrowed her big brown eyes and waved the card. "Be gracious, Bunky. You bought the show tickets and your mother bought me nice things. I'm returning the favor."

"Now, now children," Bethany chided with a giggle as Solstice dropped the card on the waiter's tray where Donny had already placed their gift credit card.

The Fantasticks was great. Even better, because Alexander knew some cast members, he was able to lead his awed companions backstage. That was wonderful—the first time he could show off to hometown people that he was truly involved with the theater.

Outside, after deciding they weren't going anyplace else, Bethany and Donny left, taking a taxi to their hotel. Because Solstice had picked up the meal tab, Alexander was determined to have a taxi to drop him off and then have the cab take Solstice home to her secret address on his dime, but before he could act, she hailed a cab.

She tugged his coat sleeve when the cab pulled over and stopped. "I'll drop you off on the way," she said. "Get in Cinderfeller, or you'll turn into a pumpkin when the clock strikes."

"You've sure got a hang-up about time," Alexander said, annoyed because she kept sandbagging his plans.

"What you don't know," she said, and they got into the taxi.

After Alexander had been dropped off and Solstice was in the taxi alone, she thought how she had learned it was important to be punctual.

When the sex trade people got into trouble, they took her to Florida and sold her to the Gastrell family. They were a crippled old man who stayed in his room, his daughter, Alvana, and his adult grandson, Alwin.

The mother was tall, with white hair, but she didn't look much older than the son. She showed Solstice around the house and told her what work she would have to do.

"You look younger than they told me and you don't look strong," the mother said. "You do a good job for us or we'll sell you to someone who won't treat you as good as us."

"Yes, Ma'am," Solstice said.

The work was difficult and non-stop but work was work. The son paid no attention to her, which was perfect. Best of all there was the Gastrells' dog, Toodles. He was little and had a curly coat. She and Toodles, locked each night in a lower room, slept curled together on an old mattress. She'd never before had something to love.

The house had a kitchen but the mother never cooked. All meals were brought in, except at night, when the mother and son went out to eat after locking her and Toodles in the lower room. Meals were also brought in for the old man. It was her job to carry his food to him and to clean his bathroom and bedroom. He didn't talk to her. She didn't even know if he could talk. She and Toodles ate leftovers from the old man and restaurant leftovers the son brought home in what he called a doggy bag.

After a while, the mother told Solstice her job included reading to the old man. He used a walker to get to his bathroom, and looked in pain all the time. His books had words she didn't know, but instead of being angry, the old man started to talk to her. He helped her with hard words. She got better at reading, but she didn't trust him to stay nice.

One day the mother told her she was to get the old man new books from a place called a library, and told her where to go. Solstice was excited. This was her chance to take Toodles and escape.

In the morning of the day she was to go out, she had windows to wash. The son and his mother interrupted. He carried a dish with a cover.

"I have two surprises," the son said. "One, the dog is in his crate with a lock you don't have a key for and he won't be let loose until you return. And also, this—"

Solstice looked at what he was holding. It appeared to be a fancy food dish, but except for restaurant leftovers, the son never brought her anything. It didn't make sense.

The son removed the cover and handed it to her like a present.

When she figured out what the strange thing in the dish was, she screamed. It was the tiny tip of Toodle's tail.

The mother spoke. "If you ever fail to return at the exact time we tell you, my son will cut off more of the dog's tail." She raised her gaze to her son, "Tell her, dear."

Solstice remembered his terrible smile as he said, "When the dog's tail is used up, I'll go for a paw, or perhaps an eye. My mother has already warned you against talking to anyone about your life here, but if you do, or if you try to run away, I'll pop the little furball into the microwave turned on high."

Feeling frightened and helpless, she left the house on foot on the book errand. She'd thought the library was a store for books. There were books on shelves, but it didn't look like a real store. A lady behind a desk had a bag of books ready.

Solstice took the bag and rushed back to the house so she wouldn't be late.

After that, she went on more errands for the old man. One time, because of a blinding rainstorm, she came back late. The son cut off another half-inch of Toodles's tail.

She was never late again.

Chapter 32

When Pilar first told Francine that Jessi would be asking her help in finding a stylish evening gown for a Fergusson event, Francine said she wouldn't do it. Later, she changed her mind, realizing that Jessi could be used to gain information about the senator.

At an informal meeting at Nancy Lou's house, Francine told the members of the Voodoo Club about the shopping jaunt. "Jessi is a size zero, as low as the little egg-sucking snake's ethics."

"So you steered her all wrong?" Amy said.

"Francine wouldn't do a mean thing like that," Iris said.

"Because she has too much pride," Darlene said, busy helping Nancy Lou set out refreshments. They spoke as if Francine wasn't there. "She wouldn't want Jessi to be embarrassed and think Francine didn't know what she was doing."

Francine sniffed. What they said was true, but that was beside the point. "Jessi's our way in to learn what we can about State Senator Fergusson. He snubbed us, but in retrospect, that's not enough reason to try and cause him trouble."

She didn't say it, but her husband, Bob, who acted as if he wasn't even listening half the time, had said that revenge on the man was going overboard.

"I've learned something," she continued. "Jessi says Fergusson eventually wants to be president."

Iris's mouth dropped. "Of this country? Of the United States of America?"

"Yes. He's first aiming for a congressional seat to move him to Washington, That's why he's scrounging for funds—to win that seat."

"We figured he's interested in Acer Wolfgang as a possible supporter but I'm always seeing scandals about politicians," Nancy Lou said. "Does he also hobnob with criminals?"

"That would be valuable to know," Francine said. "I asked Jessi to take cell phone photos—supposedly to let me see how the other women dressed, but really to see who else attends."

"We won't necessarily recognize anyone," Toria said. "Certainly not criminals. And not moneyed people from New York City, either."

Darlene sniffed but said nothing. Acer Wolfgang was from New York and they recognized *him.*

"Holly doesn't like Fergusson, either," Toria said. "He sees him as an opportunist. He doesn't like the idea that the town might be used."

Amy giggled. "Jessi's being used by Fergusson and doesn't know it, and now she's being used by us and doesn't know that either."

"Can we trust Jessi?" Nancy Lou said. "Suppose nobody at this shindig pays her any attention. She'll make up a bunch of lies to cover herself."

"Of course we can't trust her, but she's the best we've got," Francine said, her head bobbing on her short, stubby neck. "We'll try to see our way through her lies." She held up a finger. "Also, her first committee meeting is this week. Let's attend. I bet she'll do nothing but brag about the fancy fundraiser she'll be attending for her marvelous personal friend, the state senator."

Chapter 33

Slim muttered under his breath. He stood along the wall of the almost full committee room. It was the first committee meeting after Jessi Spellman had been sworn in at the reorganization meeting. She was speaking. What she was saying about the police department made him mad enough to spit bullets.

"As you know," she said to the assembly, "police cars are damaged in high-speed chases over rutted roads. That's why it's so wonderful that State Senator Fergusson is giving us"—she checked a note before continuing and then looked up with a brilliant smile—"a fully equipped, Ford Police Interceptor with a specialized police package."

She said it as if expecting applause and a number responded.

When Holly, who led the meeting, asked for comments, Slim moved forward and was recognized. He said, "First, I would like to say that my officers treat police vehicles with respect, and, as most everybody here in this room knows, the township keeps the roads in good repair. While we appreciate Senator Fergusson's generosity, he doesn't know our town. What our police department *needs* is an updated computer system, both inside the station and in our current, well-maintained, vehicles."

Slim's gaze arrowed in on Jessi as he said, "Committeewoman

Spellman, with your excellent contacts, do you think you can swap that car for what we need?"

Jessi's tilted green eyes widened and she jerked her chin high. "State Senator Fergusson worked very hard to get a grant for a new cruiser. He's being incredibly generous."

"From his personal bank account?" someone called from the audience.

"He wants the credit, but it's my tax dollars," called someone else.

Hiding a smile, Holly tapped his gavel. "Please hold comments and questions until the public session."

At the public session, Max Osterhagen rose to his feet. He gave his name and address and then said to his former political rival, "Committeewoman Spellman?"

"Yes?" Jessi's eyes narrowed in obvious annoyance. She started bending the pen she held between her hands back and forth.

"Just for clarification, Committeewoman Spellman," Max asked, "was the state senator's grant for the police vehicle originally slated for another community? I ask because there was a recent *Monitor* article in which a neighboring town that was promised a Ford Police Interceptor has been told there would be a lengthy delay. They have accused the senator of political string-pulling."

"What horrible nonsense!" Jessi's pen broke into two pieces with a vicious *snap* as if she wished it could be somebody's neck. "I only know that when a car became available, Earl—excuse me, State Senator Fergusson—said he immediately thought of JumpRope Township." She tossed her head. "He's *very* impressed with us."

"Should have told him to talk to the police chief," called someone. "He knows what we really need."

Later, in Slim's office, Holly said, "But of course, we *are* accepting the new vehicle."

"Sure, value, what, 35K plus? What Max said was right. Fergusson made a deal and there's no going back. And let me tell you, if I caught one of my men jockeying around, bucketing through swamps and taking corners at high speed like a kid on a bumper car ride, he'd walk detail until he got his head straight."

Leaning forward, he moved items on his desk, including packets of snacks. "On another subject," he said, "Fanshawe—Alexander—told Donny he thinks there was gunfire at his mother's house on New Year's Eve."

"He just thinks of it now?"

Slim settled back in his chair. "It was probably kids with illegal fireworks, but something flew through the air with enough force to shatter a hair gizmo that Alexander's girlfriend was wearing. Donny and Bethany had dinner with Alexander and the girl. Alexander told him that bullets hit his mother's house on New Year's Eve."

"Whoa!" Holly's eyes widened.

"The girl apparently doesn't believe it, but Alexander seemed convinced." Slim shook his head. "If there were bullets, I sure don't like it, but did you ever read that stuff of his that his mother sticks in her newsletter? The play he can't get published? I figure he's got more imagination than common sense. Still, we're checking with a metal detector around Alexander's mother's house where he told Donny the shots hit. If there's bullet evidence, the county may want to investigate further." Slim shrugged. "I'm not worrying about it until I know more."

"The girl was with Alexander when they were crowded off the road by Neil Bannister," Holly said. "We never learned why he was here, and since he had a rifle . . . well, any chance, you think that—"

"That there really were bullets fired and the girl was the target?"

"Well, what do we know about her?"

"Not much," Slim said. "According to Iris, Alexander just met her recently. Vivian Mather apparently knows her from years back. First name Solstice, last name Windsor. Donny got it with his glance-and-get technique."

"His what?"

Slim laughed. "Seems Donny was self-conscious about getting through school by memorizing stuff. He thought it meant he was dumb. It also explains why it sometimes sounds as if he's quoting from a police manual—he actually is. Bethany made him see the advantage for a cop. When Solstice used her credit card at dinner, Donny gave it a glance and, zingo, he had her full name. Alexander had admitted to Donny that she'd never told him her last name. Strikes an off note, like she's hiding trouble in her past."

"Didn't get the card number?" Holly asked. "That would have led to a lot more information."

"Nah. Donny said Solstice was waving it around and he felt he was lucky to have gotten the name."

"It might be smart to ask Vivian about the girl," Holly said. "Especially if you find proof of bullets striking the Fanshawe house."

"What I was thinking, mind reader."

"That's me," Holly said.

Slim grinned. "Maybe you could be a guest speaker at the ladies' spook club."

Holly gave a mock shudder. "I'm interested in what Toria's interested in, but an evening with those ladies and their whatchamacallit clairvoyant, Mar-see-ah, doesn't sound like fun."

Slim chuckled. "Speaking of the Voodoo gals, Iris, who's in the club, told me Jessi's attending a New York City fundraiser for Fergusson. They hope to learn more about him through her." He tapped on his desktop, the sounds seeming loud in the otherwise quiet room. "I'd like to know more about Fergusson myself. A politico interested in little JumpRope? Not likely."

"The club members think Fergusson sees Jessi as a conduit to Acer Wolfgang."

"Hotshot developer," Slim said. He had never trusted Wolfgang to have the town's best interest at heart—too smooth, too much money.

"If the ladies find out anything, Iris will spill it," Holly said.

"Yeah," Slim said. "She's a sweetheart, but anything she knows spills out like water in a sieve."

Chapter 34

*V*ivian chanced to meet Iris at the hardware store. She knew Iris from the previous year when she'd been invited to a Voodoo Club dinner.

"Hi, Vivian. Happy New Year!" Iris said in her bubbly way.

"The same to you," Vivian said. When she and Nero came home after visiting the families of the men he'd known in the war, he'd followed through on the decision to meet with Father Tom. Vivian was hoping for the best. She had now started redoing the rooms in the Gibeau farmhouse. Nero said he would help with anything she wanted to do except choose paint colors.

Iris gave Vivian advice, which included how helpful painter's tape was to give a nice straight line, and how using the tape could also avoid getting paint where you didn't want it. Iris then moved to the topic of State Senator Fergusson.

Her plump face earnest, she said, "Francine says the state senator is ambitious. He wants wealthy people to help send him to Washington. I know Mr. Wolfgang is your friend. We don't want to see him taken advantage of."

Vivian thanked Iris for the information, thinking that Fergusson would have to get up plenty early in the morning to catch Acer off guard. Still, when she returned home, she gave Acer a call.

He answered at once and chuckled when she told him about the club members' concern.

"This warning comes at an interesting time," he said. "I've received an invitation to a Fergusson affair to be held in New York City. Darlene Gage is one of those club members, correct?"

Vivian smiled. "I believe I mentioned that when I was once the club's dinner guest." Teasing, she added, "I wouldn't have thought you would remember."

"Some items stick in my mind."

"Uh-huh," she said, amused by his continuing interest in a woman who'd like to wipe the floor with him.

Acer entered the Housing and Property office where Darlene Gage reigned supreme.

Startled, she said flatly, "If you want to speak with the construction officer, he's out." She was full-time, but the construction and zoning officers were part-time, and she was alone in the room. She glanced at the wall clock. "I'm busy. I have things to finish."

"It will only take a moment," he said, and confidently stepped around the corner of the counter which served as a room divider. Uninvited, took a seat by her desk chair.

Boxing her in, was he? Well, it was *her* office. She'd soon teach him who was in control.

He said, "Vivian has learned from Iris that a club of which you are a member bears resentment against State Senator Fergusson."

Admitting nothing, Darlene noticed his jacket fit better now that he'd taken weight off his midsection. She liked a man who looked trim. Not him, of course. Just on general principles.

Figuring all those money types swam in the same stream, she said, "So you've come to drop a few good words about your pal?"

Acer smiled. "Actually, he and I have never met."

"Actually," she repeated his word deliberately, "I heard him say he'd never heard of you." *That should put him in his place*, she thought. He probably thought the entire solar system had him on speed dial.

Smiling at Darlene, Acer crossed his legs, the trousers of his beautifully tailored grey wool suit impeccably creased. He wondered if she had any idea of the appeal she held for him. He had first noticed her because he found her attractive—blonde, slender, classical features. Surface attributes pleasing to his eye. When he'd made his approach, her bristly manner had intrigued him. He enjoyed a challenge.

But when he'd seen her again in this office, his interest had taken a deeper turn. She was bright, accomplished and meticulous in every way. He had since learned that she'd been alone since a long-ago divorce and that her social life apparently consisted of town activities, her involvement in this club and visits to her daughter and infant grandchild in a nearby state. A constricted life for such an attractive woman. She wasn't shy, but to say that she was guarded was an understatement. There was some mystery there. She was a puzzle that came into his mind in unexpected moments, and each time he saw her, his interest only deepened.

Answering her last comment about Fergusson not knowing him, he said, "The Senator is planning to correct that oversight. I've received an invitation to a Manhattan event being hosted for him tomorrow evening by his New York supporters. Short notice, but I thought that since your club is interested in his activities, you might enjoy being my guest. You could be their representative."

Darlene was stunned. That was the event Francine had helped Jessi prepare for. She knew she would be far better than Jessi in learning more about Fergusson. But was attending with Acer Wolfgang worth it? He was so damnably handsome, so polished, so self-assured. She was never sure how to behave with him. She always felt on the verge of making a fool of herself.

She said, "There are rumors that Fergusson is interested in moving from state senator to Congress." She kept her voice cool, ignoring his invitation. "Why would New York people support him?"

"Excellent question. We shall learn more at this black-tie event." When she reached toward her desk calendar, he said, "This event won't disrupt your business hours." He sounded amused. He told her the date and the time he would pick her up.

He hadn't even asked where she lived, she thought, but of course, he'd made it his business to find out.

He said, "I read in the *Monitor* that Senator Fergusson's reason for attending your town's reorganization was to swear Jessi in as committeewoman." He smiled as if they were co-conspirators. "I question the senator's judgment."

Darlene tilted her head, her long hair shifting to one shoulder. "His questionable judgment? So what do we make of his invitation to you?" *Finally*, her brain was in gear.

He chuckled, his sea-blue eyes twinkling. "You never fail to delight me." He stood, smiling down at her from his broad-shouldered, well-tailored height. "We shall have an enjoyable evening."

Wait!" she said as he turned to leave. "I should have your number. In case something changes." Like telling him to take a hike.

He drew out a business card and a pen and wrote on the back of the card. "My private cell." As he placed the card on the counter, he added with that appealing tilted smile, "You might find it's already on your phone. It's the number I've used whenever I've called you."

Chapter 35

*D*arlene paced inside her entryway. She hated surprises and Acer was a master of them. She was determined to be ready and waiting when he came to the door. Her cell phone rang from her evening purse. A text from her daughter, Marie. She wanted the phone number of the repair person Darlene had called the last time she'd been babysitting.

"I'll get it," Darlene texted back, heading for her everyday purse in the bedroom. She found the number and sent it back. Why didn't Marie ever call so she could hear her voice?

The doorbell rang. Darlene cursed under her breath. Acer, catching her by surprise.

She hurried from the bedroom, the heels of her silver evening shoes rapping on the entry's ceramic tiles. She threw open the door and there he was, looking splendid in his tuxedo, but she had seen him in one before and refused to be impressed.

A gust of freezing air swirled past him and into the entry.

Recapturing her manners, she moved back to allow him inside.

He thanked her, his eyes showing pleasure as he stepped inside and gazed at her.

Now, she thought, sourly, *here comes compliments I can't trust.*

"I like seeing you in blue," he said.

Not what she'd been braced for. Did he recognize it as the same gown she'd worn to the banquet last August when he had first come into town? Tonight, she had topped it with its matching silver-trimmed jacket—she had bought the set because of its versatility. Was he wondering what kind of backwoods woman wore the same gown twice?

Switching her phone to *vibrate*, she slid it into her evening purse and reached toward her cape.

"Excellent choice." He lifted the black wool cape from its resting place on a chair back. "It's bitter outside, but you can slip this off easily in the warmth of the car." He held it so that when she turned, he could drape it around her shoulders.

Feeling helplessly manipulated, she turned. He settled the cape about her shoulders with practiced expertise and lifted her hair from where it had been trapped under the collar. As his fingertips grazed the back of her neck, she involuntarily shivered. Even with her heels, he was noticeably taller. For an instant, she wondered how it would be to relax and lean back against him.

Coming to her senses, she mumbled a thank you and took a jerky step toward the door. She would have opened it, but he was too quick. Outside, he closed the door behind them. She heard it click, but feeling defiant, she checked to make sure it was locked. She turned and saw a Bentley with a chauffeur.

"Goodness," she said. "You could have sent your man in to fetch me like a package."

He smiled. "Never," he said.

Something in his smile made her feel that he understood her entirely too well.

Riding with him on the New Jersey Turnpike, Darlene remembered how her Voodoo Club members were delighted that she had this opportunity to spy on Senator Fergusson. They had talked about Acer.

Iris liked him, but then again, Iris liked everybody. Francine was awed by his polish and wealth. Toria thought he was pleasant and gracious, and besides, Holly liked him. Nancy Lou and Amy appreciated his good looks. Not as good-looking as Nero Gibeau, but as Amy had said, "Nero being so handsome doesn't count as much because he isn't anybody. He's just a heartstopper who's lived in JumpRope all his life and not a somebody like Acer."

It was Acer's being a *somebody* that furthered Darlene's distrust. That, plus his apparent interest in her. He had won board approval for his development and would break ground as soon as weather permitted. What more could he want?

She looked at him as he took out a folder that he said contained research material about Fergusson, and made comments as he read.

When he paused for a moment, Darlene said, "You mentioned Fergusson's stepdaughter. I'd supposed he was a bachelor."

"He's apparently a fan of committed marriage as long as it's handled in a serial fashion," Acer said.

Darlene thought she heard a hint of disapproval but decided she was wrong. Serial marriages were the norm with people of his class.

"Fergusson and his first wife were divorced after five years," he said. "No children. A year or so after that, he married a widow with a young daughter, Leslie. After five years, Fergusson and his wife separated but never divorced. Leslie's mother died and he took custody of the girl, who was then aged fourteen. He's now forty-two. His third marriage was annulled. Technically, he's had one divorce, and that's well in the past."

"How did Fergusson become a state senator? " Darlene asked. "Was he a lawyer first?" If things had worked out differently, she would have been a lawyer.

"Yes," Acer said, referring to the document. "First, he was a lawyer in his family's firm, an insurance conglomerate in West Jersey. He went from serving as a municipal solicitor to winning a contested race against an incumbent state senator and kept that seat this past November. Now, there's an opportunity coming up in Congress because a New Jersey Congressman is looking to retire. That's the spot

Fergusson's supposedly aiming for next. He's working to lever himself up, raising funds to beat out contenders.

Darlene's gaze moved to the windshield. There was nothing ahead she could see except lights from a wide overhead turnpike sign that appeared and then was gone as if it had folded under the pressure of the moving vehicle. She wondered at their speed. The Bentley's smooth ride gave little impression of motion.

The driver, Ritter, spoke to Acer. The two men exchanged a few words. Acer laughed.

With that laugh, seen at a new angle, Darlene saw what had bothered her from the start about Acer's oh-so-appealing yet somehow not perfect smile. The angle of the overhead lamp allowed her to see that one tooth bore a slight chip. She couldn't believe it. Her own smile was as perfect as modern science could make it. When she chose to smile, that is. And if there was a problem she was knocking on her dentist's door.

That's when she saw a faint scar on Acer's cheek to the one side of his mouth. *That's* what gave his smile that charmingly lifted corner. Damn! The man even made injury work to his advantage.

Noticing her gaze, Acer gestured toward his face. "A skirmish of sorts, from way back. The damages serve as reminders."

"Reminders of what?" Darlene said, at the same time noticing that something about his left hand didn't look quite right.

He caught her look. There was a pause, and then, as if he'd come to a decision, he held up the back of his hand. It was broad, the fingers long, but the last three fingers were not entirely straight. He reversed his hand and she saw the shocking web of white scars lacing the underside side of those three fingers.

The manner in which he seemed to await her reaction, struck her as uncertain. When she said nothing, he smiled faintly. "Reminders of where I've been and where I've come since then." He flexed his hand into a fist and straightened it out again as if reassuring himself it still worked properly. With his eyes meeting hers, he said, "We all have a history of where we've been and what has made us who we are now."

Darlene could frame no reply. For a moment, she imagined him as young and rough and brash. No caution, no elegance, just fit and primed for a thumping brawl. Dangerous. An answering visceral sensation trembled deep inside of her that she immediately denied.

She'd never been attracted to bad boys, not even in high school.

Closing her eyes, she saw herself as a teenager in rural Pennsylvania. She'd been quiet and serious and convinced that dating would distract from her plans of a career in law. Her uncle, a lawyer, encouraged her by hiring her to work in his office during high school and promised to help financially with her higher education.

Then she met Keyton Gage and fell in love. As soon as his divorce was final they married. She took off with him as he moved from one job to another, each position, he claimed, better than the last. It wasn't until after Marie's birth and their last relocation that she learned the truth about him and their marriage ended. The only good thing was that their last place had been in JumpRope. That's where she stayed, but she was no longer the same person she had been. She was tougher and smarter. No man would ever again play her for a fool.

Looking out the window, she saw lights ahead leading to the tunnel that would take them into the city.

Not believing Acer could walk into a fancy New York crowd and not see somebody he knew, she said, "Tell me about the people you think we'll be meeting tonight."

They had a bit more time to kill before they reached their destination. She might as well allow him to entertain her.

Chapter 36

Jessi Spellman delicately finished another appetizer, little finger upraised. *Yum!* Rolled up dates and bacon with some sort of cheese. The food for this Fergusson deal probably cost a bundle. The Lawrences always did things right. In her head, that's how she thought of the host and hostess, Frank and Madelaine Lawrence, whom she had just met. *The Lawrences, her very good friends.*

She snagged another treat from a passing tray. The women servers wore dresses with aprons and the men wore tuxes. How could anyone tell the male guests from the hired help when they all dressed like penguins? Actually, she *could* tell. If a guy was young and good-looking, he was rented for the evening. The husbands were middle-aged or even decrepit. Even so, their hair, if they had any left, was cut just so, their fingernails buffed, and they had cufflinks bigger than eyeballs. Most of the wives were a lot younger and they all looked terrific.

Lifting another glass of champagne from the tray of a passing server, she thought, *I could get used to this.* She slid an eye across the grand room to Arnie and the food people. Earlier, he had been talking with one of the husbands who yammered about his properties on Emerald Cay and Turks and Caicos. Private islands weren't in Arnie's skillset, so he'd swum back to shore to hang with the chef and caterers. But didn't he look sharp? All dressed for the occasion.

Everything here was just so special. Except, she didn't understand the interest in her dumb little New Jersey town. The Lawrences and others had asked about it. They really seemed interested. Maybe these people were like that old French court that held parties in cow fields. Women in fancy wigs and swinging on swings, like on the printed curtains that Pilar had in her family room. "Twall," she called it, only it was spelled a funny way.

Jessi moved around, on alert for a roaming waiter with some snack she hadn't tried yet. Mixing it up with all these fancy people—she felt right at home.

And now, Senator Earl was over on the other side of the room sucking up to a new couple who had just stepped in—

Jessi let out a squeal.

What was *she* doing here?

Her nemesis, Botox Barbie.

As soon as Darlene stepped into the huge room in the penthouse, she knew she didn't belong. They had entered a space as large as the town hall court/committee room. Her gaze rose to the spectacular ceiling. What sort of people had a rotunda in their private home? The chandelier suspended from its center was one of two other such fixtures, each one positioned over seating arrangements composed of couches and upholstered chairs

She realized she was clinging to Acer's arm, Acer, the only familiar warmth in the room. She managed to force herself to step away from him as their host and hostess, Frank and Madelaine Lawrence, who Acer already knew, came up. Darlene responded automatically, saying, she prayed, all the right words. With a sinking sensation, she realized that her prime wish had become—other than transforming into vapor—to avoid bringing embarrassment to Acer. Lord! How had everything become so twisted?

Madelaine introduced her to Philip Dartmore, another person Acer had mentioned ahead of time. Philip sat with him on two corporate boards, one the North American division of a luggage concern located primarily in South America, and the other an international fashion conglomerate. Philip's wife, Evelynn, was a women's wear designer. With Evelynn was Robin Harley, also a member of the fashion world.

Fergusson and his stepdaughter, Leslie, an auburn-haired young woman, joined them. Fergusson, with his billboard-sized smile and perfectly coiffed hair, told Darlene it was good to see her again, and then he greased his attention over to Acer. He spoke of his enjoyment of Acer's presentation at a recent financial meeting.

When someone drew Fergusson's attention, Acer whispered to Darlene, *"He was never at that meeting."*

Before Darlene could think of how to react, Madelaine turned from speaking with Leslie, and said to her, "You have no idea how enamored the senator is with your hometown. He's made it sound so deliciously quaint."

Darlene smiled and told herself to stop thinking of the difference between her and these impossibly wealthy people and remember her mission. She was there to discover what she could about Fergusson.

That's when she saw Jessi. She was coming at a fast clip, her up-tilted green eyes smoking like malfunctioning lasers, the hem of her lavender gown swirling and twitching around her ankles like the tail of an angry cat.

"Here you are, Jessi, dear," Madelaine said, enfolding Jessi as she reached their group. "Look, dear, we have another guest from your darling little community."

"Yeah, fancy meeting you here," Jessi said poisonously to Darlene.

Darlene disregarded the venom. "Jessi, you look lovely, and what adorable shoes!"

Jessi blinked and looked down. Her shoes, in a darker lavender shade than her gown, had four-inch heels and tiny silver buckles on the delicate straps that held them to her doll-sized feet.

"Oh, yes, aren't they adorable?" said Madelaine. "You can always depend on Armani."

Madelaine then said to Acer and Darlene, "Perhaps you two might wish to select something from the buffet. A waitstaff member will bring your choices to wherever you're sitting, but I do hope you'll join us in that corner over there." She gestured, a space with two full-sized couches and three big armchairs placed around an oriental rug and under a chandelier. "I'd love to have a comfortable chat with you before the senator speaks of what he hopes to accomplish as a congressman. And—" she winked, "once he's in Washington, we'll look forward to his even more promising future."

After having made their food choices, Darlene and Acer were on their way to Madelaine's "corner," when Darlene paused to study a sprawling arrangement of tropical flowers. She would have sworn they were artificial, but they were real. A glance through the stems and branches revealed Fergusson and Leslie in an alcove in the opposite wall. A waitress placed two champagne flutes on a shelf before them and moved on.

"Appears they've found a private location," said Acer, who had paused with Darlene and was also in a position to see through the flowers.

Darlene was about to say it wasn't so private if they could see them and then she realized that the depth of the alcove hid the room from Fergusson's and Leslie's viewpoint. The floral arrangement seemingly screened them from anyone on the opposite side.

Darlene watched the pair, their backs to the room, stand with their shoulders and hips together. They turned to face one another and lifted their champagne in a mutual toast. Leslie smiled up at Fergusson, tossing her auburn hair, her smile teasing. Their bodies touched from their waists downward and then their lips touched.

Eyes wide, Darlene murmured, "That's a man with his daughter?"

"Stepdaughter, but even so . . ."

Darlene nodded, thinking that this moment between Fergusson

and Leslie was something her fellow club members would be interested in hearing about.

"We'd best move on," Acer said. Darlene nodded.

They were soon taking their seats in the company of Madelaine and several others. The servers arrived with their plated food and beverages. They were greeted for a second time by Acer's fellow board member, Philip Dartmore, and his wife, Evelynn, who sat next to Robin Harley. Robin's husband was a scrawny, balding fellow, who sat with his hands on his bony knees. His expression was pleasant but vague when Robin introduced Acer and Darlene. Robin, at least twenty years younger than her husband, was glamorous in a pale yellow silk gown, her sleek blond hair swept back to show off elegant diamond and emerald drop earrings and a matching necklace.

Darlene felt acutely aware of the plainness of her own attire, even more so when Evelynn mentioned a recent runway event that the other two women had also attended, mentioning apparently famous designers Darlene had never heard of. *Francine*, she thought, *where are you?*

The conversation moved to the subject of how the Internet had changed business and design ventures. Evelyn gave examples of how it had brought her new clients. Robin agreed, saying how her talented webmaster, Gregory, had enlarged the online subscribers to her husband's magazines. Madelaine, who also used Gregory, spoke of his graphic designs, saying they had increased the outlets for her husband's luggage business.

As the insider talk swirled on, Darlene felt increasingly out of place. To her, the Internet was for research. It also offered a municipal page that gave residents a way to keep up with notices and meetings, plus downloadable information about construction and building regulations and the like. Nothing resembling what these women spoke of.

She was almost relieved when Jessi showed up and changed the focus.

"Hey everyone, I'm here," Jessi said as if they had all been waiting for her.

"And always welcome," Madelaine said.

Jessi took a seat. The following waiter placed her plated food on a handy side table, spread a napkin over her lap, and handed her a flute of champagne. He then asked if she needed anything more. Jessi waved him away and cast an evil glance at Darlene as she sipped champagne.

Amused, Darlene figured Jessi had made a silent toast to her future downfall, maybe death by dismemberment. She decided that feeling out of place was nothing but whining and she wasn't a whiner. Maybe these wealthy women, who seemed so sophisticated, hadn't begun life as privileged. Maybe they had married into it. There was no way to tell, just as it was with that scene between Fergusson and his daughter. Was there any way to be sure about anything?

From what Acer had said in the car, if he could be believed, made it clear that he hadn't been born to privilege, either. But why had he told her about his hard knocks and shown her his damaged hand? It was as if he were sharing something that he might not share with everyone.

She glanced his way. He was the only one in the vast room with whom she felt even halfway comfortable, yet she trusted him about as far as she could throw him.

Their business discussion having come to an end, Robin said to Darlene, "Jessi told us all about your little town before you arrived."

The women began replaying things Jessi had told them. Frank and Philip, who had finished eating, invited Acer to join them for a drink and a chat with Earl before he gave his presentation. Acer said he would catch up with them. That left Acer the only man with the women except for Robin's husband, who had not participated in the conversation and still sat smiling at nothing. Darlene wondered if he'd suffered a stroke.

Jessi began to expound on the marvels of her upcoming restaurant and how excited she and the senator were about her plans. She made the restaurant sound as if it would be the centerpiece of the town if not all of Melton County and perhaps the entire East Coast. Next Houston, then Los Angeles then on to the moon. Darlene thought she would gladly wave when the rocket ship took off.

Jessie, basking in the attention of the three women who seemed to be hanging on her every word, said, "Of course, you'll be my special guests on the restaurant's opening night."

"Delightful," Robin said. "When will this grand opening be?"

Jessi's face wrinkled in a pretty moue of sorrow. "I wish I could give you an exact date, but there are delays with inspections, approval, rules and regulations."

Knowing Jessi cared nothing for rules except bending them to her advantage, Darlene felt her shoulders tense.

"But surely, with you being a committee person, there should be no difficulty," Madelaine said. "They know you. And you certainly know all the requirements."

"So true," Jessi said. "But there's always someone . . ." Her eyes flickered to Darlene. "Someone less accomplished, who—"

"Bears a grudge?" Evelynn said. "Oh, my dear, the fashion industry has similar problems."

"I can't believe these matters can't be easily resolved," said Robin. "Earl wouldn't otherwise speak so highly of the community."

"Earl is correct, Robin." Acer's voice, while quiet, was rich with authority. He turned his attention to Jessi. "This is your first time in business and in your inexperience you're anxious. But after your marvelous presentation to the planning board last year, you received unanimous approval and even applause, if I recall."

Jessi *had* gained approval, although Darlene remembered no applause, however, she was delighted to see Acer's words had left Jessi not knowing what to say. From her expression, she was enraged over his use of the word "inexperience," yet flattered by the words "excellent presentation" and "applause."

Acer spoke again, this time to the group. "It's a splendid community. I never would have considering building upscale homes there otherwise." He then described the community's finest features, which Darlene figured could have done service as a travel advertisement.

"It sounds like a little village in Scotland or Britain, a place that time hasn't touched," Madelaine said in a dreamy voice.

Darlene nodded at the idyllic description, but for some contrary reason, the memory of the house with a blood-stained kitchen came to her mind.

"It sounds lovely," Robin said with a sigh.

Evelynn turned to her. "Robin, haven't you been speaking of a place that would be, well, pastoral, but still close to the city? I mean, dear, you have that . . ." She paused, and then clarified, "That relative who's been having difficulties."

Robin looked startled, then brightened. "Oh, I see what you mean."

It went through Darlene's mind that this unnamed "relative" was probably her husband.

"There is someone dear to me who could benefit from a time away from the stress of ordinary life," Robin said. She placed a hand to her heart, her fingertips brushing her diamond and emerald necklace. "Rest and seclusion, with attendants to see to all needs, of course." She turned to Acer and Darlene. "Is there a guest house or a charming little hotel where my relative might stay?"

"There's Juan's Hacienda," Jessi said, cutting a glance at Darlene and digging in a claw, knowing that Juan's was a constant thorn in Darlene's side.

"Hacienda?" Robin said. "I didn't realize there was a southwestern flavor to the town."

"There isn't," Darlene said, managing to avoid looking at Jessi as she added her fondest property inspector's wish, "It's even possible that the mentioned establishment might be closed down."

Having heard of Darlene's running battle with Juan's Hacienda, Acer smiled at her reply. He was also thinking that she must be drawn to him on some level or she would never have agreed to come. It didn't matter that she was furthering the interest her club members had in Fergusson—she was too independent to do something she really didn't want to do. She was attracted to him, he was certain, yet not ready to admit it, perhaps not even to herself. But he could wait. He was a patient man.

His attention shifted to the conversation between Madelaine and

Robin. Madelaine was clearly familiar with Robin's problem with the ill person she had spoken of. Who was probably her husband, he thought. This reminded him that Grace Mather had once fled in a troubled time to the Mather house.

"I may be able to offer a possible solution to the difficulty you mentioned," he said to Robin. "To serve my housing development, I have a house with a first-floor office, but there are refurbished bedrooms and baths on the second floor. Locals call it the Mather house and I'll keep the name. It's not handicapped accessible at this time, but if that doesn't rule it out, it may suit your relative and the attendants you feel are needed."

"Mather house?" Robin stroked her lower lip in thought. "Is there any connection to the delightful Elizabeth Mather, the artist, who works with disadvantaged Manhattan youths?"

"Yes. The development is on a farm that belonged to Elizabeth and her heirs. The house I'm speaking of was the former Mather family home."

Robin frowned, and then said, "Would it be possible to come and stay there for a few days to see if it would be suitable?"

"Certainly. Simply advise me of when."

Smiling, he was thinking that when he no longer needed an office for the development, the house might make a bed and breakfast. Even though Vivian had found a place for herself at the Gibeau farm, she still had affection for the old family home. She would be pleased to see it utilized.

Chapter 37

At the Gibeau farm, Vivian was in bed and looking through a decorating publication that had a section for new homeowners that might be basic enough for someone on her level. One thing for sure—she didn't want a lot of "stylish" items that would be proclaimed *dated* in the next breath. She'd watched TV programs where people looked for a perfect house. The realtors most always said that the house being shown was totally renovated before going on the market. The wives, always the wives, said that the kitchen or the bath was outdated and would have to be torn out and redone. Were they showing off their high standards? Trying to wiggle the price down? Maybe both.

She turned a page and saw a kitchen with a "country-style farmhouse sink." It was a sink with a deep apron built into a row of cabinets with a quartz countertop. Hmmm. She was living in an authentic farmhouse with a kitchen sink that was a free-standing porcelain piece with a sink and drain board standing on legs. Underneath, on the floor, was a bucket for collecting food scraps to feed the chickens.

Now *that* was a farmhouse sink.

She turned to a section about bedrooms.

Pink rooms and blue rooms.

Rooms meant for a nursery.

Nero, lying next to her, wearing his customary nightwear, which was underwear, read a magazine about engine repair. Vivian had her hand on his thigh, idly stoking every now and then, enjoying being next to him, touching him.

She thought again how she'd never told him she loved him, but she did. How he had never told her he loved her, but she knew he did. Maybe she had more of a male attitude—actions speak louder than words. A future together was accepted. Promised not in words, but in a multitude of small actions that signified they were each thinking, *forever*.

Forever in a town called JumpRope. She had never before had a permanent home. Here, she had a place and people she liked. She even had a community responsibility, like meeting with the police chief, who had questions about Solstice. What was that about?

Nero closed the magazine and set it aside. Vivian's hand still rested on his thigh. He placed a warm hand on top of hers.

She looked over at him quizzically and tried to lift a single eyebrow—their running joke, that he could lift a single eyebrow and she couldn't.

He grinned, lifted a single eyebrow, and then moved her hand to a more strategic position on his body.

Remembering what he once said to her, she said, "Aren't too subtle, are you?"

He mimed a sheepish smile. "I try."

"Oh, sure. Trying—" she mimed disgust— "really hard."

He grinned at her inadvertent word choice. "Well, now, since you've brought that up . . ."

Soon she was sans nightgown, her long wavy hair free from the braid she wore at night. She rested against his now naked body, his hands cupping the fullness of her breasts.

"You're so pretty," he whispered, snuggling his face against her neck.

She leaned further back to give him better access, aware of a slight but not unpleasant tenderness in her breasts and wondering if he noticed any change as she said—as she often did—exactly what she was thinking, "If I'm as fertile as your grandmother hopes, then considering my full figure, what you're fondling may someday be kissing my waist."

Smiling, his head bent, he nuzzled her shoulder where it sloped into the curve of her throat. "Is this where I'm supposed to say, 'Not if I kiss them first?'"

"You can say anything, but if kissing could stop gravity, we'd all be flying to the moon."

Moving so he could lower her gently to the bed, he leaned over her, gazing into her eyes. "How about if we try flying there now?"

She looked up, softly touching his face. "Sounds like a plan."

He smiled and started to speak, and then something broke in his voice as he said, "Vivi, Vivi . . . where have you been all my life?"

"Doesn't matter." Her arms pulled him close. "I'm here, now, and here to stay."

And as she spoke, she smiled a secret smile.

Should I tell him?

No, she thought as she joyfully surrendered. *I should wait until I am absolutely sure.*

Chapter 38

Each Sunday, Darlene prepared five main meals for the coming work week. That way, her nightly dinners only needed to be heated up. A freshly made salad each night would provide variety. This week, the main meal would be beef stew: her own recipe prepared her own way. When she'd come home from church, she'd put on old jeans and an equally old knit shirt. Her hair was swept back with a clip and her face was bare. Slicing onions made her eyes water and made a mess of her mascara. She'd washed off her mascara and all the rest of her make-up as well. Didn't need it to cook.

She answered her ringing phone. The caller was Acer.

"Do you have time to see me shortly?" he said. "I have some information your group might find interesting."

She hesitated, but the word *information* was a draw. "I'm busy, but I suppose so."

"A half-hour, then," he said.

She decided to do nothing about her appearance, not even a swipe of lip-gloss. Acer would be invading her territory. If he didn't like what he saw, too bad.

The cubes of beef were starting to brown when her window revealed a dark green Audi stopping at the curb. Acer emerged from the driver's side. Turning down the heat and wiping her hands on a towel, Darlene met him at the door.

"Happy Sunday," he greeted.

He stepped in, took off his mid-length coat and she hung it on the rack by the door. He wore dark slacks and a grey pull-on sweater. On his feet were black canvas shoes. She'd never seen him in such casual garb, but as he moved further into her foyer, she became aware that the lack of a suit and necktie did nothing to diminish his easy grace and power.

She was appalled at the mistake she'd made. How could she appear before him like this? A woman shouldn't dress down with such a man. She groped for something to say to help her regain a sense of command.

"Where's your driver, Ritter, and the Bentley?" she demanded. "You're driving yourself in an Audi."

That at least showed him she knew something about cars, which many women didn't. Recognizing vehicles was a plus in her job, although the Audi logo with its four interlocking rings emblazoned on the radiator grill should be easily recognizable to anyone.

He smiled. "I sent Ritter back to the city. I keep a car here for conducting local business." He paused and then added, "I'm exploring different possibilities for the addition of a pond and landscaping for the Mather development."

Darlene stiffened. "That wasn't included in your land use board presentation."

"Back then I believed I could purchase the property that belongs to Jessi and her partners. Since that failed, I now believe a small body of water and plantings will provide a buffer between her property and mine. I doubt she would make a good neighbor."

Darlene agreed with him about Jessi, but she narrowed her eyes. "Why give me advance notice?"

"Perhaps it's my pleasure to watch you reach for your shield and sword at any mention of a late addition to my plans."

Not knowing how to respond, she snapped, "I'm busy in the kitchen. Since you're here, you might as well come on."

Unbidden, he took a seat at the kitchen table.

Putting her back to him, she upped the heat under the pan. She turned the meat and saw to her satisfaction that the minced onions were caramelizing nicely.

"You'll have to amend your plan and get approval for any change," she said, setting him straight about the planning board.

Ignoring Darlene's planning board remark, Acer leaned back in his chair, thinking how pleasing it was to see her wearing at-home clothes, and yet, as always, she looked trim and polished. She wasn't wearing make-up, but it didn't diminish her classic beauty—that was bone structure and a lovely complexion. Someday, when she trusted him, they could spend comfortable times like this, lounging around and perhaps planning a pleasant activity. He could take her sailing when the weather was suitable, or when it was cold they might ski. Had she ever done that? If not, he could teach her.

"What is your granddaughter's name?" he asked.

She turned. "What made you think of her?"

"The photo of you holding an infant." He gestured to the display on her refrigerator. Her refrigerator, unlike her plain desk at work, was like a Facebook page, full of photos and memorabilia.

"Her name is MacKenzie," she said, her voice softening. "Her great-grandmother, my mother, called it a 'modern unisex name.' She likes to think she's on the cutting edge." Abruptly, she stiffened. "Enough about my family. Back to last night. Fergusson's supporters seem enthusiastic. What did you think of the spiel he gave that evening?"

Acer remembered that they hadn't discussed the evening on the drive home. As soon Ritter picked them up, urgent overseas calls had come in. She'd said to go ahead with his calls. She had then retreated into the corner of her seat, pulling her cloak to hide her face. She didn't answer when he spoke to her later, but he suspected she played possum.

When finally reaching her house, she'd awoken, or at least appeared to do so. When he'd walked her to her door, she'd thanked him for the evening and cut short anything else that might have been said.

Answering her question, he said, "Fergusson offers no new ideas. He imagines his strength lies in pointing out deficiencies in the man who will surely be his opposition. As a New York State resident, I'll have no vote either way, but as I told you, I have new information."

She turned from peeling carrots to look at him. "Yes?"

"Madelaine confided that being married would make Fergusson more appealing to voters. That may or may not be a fact, but if Fergusson wins the congressional seat, he intends to marry again, a woman his age, a longtime acquaintance who's receptive to the idea of his continued move upward and to someday becoming the First Lady."

"A marriage of convenience," Darlene said. "And would Leslie be content to stay in the background?"

"Not necessarily. The daughter figure, or rather, the stepdaughter, could find power of her own."

"Do his supporters suspect anything between him and Leslie?"

"I don't know. That's for insiders and I'm not yet seen as that."

Darlene turned and added water and to the beef cubes and then added the vegetables she'd prepared: carrots, cubed potatoes, sliced celery and herbs. "How do Robin and her husband fit into this?"

"Harley, that's what his friends call him, although his first name is Owen, started his career at his father's firm. The family business is publishing. There's no relationship to the family of the motorcycle name. When Harley came into his own, he furthered the family fortune with fashion publications. He and his first wife were close friends of Frank and Madelaine Lawrence. Harley knew Robin because she appeared as a model in his magazines. By the time Harley's wife died, Robin was divorced and starting her own fashion company, continuing ties with industry magazines. One thing led to another, and she and Harley married. She gets along with Harley's friends as well as the first wife did."

Darlene turned to face him again. "When Robin spoke of an ill relative who needed peaceful surroundings, I'm sure she meant her husband. What's his problem?"

"Philip Dartmore, who you met, said that Harley was vigorous until last year when he suffered a stroke. He recovered, then relapsed and continues to lose ground. It's a difficult matter in business when a leader suffers a decline and there is no direct successor. A stay at a country retreat makes a problem sound temporary, unlike the darker message of a nursing home or assisted care. It gives those in charge time to make decisions without the bright light of public scrutiny."

"His stay here would give Robin more time to pursue her own responsibilities," Darlene said, turning up the heat to simmer the stew. "She's apparently busy with her career, which involves travel and entertaining."

"I never knew Harley in the past, but Philip and Frank are concerned about him," Acer said. "For their sakes, I'm more than happy to assist Robin. Perhaps you know of someone in town who could pull together a small gathering so she can meet a few people. It might also present an opportunity for your friends to learn more about Fergusson."

"I'll see what I can do," she said. "And now, if you don't mind, I have other things on my schedule for today."

"Of course," he said, standing.

As she saw him to the door, she said, "Robin and her friends would have never heard of this town if it hadn't been for Fergusson. Going back to our earlier conversation, we know he's only looking for a way to your checkbook. His interest in Jessi is for the same reason, a way to get to you."

Acer smiled. "If that's his aim, he's gone after the wrong woman. It's not Jessi I keep coming to see."

Chapter 39

Despite the cold, Alexander rode his Yamaha in the city. It was more fun than the bus and he didn't need to travel a great distance. His longest trip had been his first one when he and Solstice returned to the city after the bridge accident.

Maybe he should go home again.

For some reason, going home no longer seemed so awful. Besides, he deserved a break. He'd been making money working with ad agents, dreaming up material for the Academy Awards in March, cranking up hype about the films and actors that people swooned over. If he went home, why not take Solstice? His mother was delighted to think he had a real live girlfriend. Why not please her?

"I'm having a party this Thursday," his mother said when he called her. "Why don't you and Solstice come and stay overnight?"

"A party for a client?" His mother liked combining work with social occasions, using them to discover what clients wanted in a decorating scheme. She often said that what people *thought* they wanted and what they *really* wanted could be two different things. She got credit for being magical when she simply made the effort to understand them.

"A society woman is visiting the town and I'm throwing a welcoming affair. It could lead to a new client."

"I doubt Solstice is free in the middle of the week," Alexander said. "Are you free next weekend?"

"Do you mean do I have *personal* plans?" Pilar asked.

Alexander cringed at this reference to her love life.

Pilar laughed as if she knew what he was feeling. "Try to come on Thursday," she said, sidestepping her possible weekend activities.

"Okay, but if we come, and we stay over, we need . . ." He hesitated. "We need separate bedrooms."

"Oh?"

Dissembling quickly, he said, "I snore. Really loud."

"My goodness!" Pilar exclaimed, exaggeration in her tone. "How dreadful! It must be a recent affliction. An allergy? Maybe because of carbon monoxide in the city? Even worse for you now because of the bike. All that polluted air rushing up your nose."

He knew she was teasing. She knew he'd been lying. She always knew stuff.

"I deal with it," he said shortly and disconnected.

That felt good, he thought. He didn't think he'd ever hung up on his mother before.

Glad that plans had been made, Alexander wished he could simply call Solstice, but she still refused to give him her phone number or address. She was just so weird!

He emailed, *"How about a motorcycle ride to JumpRope this Thursday? My mother asked us to a party."*

She emailed back, *"the office is closed from Wednesday through the weekend. A bigshots retreat."*

He felt a thump of excitement. "That means you can go?"

She wrote, "you're saying i'm not a big shot? HA! *when should i be ready?"*

Still the lower case letters girl except for shouting, he thought, and wrote: *"Ten o'clock Thursday morning. Tell me where and I'll pick you up at 10 sharp. We can stay overnight at my mother's after her party. Separate bedrooms."*

She didn't answer.

He knew it wouldn't do any good to email again because she wouldn't reply. He knew what would happen. Sometime before ten o'clock, she'd be at his door. They would walk to where he garaged his Yamaha because there was no place on the street for it.

For some reason, he started thinking about his conversation with Donny when they'd been at the Glass House Tavern—the feeling that Donny had been about to say things he'd rather hold back.

Alexander frowned, remembering that when he'd told Donny about bullets hitting his mother's house, Donny had been interested enough to say he would check it out. He didn't think Donny would have forgotten. Still, it seemed he should have said something. Or, maybe he hadn't checked yet. Even so, Donny's silence made him feel uncomfortable.

Or maybe, he thought, he was just getting antsy because he was taking Solstice home with him? With her, he never knew what to expect.

Chapter 40

That same day, with the noon sun doing nothing to warm up the January weather, Holly was already seated in Sean's Pub when Slim came in, wearing a grin.

"Something good happen?" Holly said.

"Sure did," Slim said. He hung his fleece-lined jacket on a hook and fit his lanky form into the seat across from Holly. They were in their usual booth toward the back where there were no nearby tables to attract listening ears. "The detective over at the county, Isaac Ellis, says they found bullet traces on the front of the Fanshawe rancher. They searched where the tech guy estimated the shooter stood and found discarded casings. He stood on the far side of the road, probably bracing on his vehicle. It was dark, but if a bullet smashed the girlfriend's hair ornament, it was a darned close miss. The gun was the one found in Neil Bannister's car."

"Whoa! So Alexander was right about gunshots," Holly said. "They came from Bannister's rifle and when that didn't work, he tried to run Alexander and Solstice off the road. Does Alexander know?"

"Donny's going to tell him as soon as possible and talk to Solstice, too. With the shooter dead, we can't ask who he was after or why."

Holly looked thoughtful. "I'm betting Solstice is the target."

"Sounds like a sure bet. She comes to town, and trouble starts. There's gotta be a story in her past. I'll talk with Vivian. Iris said she and the Colonel took Solstice to the Gibeau farm. The girl and Vivian had a private pow-wow."

Tim, one of the waiters, approached to refill Holly's coffee mug and to set down one for Slim. He asked what they wanted for lunch.

"Pub House Special Burger," Slim said. "Plus extra blue cheese and more onion rings."

"Same here, except regular blue and rings," Holly said.

After Tim left, Holly asked, "What did Pilar think of the police snooping around?"

"Donny told her Solstice lost a hair ornament and Alexander asked him to look for it. Pilar was on her way out. She waved and was gone."

"For now, you're keeping it quiet, right?" Holly said. "Pilar's involved with a party for Thursday. Wouldn't do to think somebody's taking potshots at her house."

"You going?"

"To the party? Yes, Toria and me. You?"

"On duty."

Holly nodded. "Some woman from New York City is coming to the Mather place to stay a few days and she rates the VIP treatment. Toria says she's one of Fergusson's supporters. The Voodoo Club members are hoping to hear things about him, preferably bad."

"They're still steamed?" Slim said.

"Aren't you?"

"Hell, yes," Slim said. "That police car is scheduled to be delivered any day. Fergusson will show up to grin for the *Monitor* along with politicos from the county, whoever is available from the committee and yours truly—a command appearance."

"Jessi will be there with bells on, hoping to persuade JJ to do an interview on her first week on committee."

"JJ might not be there," Slim said. "Remember her dead writer friend's paperwork was swiped? JJ's learned that a retired editor in

Connecticut who proofed her first book has copies of the draft for her second book. JJ's going there hoping for a clue to tell her why her friend came here."

"And got stabbed in an empty house."

"Yeah," Slim said.

Their food arrived. For the next few minutes, there was no further talk, until Slim, having finished his own double order of onion rings, snagged one of Holly's.

"Be my guest," Holly said.

"What are buddies for? Who's the VIP coming to town?"

"I don't know that she's actually a VIP, but she probably has money," Holly said. "She and other New York society people are on the bandwagon to see Fergusson eventually run for president."

Slim made a rude sound. "He's a Cheshire cat, empty smile glowing in the dark." He snagged another of Holly's rings.

"Jessi is impressed," Holly said, edging his plate further away from Slim. "She came into town hall this morning with cell phone photos from a Fergusson event." He noticed Slim checking his watch. "Someplace to go?"

"Sable Kilgallen has a card shop problem. Couple of teens came in carrying open bags of chips and drinking from cans of soda. Sable told them to go out until they were done eating. Instead of leaving they started fooling around pushing and shoving and on purpose or not, one kid dumped his can of soda over a card display."

"Oops!"

"Yeah, a high school sophomore. The kids ran, but Sable knew them. She called 911. I'm meeting with Sable and the kid's father in her shop. He's a good guy. Any damage, he'll make it right. He'll also make sure his kid's learned a lesson."

"Glad it worked out," Holly said.

"It doesn't always, but good when it does."

For dessert, Slim had Chocolate Death cake with two scoops of fudge ripple ice cream.

Holly, who had a slice of lemon meringue pie, looked at Slim and said, "You eat like that, but you're no heavier than when Lana was keeping you on a no-sugar, no fat diet."

"Lana?" Slim grimaced. "Trying to wreck my appetite?

"Sorry." Holly wasn't sorry—he could have eaten more of his onion rings, but he guessed Slim didn't need to be needled about his broken engagement. He changed the subject. "Does Darlene know you have proof that Juan's renting rooms again?"

"Juan says he was just doing the guy a good turn. No way to prove otherwise. I'm keeping my distance from the Empress. It's January. I get my frostbite by stepping outside."

Chapter 41

Darlene was the last to arrive when the six members of the Voodoo Club gathered informally at Toria's house to discuss the party to welcome their New York City guest, Robin Harley. Darlene had told them Robin was coming because she hoped to provide a peaceful retreat for her sick husband.

Toria served refreshments on her Christmas gift china and received rave compliments. Francine correctly identified the pattern. "Royal Albert Old County Roses."

Toria smiled and nodded. Francine was always right.

Nancy Lou said, "This Thursday should be when we have dinner at Teddy's and meet with Mar-see-ah. Pilar's party is the same night."

Amy said, "Why not go to Teddy's tomorrow night, and see if Mar-see-ah can make a space for us. Dinner one night, party the next night. Win, win."

They laughed and all agreed.

"We're inviting Robin to the dinner too, aren't we?" said Iris.

Again, they all agreed.

"She should know all of this ahead of time," Toria said.

"Oh, gosh, yes," said Nancy Lou. She turned to Darlene. "Since you've already met her, will you call her?"

"Yes," Darlene said. She didn't have Robin's number, but Acer would, or knew how to get it. She hated to ask him for a favor. Then she realized that asking him to call Robin to inform her of the arrangements wasn't asking him for a favor. He'd asked her to set up an evening to introduce Robin to people in the community, and she had. Which set up the party they were discussing, and she'd let him know about that. So there! She'd already done him a favor. This would be another one.

Feeling satisfaction, she joined with the others who in discussing how they could help Pilar with the party, but Francine said, "She told me she prefers attending to it herself." There was disapproval in Francine's voice about those who thought they didn't need her help and advice.

Without comment, the rest of the group turned to the purpose of their meeting: reviewing the photos Jessi had taken at the Fergusson event. Darlene was the only one who had been there, but Francine took over, thanks to her conversation with Jessi who had shown her the pictures on her phone. She had printed them out on the color computer at town hall. Taking advantage of Committee woman's privilege?

"Which one is Robin?" asked Toria as the pictures were passed around.

"The blonde." Francine pointed to the woman. "Jessi raved about her diamond and emerald jewelry. She told me Robin was a model until she married an older man who bankrolled her fashion design business. Now, Jessi says he's gone gaga and Robin is probably—Jessi's words—'tweeting for a new worm.'"

"Funny, but not really," Toria said.

"Maybe there's a rich doctor at the county hospital who's right for her husband." Nancy Lou said, running a hand through her tight, newly high-lighted curls. "When he passes, the doctor will be right for her."

"Seems there would be richer pickings in high-flying New York City," Amy said. She lifted a photo. "Darlene, Jessi cut you half out of this one, but it's a great shot of Acer Wolfgang. He's even better than I remembered. I bet you were smiling your head off."

"Being together was merely a convenience," Darlene said.

"Mr. Wolfgang is so nice to help this lady," Iris said. "Did he know her before?"

Darlene explained how the invitation came about. "Our hostess had talked with Jessi about the town. She thought it sounded like a little Scottish village and figured it would be a good place for Robin's husband to recuperate. With that, Acer invited her to use the Mather house."

"Which brings her here and helps our plan to learn more about Fergusson," Nancy Lou said. "If we invite her to the club dinner tomorrow, maybe we should hint to Mar-see-ah ahead of time that we're interested in Fergusson and that Robin's one of his supporters."

"Mar-see-ah doesn't need us guiding her," Iris said. "She's psychic."

Amy laughed. "Doesn't matter, not when Toria makes Mar-see-ah's mysterious messages understandable, like last month when Mar-see-ah quoted that rhyme about Miss Muffet and the spider. It sounded bad, but Toria decided it simply meant there's going to be a surprise."

"Mar-see-ah doesn't say bad things," Iris said.

"How a spider can be good is beyond me," Nancy Lou said with a mock shudder.

Darlene didn't believe in Mar-see-ah as Iris did. Still, the psychic did say things that worked out in ways that seemed uncanny. She hadn't told them yet about a possibly more intimate relationship between Fergusson and his stepdaughter. She was curious to see if Mar-see-ah might say something that alluded to it.

Amy pointed to the picture of Acer. With mischief in her voice, she said, "I could go for him even if he is so old, at least fifty. If Robin's searching for a new man, maybe it's him. That would explain her jumping to his invitation." She slid a teasing glance at Darlene, who had recently celebrated her fiftieth birthday, only her friends knew she was really fifty-three. "You've made it clear you don't want him, so Robin has a clear field, right?"

Anticipating a testy retort from Darlene, Nancy Lou quickly changed the subject. "I saw Vivian Mather coming out of the doctors' office complex last Friday." Nancy Lou was a pediatric nurse at the Melton County Hospital. "Anybody know if there's a problem?"

"Pfft," said Francine. "Vivian was probably seeing an obstetrician. She's probably pregnant. No better than Bethany. Just wait and see. Vivian will have our next hurry-up wedding."

"And she'll be getting Nero Gibeau," Amy said, patting her heart.

"If anyone heard you, they wouldn't know you were already married," Darlene said.

"Being happily married doesn't mean I'm blind," Amy said.

The others laughed, and they were soon all out the door,

Darlene couldn't wait to get home. She knew Amy had been teasing her and she hated to be teased. But could there be a kernel of truth about Robin being after Acer? Looking through the eyes of the club members, she saw that Robin's thought to bring her ill husband to JumpRope *had* been awfully sudden. Robin knew Acer was wealthy because Senator Fergusson wouldn't have been interested in him otherwise, and Madelaine had probably mentioned how charming Acer could be. Then Robin saw him for herself. If she had an eye out for a future husband replacement, she would have been alert for any opportunity to bring them closer. The drift of the conversation and the resulting invitation to the Mather house would have struck her as ideal. No wonder Robin had jumped on it.

Darlene decided to call Acer from work in the morning to ask him to tell Robin about the club dinner and the party. Phoning from her office would make it more like a business call.

Telling herself to think no more about it, she turned on a cable travel program and settled down to enjoy seeing exciting places she would never have a chance to visit.

Chapter 42

The stars outside the Gibeau bedroom window glimmered against a navy blue background above bare-limbed trees. Looking from her position in the bed and resting on Nero's shoulder, Vivian gazed at the top of a tall pine silhouetted against the velvet sky. She imagined the air outside would smell fresh and sweet but she knew that was foolish. It was January, for heaven's sake. But she wanted to whirl and dance as if it were springtime. Everything seemed so special, so beautiful. She was giddy with the wonder of it.

They had just finished making love and were basking in the afterglow. Vivian tilted her face toward Nero. "There's something I want to tell you."

He chuckled. She could feel the vibration in his chest. "Umm," he said in a teasing tone, "we do okay together, don't we?"

She smiled. "I guess we do." It wasn't what she'd meant, but his response had delighted her. He'd only had one session with Father Tom, but the next day he'd gone to a diner in Melton with other veterans he'd met at the session. She didn't know what they had discussed, but she knew it made a difference to share experiences with people who truly understood.

Not that she'd had much of that in her own life.

As a young person, she'd never had a girlfriend, and as an adult, not a woman friend—except maybe Aunt Elizabeth. But even with her, she hadn't shared her innermost thoughts and feelings. For that, there'd been two men: Acer, like an older brother, and Cousin Barry, whom she related to as if he'd been her father. Her own father had been a complicated, troubled man. Not understanding his torment, she had resented him. Recently, she had learned of his injuries during the Vietnam War, physical as well as emotional, resulting in post-traumatic stress disorder—PTSD. And that's what afflicted Nero. It was too late for her to help her father, but with Nero, she felt she'd been given a second chance.

"What I want to tell you," she said, "was that I went to the doctor and—"

He tensed and looked into her face. "Are you all right?"

"I'm more than fine. What I wanted to tell you is news that I think is wonderful. I'm pregnant."

"What?" Sitting up, he turned on the light and stared at her as if he didn't understand what she'd said. Looking at his strong features sculpted by lamplight, Vivian remembered her Aunt Elizabeth looking at him with her artistic eye and calling him a *beautiful man*. If they had a daughter, Vivian hoped the child would inherit his clear grey eyes and long dark eyelashes—those lashes, probably a remnant from an ancient time when women ruled and men needed to bat their eyes to win attention.

"You're pregnant?" he repeated. "We're going to have a baby?" His joyful expression almost immediately turned to anxiety. "You want it, don't you?"

"Of course I do. Didn't you hear me say it was wonderful?"

His distress didn't lower. "You have a career that takes you everywhere. How can . . ." His voice trailed off. "I should have been more careful."

As if she didn't bear responsibility, too, Vivian thought with a smile. "I don't care about my career," she said. "This is where I belong."

She had realized that traveling all over the world had just been marking time until her real life could begin. The psychic Mar-see-ah had once told her, You'll lose the air but gain the ground. She had scoffed and turned it into a plane crash joke, but later, she'd realized what it meant: her existence before had been as airy as the clouds, but what she had now was solid and secure. All that mattered was Nero and the life he'd given her here at the farm, and now, the life growing within.

"Our child," she'd said softly. "Ours. Together." Seeing that his doubt remained she leaned forward to kiss him and then to look into his eyes. She had thought before that feelings didn't have to be spoken, but now she knew they did. "I love you, don't you know?"

His smile was like the sun coming out. "You never said. I never wanted to tell you I loved you. I was afraid it would push you away."

"I love you," she repeated, likening the taste of the words on her breath and writing them on her heart. "I love you."

Laughing, he repeated the words back to her and then said, "We're getting married, of course," and then he started looking worried again as if she might not go along with it.

"Of course we are!" Suddenly she couldn't wait. She didn't worry about details—they could come later.

Right then and there, they decided that their wedding would take place on the second Saturday in February, which was only a little over two weeks away. And there she was, a most unconventional woman becoming the bride of a most conventional man, and nothing could have pleased her more. Who could have guessed the way her life would turn out?

That morning, they told Yvette, who, as usual, down-played her emotions, although a sparkle lit her faded eyes. "Good," she said. "I'd made up my mind not to die until there was somebody else here for Ro."

"You better keep hanging around for a long time," Vivian said to her. "I have a lot yet to learn."

"That's the truth," Yvette said with a nod, finally showing a smile.

Vivian smiled back at the no-nonsense, heavily wrinkled, white-haired woman she'd grown to love. Maybe, she thought, she had finally found a girlfriend.

Chapter 43

Acer called Vivian that morning. He explained about his guest, a woman named Robin, who would stay at the Mather house for a few days. The connection was bad, but Vivian understood she was to meet his guest at two o'clock and give her the keys she would need for her stay. Robin would also be a guest at the party at Pilar's the next night, which Vivian already knew about because she and Nero were also invited.

"I have news," Vivian said. "I want to talk with you when I can." She was eager to tell him about the baby, but not over the phone.

Immediately concerned, he asked, "Are you all right?"

She laughed. "Definitely. But I want to tell you my news in person."

The call completed, she returned to the work she and Yvette were doing in the kitchen. If Iris hadn't told her about shelf paper, she would never have thought of it on her own. It was amazing to realize she had done so much in her twenty-seven years, including keeping trailers and temporary campsites clean, yet she didn't have a clue how to manage an ordinary house.

Death Spins an Indigo Web

* * *

Vivian arrived at the Mather house shortly before two o'clock. While waiting for Robin, she walked around outside, admiring Acer's new landscaping and the house itself, everything looking fresh and new. Inside, the development office was located where the living room had been. The former dining room would serve as the showroom. There were model houses pictured on a big map, plus drawings of various interiors. There were also samples of, tiles, carpeting, fixtures, cabinet faces, and such so that buyers could tailor-make their homes. Acer's next step was the construction of the model homes.

It wasn't until after three that a lipstick red Maserati drove up and an elegant woman with blonde hair stepped out from behind the wheel.

"Hello, you must be Vivian," she said cheerfully. "I feel like I know you already. I've met your Aunt Elizabeth at a charity event for children she sponsors. She's wonderful! As you probably already know, I'm Robin and this—" she gestured to her companion, who'd stepped from the passenger side, a sturdy, big-hipped woman, also a blonde. "This is my friend, Genna Benton. She's a nurse."

Vivian noted that Robin offered no excuses or explanations for being over an hour late. Vivian, who was experienced with the world-revolves-around-me personalities, took it in stride.

Having already shaken hands with Robin, Vivian reached out a hand toward Genna, but the nurse shook her head, touched her throat, and said in a hoarse voice, "I have a bad cold."

"Germs, you know," Robin said. "Nurses are so particular. This place has to suit her as much as me because she'll be the one who will be staying here with—" She broke off and with a catch in her voice said, "I've hated to admit it out loud, but it's my husband, Owen, who needs care."

With a tissue, Robin dabbed her elegantly fashioned eyes. "He had a stroke and came home after rehab, but after a relapse, he hasn't been the same." Straightening, making an obvious effort to get herself back in hand, she took in the surroundings. "This setting is so nicely isolated, yet I know it's part of your little town. From all I've heard, I adore it already."

Vivian found Robin stagey, but there was no question that her feelings about her ill husband stirred deep emotion. She led the two women inside and up to the suite they would occupy for the next few days, the suite where the nurse and the patient would eventually be situated if that was the decision they made. Robin and Genna oohed and aahed over everything, including the tiny kitchenette that now adjoined the new bathroom.

"So convenient," Genna said hoarsely, then apologizing, she turned her head away and coughed.

"I think you should get into bed and rest," Robin said.

"I'll bring in the luggage first," Genna said.

As the nurse left the room, Robin said, "Poor Owen seems to have recovered physically. His mental state is the problem. Things confuse him so." She sighed dramatically. "That's why I thought that once he became settled in a quiet place, he might start to . . ." Her voice broke again, and she made a pained gesture. "Might start to come back."

Genna trudged up the stairs with a large suitcase, a small travel bag and a garment bag. Vivian thought it was a good thing that generous new closets had replaced the old-fashion shallow originals.

She handed Robin the house keys. When Genna came downstairs again, Robin told her not to forget her cosmetics case. She then turned to Vivian.

"Darlene invited us to share dinner with her friends tonight. I can't wait to meet more residents of this darling community. Will Jessi be there? She's such a dear."

"I wouldn't know, it's not my group," Vivian said, "but I'm sure you and Genna will enjoy yourselves." She doubted the group would have invited Jessi. She'd never had trouble with her, but she'd heard plenty.

On her way out, Vivian said goodbye to Genna, who was returning with a stylish-looking case.

Thinking of the numerous items of luggage, Vivian mentally compared Robin's elegant silk outfit and high-heeled pumps with Genna's plain long blouse worn over slacks and wedge-heel white shoes. Her only jewelry was a large-faced watch with a gold-colored background. Vivian bet it had a touch screen for different functions, like a fitness watch. Or maybe, something special for nurses. One to one to read a patient's blood pressure or take a temperature. There were all kinds of tricky instruments in wristwatches today.

She'd tease Acer—ask him if he had a medical watch in his collection.

Chapter 44

That evening, Alexander called his mother to tell her for sure that he and Solstice were coming. She said something about Donny that disturbed him, made him angry. He was about to call Donny, when Donny called him!

Gripping his phone, Alexander responded to what Donny had just said. "You saying you want me to set up a meeting tomorrow between you and Solstice?""Yes," Donny said. "It's important."

"I bet it is," Alexander said harshly, knowing for sure that Donny was calling because of the shots fired on New Year's Eve. He recalled the feeling that Donny was holding something back. With what his mother had said, it had all came together like the big scene at the end of Act One when the characters suddenly realize the trouble they're in.

"You knew!" Alexander said into the phone. "You knew all along that Solstice was in danger. That she was a target for murder! You knew from the moment I told you about the bullets hitting my mother's house."

"Hey, hey," Donny said, "Calm down. It wasn't like that."

"Yes, it was!" He'd raised his voice. "You have been trying to figure out why that Bannister guy was in town. As soon as I mentioned bullets just missing Solstice, you knew because Bannister had a gun. Right?"

"Well, yeah, he did," Donny said.

"Right! And you went to my mother's house with a story about hunting for something Solstice lost, My mother thought I'd asked you to look and she asked me if you'd found it. For a hair barrette, that's what she thought, not bullet marks. You found them and then you knew the reason Bannister was in town was to kill Solstice."

"Okay, but calm down," Donny said. "You're right, but I couldn't be sure at the time."

"You still could have warned us. My God! That guy wasn't driving us off the road because he was having a heart attack. He had a heart attack because he was the one flying off the bridge instead of Solstice and me. It was his second attempt, Donny, and whether you were sure or not, you could have warned us."

"Okay," Donny said. "Suppose I warned you and it turned out to be a big nothing. Suppose it was like you thought, stray bullets fired on New Year's Eve with no connection to Bannister. You and Solstice would have been upset for nothing. Next thing, you would have yelled about me to the Chief. Then he would have yelled at me because I couldn't keep my mouth shut about an ongoing investigation."

Alexander sat back. He didn't get mad often, and he didn't think he'd ever been as angry as he was a few seconds ago, but he could see Donny's point. He wouldn't have ratted him out to the chief, but . . . He drew a breath. "I didn't think about your side of the story."

"Thanks," Donny said. "I've made a lot of mistakes since I've been on the force—stupid stuff I'll never tell anybody, so I wasn't taking chances. But now, I *can* tell you. There were bullets smashed against your mother's house and casings not far away that matched Bannister's rifle. What I need to do now is talk with Solstice and find out why her life was in danger."

"And still is," Alexander said.

"Maybe yes, and that's why talking with her is so important."

"Okay," Alexander said, "I'll get back to you."

Alexander knew if he said the wrong thing to Solstice she'd shut him off. He sighed. He could only do his best.

"*Donny is coming into the city tomorrow around 5:30 and wants to have dinner,*" he wrote. "*Can you come to my place? I'll order Chinese.*"

"*i 'm not sure when i'll be done at work.*"

"*Well, get here when you can.*"

"*i'll be there at five-thirty.*"

Alexander called Donny back with the arrangement, and then sat with his fingers nervously working through his beard. So far, nothing bad had happened to Solstice in the city, but he knew one thing for sure. Two attempts had already been made. There was bound to be a third.

After a night of barely sleeping and a fingernail-gnawing day, Alexander started looking out the window early Wednesday evening for Solstice. He knew the information Donny was bringing would frighten her. It would be just like her to grab her coat and run. The time for both their arrivals was five-thirty, but considering her obsession about never being late, he expected her to be early.

Time seemed to crawl. It was getting dark and the streetlights came on. Alexander kept glancing from the window to the clock. A *Waiting for Godot* clock, it was never going to get anywhere. But then, at 5:16, he saw her from the window.

Illuminated by the nearby lamp, she sat on an overturned trash can and was eating an orange Popsicle. Popsicle in January? She wore a fluffy hat and a scarf. Her long gray coat dragged on the sidewalk.

He opened the window and called down. "Push the bell in the entry. I'll let you in."

She raised the Popsicle, pointed at it with her other hand, and then stuck up five fingers, meaning, he guessed, five minutes.

He called down, "I'm supposed to stand at the window watching until you're done?"

She gave up her mime act and called up, "You got something better to do?" She waved the Popsicle like it was a sparkler on the Fourth of July.

A car driving by tooted and waved. Alexander tensed until the jerk in the car kept on moving. Somebody could have pointed a gun at her out of the car window. He hoped Donny could convince her she was at risk.

Alexander closed the window with a bang on the freezing air coming in. Still looking outside, he saw Solstice laughing.

He closed the lid of his laptop, which he'd been using to research modern-day slavery and human trafficking in this country. Mostly women and children from foreign places thinking they'd come for a better life. But it happened anywhere there were helpless people and greedy, cruel monsters to take advantage. If that's how it had been with Solstice, how wonderful it must be for her to be able to boss somebody around without fearing punishment, to buy a Popsicle with her own money, to sit on the street shouting and waving her hands in silly fun.

But it was risky and she didn't know it. Was the danger from the *Legal But Don't Look It, Daddy's Girls* outfit?

Back at the window, he was relieved to see Donny on the sidewalk, his red hair flaming under the streetlamp. Alexander buzzed them in together. He greeted Solstice and shook hands with Donny. Solstice shed her coat, tossed her backpack in a corner, and headed for the bathroom. "Sticky hands from the Popsicle, Cervantes," she called over her high shoulder.

Cervantes, another playwright, sure, rub it in, he thought, but he grinned. Her itchy ways could be sort of cute.

Donny took off his coat. He wore regular clothes, not a uniform. Good. Less scary for Solstice.

She came out. Alexander saw that she'd chopped her hair short and a bit raggedy. Alexander thought it looked good—not so flat to her head. It went better with her big brown eyes and rosy mouth. His Cosette with a smile.

His Cosette? Oh, boy, what was he thinking? He led his guests to the desk table that he'd cleared of papers so it could be used for dining. They took seats and made food selections from the takeout menu Alexander had ready.

He phoned in the order, thinking that if the ensuing conversation made Solstice bolt, he'd have enough rice and Szechuan delights to hold him for the rest of the month.

Donny started off by saying to Solstice, "I need to ask you about New Year's Eve at Pilar Fanshawe's house. Alexander said firecrackers went wild and struck you."

"Ha!" Solstice jabbed a thumb toward Alexander. "Chicken Little thought it was gunfire."

Donny cleared his throat and sat up straighter. Alexander saw something familiar about the gestures and he realized that Donny was like an actor preparing himself for a scene: a formal police interview.

"Actually, Miss Windsor," Donny said, "Alexander was—"

Solstice surged forward and cut him off. "How do you know my last name?" Her face had gone pale, her freckles standing out like orange sprinkles on vanilla icing.

Taken aback, Donny said, "Alexander must have told me."

"A filthy lie! I never told him. I knew spending time around a cop was bad news." She looked angry, but also scared. "Rotten bloodhound! How did you nose out my name?"

Alexander was thinking, *Windsor . . . that was her last name*? He was glad to know it and relieved that she looked ready to fight instead of running.

Floundering, Donny said, "I saw it on your credit card when we were out to dinner. I didn't know it was a secret."

"I bet. You asked Ditsy here and he didn't know, so you made it your business to find out." Scowling, she folded her arms.

Donny got himself back in hand.

"Solstice, your last name doesn't matter. What matters is that Alexander was right. We found two spent bullets in the front of his mother's house and cartridges across the road, enough to prove they came from a gun that was in the room of the man who tried to run you and Alexander off the road. Both incidents appear to be attempts to kill you."

"*Appear to be?*" Alexander said in a loud voice. "Of course he was trying to kill her."

Looking over at Solstice, he saw her face now looked even more bloodless. He wished he could put his arms around her but that would make it worse.

The food came. He distributed the cartons and everything that went with them, including plastic cups and soda. It all sat ignored.

He sat down again as Donny continued his questioning.

"You said you didn't recognize the man who tried to crowd the cycle off the road. Maybe he was hired. Do you know of anyone who might want to see you harmed?"

Solstice sat with her head down, looking totally withdrawn from the room and everything in it. Alexander noticed she had her right hand deep in the pocket of her skirt. So deep that he wondered if she had worked her hand through the seam and made a hole.

She lifted her head. Suddenly defiant, she met Donny's eyes. "There were bad people in Florida before I came here. They'd love to see me dead." Without further prompting, she continued speaking, as if the words had been backed-up in her throat and the dam had broken.

The story that started coming out stunned Alexander. It wasn't what he'd been prepared for. What she spoke of was domestic servitude. He listened as she told Donny about a mother and adult son in Miami and their grandfather. They made her work for them and used a little dog to keep her in line. They threatened to torture and kill the animal if she tried to expose them or to escape.

"Back up a bit," Donny said. "Where were you before that?"

"My parents ran from their wicked families. We lived on the road. We kept moving so they couldn't find us."

"Your parents' names?"

"They made up names for themselves so they couldn't be traced. Their actual names were Solstice and Earnest Windsor." She folded her arms. "That enough to satisfy you?"

Donny paused, as if not sure what to ask next. "Ah—where are your parents now?"

"You got time?" she said. "Their story is pretty sad."

"Well, sure," Donny said.

"Okay," Solstice said. "Here it is. When my mother got sick, my father left her at a hospital emergency room. He didn't stay because he'd have to answer questions that might allow her wicked parents to find her. Then he left me with some people. He said he'd come back only he never did." She looked down for a moment. When she looked up, her expression was unreadable. "I never saw either of my parents again. And the people I was left with were bad. They rented me out to work. I was put in different places. Then they sold me to the people in Florida."

"*Sold?*" Donny's eyes went wide.

"You want me to repeat it? Yes, sold."

Solstice was proud of herself. Instead of acting limp and frightened, which she really was, she had used that take-charge gutsy attitude she used with Alexander. On the other hand, if she wanted to keep herself safe, Donny needed information, at least what she felt was smart to tell him.

"About the Florida people," she said. "They said their last name was Gastrell. Their grandfather was crippled and mostly stayed in bed. Part of my job was cleaning his room and bathroom and taking meals to him."

She shifted in her chair as she spoke. "The old man and I learned to trust one another. I learned he wasn't their grandfather. He told me that the mother and son were strangers who had made him a prisoner in his own home. They acted as if it was a game. He said he probably wasn't the first one they'd taken over."

Donny tilted his head. "You mean they were con artists?"

Solstice nodded. "He didn't think their names were really Gastrell. Maybe their first names, Alvana and Alwin, weren't real either. He wasn't even sure they were a mother and son. She was the boss and older, with white hair, but I don't think she was *that* much older. I did the cleaning. They each had a bedroom but I know they sometimes slept in the same one."

She shifted in her chair. "I couldn't go to school, so the old man said he'd be my scholar."

She wasn't going to tell Donny she could barely read before. She smiled, remembering that the old man's hair had looked like dandelion fluff floating about his kind and wrinkled face. Aloud, she said, "Because he taught me, I called him the Scholar but his real name was Darius Floye."

"I'll look him up," Alexander said and moved to his desk.

Donny waited. A few moments later, Alexander lifted his gaze from his laptop. "Darius Floye was a wealthy adventurer. He found a lost temple and explored jungles. After being seriously injured in a climbing accident, he retired to Florida. He reportedly became a recluse and cut himself off from everyone, including his doctors and legal people. When he died of pneumonia, his estate went to his adopted daughter and her son. It gives the same first names that Solstice just said and their last name was Gastrell. That's all I can find about them."

Donny frowned and said to Solstice. "How did these people take over the old man?"

"He said they forced him to sign papers and they drugged him. When he could think again, his staff was gone and he had no way of communicating with anyone outside."

"But he was well known. He couldn't just drop out of sight."

"He said that he had been happy living quietly before the Gastrells. His housekeeper drove him to the library for books. Books made his life rewarding. That was another thing he taught me. That if you read, you can learn anything. When it became a struggle for him to get around, he communicated with the library by phone and his housekeeper went for the books. After the Gastrells came, Jenny—she'd been his library contact—called his home because she hadn't heard from him. Alvana answered. Claiming to be his daughter, she said he'd gone into a coma and was in a long-term care nursing center, Jenny believed her.

"He told me that because he was worth more to the Gastrells alive than dead, he was in no immediate physical danger, except he didn't have his prescribed medicine. He was always in pain, but despite that, he made fun of the Gastrells. He said they thought they were smarter than anyone else, but they were stupid."

She smiled as she remembered. "He had a trophy room, a wardrobe closet with collections from his travels. The Gastrells considered it junk, but they were wrong. It made him laugh to think how stupid they were."

Donny frowned. "If you had to work, how did the Gastrells let you spend so much time with this man?

"Hey, good question. I brought him his meals, morning and noon, and I had to be there when I cleaned. He didn't eat at night because it hurt his stomach. When he told them he could no longer feed himself, which wasn't true, I was told to feed him, so we were together longer. Another thing the Gastrells were stupid about was books. They sent me to the library for the books he wanted."

"Wait a minute," Donny said, "If they let you go out, why didn't you tell somebody what was happening?"

She glared. "Because they said if I did anything like that they would kill their dog that I'd come to love and the Scholar. Then, they would find me and kill me too, and they would never be caught."

"But could they actually do all that?" Donny said. "If the police--"

She cut him off. "If you think I would risk it, you're crazy."

Alexander butted in. "She's probably right. We've never been in a situation like that. We can't know what it's like."

Not waiting for Donny's reply, she started talking again. She wanted to get it over with. "I told Jenny he'd come home, and that he'd gotten stronger and was able to read again." She took a breath and told the last part fast, "Then the Scholar got sick. He kept wheezing and couldn't speak. The Gastrells got scared and took him to a hospital where he died. They ran around like crazy people, pretending grief and talking to lawyers about the documents they'd forced him to sign. That's when I took my chance."

"To escape?"

"Right. The Scholar had hidden money. He said if I ever had a chance to get away, it was mine. I grabbed it and the dog and ran."

She sank back, exhausted and thinking how much she'd lied to Donny. She would never tell anyone about the sex people, she was too ashamed. And she didn't want Jenny badgered by the police. She had health problems and not much money. She was in no position to go against the Gastrells, but when the Scholar sent her notes in returned books, she helped in every way she could. Donny wouldn't understand any of that.

What she hadn't told him was that her parents never registered her birth, but the Scholar had somehow, through Jenny, arranged for a birth certificate. She'd also lied when she'd told Donny her parent's names. She'd never known their real names. The Scholar recorded her father's first name as "Earnest," because he thought the name on an official document should be more conventional than Equinox. The Scholar chose the last name, "Windsor," because she'd told him her parents said they were "as free as the wind." The last name pleased her, making her feel as if in some way, she was still connected to her parents.

She hadn't intended to say more, but then she heard herself say, "After Toodles died, that was the dog's name—" Tears choked her. She started to cry. Remembering everything had been too much.

Alexander spoke up. "She told me that after the dog died, she went looking for Vivian and David Mather, the only names she knew from the past. I answered her social media query. That's how we met and that how we got here now."

"Is that correct?" Donny asked her.

She nodded and suddenly found one last bit of strength. "I can't prove what the Gastrells did but if anyone wants to kill me, it's them!"

With that, she stumbled away from the table and collapsed on the couch. She curled up and hid her face in a pillow.

Again, Alexander wanted to go to her, but he knew it wouldn't help. At least she hadn't run. He gave Donny the Internet information about Floye that he'd sent to the printer from his computer.

"I'll take it back to the Chief," Donny said. Then he looked at the food on the table. "Guess we might as well eat."

Solstice, refusing Alexander's attempt to get her to eat, stayed on the couch and kept the pillow over her face.

While eating, Donny asked Alexander if he had anything to add. Alexander knew more about Solstice's past, but they were her secrets and had nothing to do with the Florida people.

"What she told you today was news to me," Alexander said. "I knew her parents died when she was young and she had a rough time after that, but there's nothing I knew to help with this."

When he finished eating, Donny stood. "The Chief already said he's going to talk with Vivian Mather. He knew Solstice had visited her."

Alexander said that was true, but he didn't know what they had talked about.

After Donny left, Solstice kept hiding her face, ignoring anything Alexander said. It was worse than the way she'd acted after talking with Vivian. She was totally wiped out. Turning himself into a dictator, not even trying to think of a theater role to play, he ordered:

"Move from the couch to the chair. If you won't do it yourself, I'll *make* you move. You know you won't like that."

Meekly, she submitted, moving as he'd directed. When she was on the chair, as pale and silent as a ghost, he got sheets and made the couch into a bed.

"I'm sleeping here," he said when he was done. "You can have the bedroom."

She seemed removed from reality. He figured he was going to have to take her to the bedroom, or—he cringed—maybe to the bathroom first. He didn't know when he'd felt in such an awkward situation.

He took a deep breath. "You brought your backpack. You told me you always packed a few items." The success he'd just had with her made him feel on firmer ground. "Keeping your location a secret from me is stupid now that I've heard all this other stuff. You were originally going to come here at ten o'clock tomorrow and we would go to JumpRope, but you're here already, so you'll stay here. What we'll do tomorrow is go to your place, pick up whatever else you need for the weekend, and go."

She didn't argue. Alexander thought he should feel good about being the bossy one for a change, but he didn't. He wondered if she had stopped to think that if her enemies had hired the man who died in his car crash, they might hire someone else. Maybe they already had.

He wasn't going to let her out of his sight.

Chapter 45

Darlene met Robin in the lobby of Teddy's restaurant. The woman had said she would drive herself rather than being picked up. Darlene, the only one in the group who knew her, decided it would be courteous to be there and guide her in to meet the others.

Robin was late. Either she didn't realize it or she didn't care because she cheerfully greeted Darlene and made no apology.

The other club members were all waiting inside in the club's customary small dining room. Darlene led Robin in and introduced her.

The members greeted Robin warmly, and she responded in turn, not only warm but utterly charming.

Too charming, Darlene thought, blaming her sour attitude on the things Amy had said about Robin's possible interest in Acer.

In Darlene's opinion, Amy was a generous person who would do anything to help somebody, but she didn't see the difference between teasing and causing friction. Still, when Darlene looked at Robin, she thought: *Polished Acer and glossy Robin. Perfect together*. The woman wore a smart black outfit with taupe trim and a matching coat. She shrugged off the coat and unthinkingly held for someone to take, which Amy did.

When they were all seated, Robin looked around the table. "When will Jessi be here?"

There was a silence because the club wouldn't have Jessi as a member if she came gift-wrapped, but diplomatic Toria, blushing as she told a half-truth, said, "Jessi's not too free for social occasions. You know, being on town committee."

"Yes, I understand," Robin said. "Even though this town is so tiny, there must be awesome responsibilities. I drove through earlier today. A lovely main street. The snow makes it look like a Christmas card."

There were pleased murmurs at this.

The menu was studied and orders were given. From the time they had taken their seats, members had made leading remarks about Fergusson, pretending to be impressed, admiring his brainpower and saying, with maybe a hint of a question, how difficult it must be to remain an ethical politician. To their disappointment, their techniques failed to encourage Robin to say anything that was even the slightest bit negative.

Iris stepped into a conversational pause. "I thought you might be bringing friends along."

"Nurse Genna's the only one with me," Robin said. "She's been looking forward to meeting people, but she's feeling under the weather tonight." She turned to Darlene. "I have to confess something. I'm unable to figure out how much my husband understands anymore, so when we were together in New York, and he sat right there with us, I couldn't reveal that I actually meant him when I spoke about finding a retreat for a relative."

Darlene had already told the group it was the husband. The members politely murmured words of compassion.

Poor little Robin, Darlene thought sourly.

After the meal had been served, Amy said to Robin, "You're going through such a rough time; it's so great that Mr. Wolfgang had the solution of coming here. He's so kind and generous."

"That he is," Robin said, showing a brilliant smile.

"He's a bachelor, you know," Amy said. "He's spending so much time in JumpRope planning his gigantic development that I thought someone here might catch his eye. Then, Darlene told us about the fundraiser for State Senator Fergusson. Wow!" Amy giggled. "Was I off-base! Mr. Wolfgang lives in an entirely different world."

Darlene's shoulders went rigid. Amy had clearly put the question of Robin's possible interest in Acer on the table.

For a moment, Robin didn't respond, and then she said, "Amy—it is Amy, isn't it? I can't speak for Mr. Wolfgang, but it's obvious your town has its share of attractive women." Robin then turned to someone else and asked a question that had nothing to do with Acer.

As far as Darlene could see, the exchange hadn't revealed anything, although it had seemed Robin colored faintly when Amy had mentioned Acer's being a bachelor.

Nancy Lou said, "I hope Genna will come to your welcoming party tomorrow. I'm a nurse too, over at the county hospital. I'd love to show her around our facility."

"She'll be eager to take you up on your invitation," Robin said. "It's always good to know of medical facilities close by. We'll see how Genna feels tomorrow." She looked around brightly. "Now, tell me the truth, girls. Is this affair tomorrow night really a welcoming party for little old *me*?"

Little old Robin. Darlene smirked inwardly.

The coming party became the topic, including details about Pilar.

"She gives wonderful parties and her house has antiques all over," Nancy Lou said.

"She's a seamstress and a marvelous interior decorator," Toria said.

"Her son is a playwright," Iris said.

"He'll probably be there with his girlfriend," Amy said. "You can give her fashion tips."

"Oh?" Robin looked puzzled.

Francine, who had been admiring Robin's attire, said, "The girl wears long skirts with long sweaters pulled over them."

"Retro fashion," Robin said. "So popular with the young set."

Amy giggled. "She ought to please Alexander's mother because Pilar is always showing up in fashions from the past century."

When their desserts arrived, it was time to start the sessions with the medium. Members of the group had explained the routine to Robin. The medium had an alcove in the restaurant to meet people with prearranged group appointments, as with the members of their club. The readings were individual. When they'd all had their turns, they shared with each other what they'd been told.

"I'm not necessarily a believer," Robin said, "But I find astrologers, card readers, psychics, and such, all quite entertaining.

"Mar-see-ah is more than that, you'll see," Iris said with enthusiasm. "And it helps to keep specific unvoiced questions in mind. Mental concentration aids the spirits."

The other members smiled.

Forty minutes later, when all had finished their sessions, they sat at the table to share what Mar-see-ah had told them.

Robin reported she should watch out for the physical wellbeing of a loved one.

"Your husband," Iris said with a nod.

"I'm sure you're right," Robin agreed, "but then she mentioned my musical ability. Believe me, I have none. She was on the wrong track, but it was spooky. She took my hands in hers and asked if I'd ever played the violin. It sounded cautionary, but it made no sense."

"Mar-see-ah can create a mood," Nancy Lou said.

"All will be revealed in due time," Iris intoned with solemn confidence.

Robin looked blank for a moment, then smiled and rose to her feet, saying she should get back to see how Genna was feeling. She thanked them for the lovely evening and then made an airy gesture toward the coat rack. Amy again did the honors. Coat secure about her shoulders and with a promise to see them the following evening, Robin departed.

For a moment, the club members were silent, and then Amy gave an upward puff of breath that lifted her bangs, and said, "Boy! She sure expects to be waited on."

"And you did it so well," teased Nancy Lou, then added, "However, we didn't learn anything negative about Fergusson."

Francine spoke to show where she reigned supreme, "She wore Emilio Pucci."

"Sure, she looked wonderful," Darlene said. She was sick of Robin. And Amy's needling about Robin's possible interest in Acer might have put the thought in the woman's head even if it hadn't been there before.

Sitting tall, Darlene had come to a decision. Since Mar-see-ah had given no hint to it, she rested her elbows on the table and said, "Now that the outsider has gone, I have something to say about Fergusson that you may find interesting."

Launching into what she had witnessed between Fergusson and his stepdaughter, and what she's learned from Acer, she said, "And, if Fergusson is on track for president, a contrived marriage could keep the relationship with his stepdaughter a secret."

The others were enthralled by the gossip, but Toria said, "We can't do anything about it now, if ever. If Fergusson intends to run for Congress as a step toward the presidency, it's in the future. Right now, it doesn't have anything to do with our town."

"Except," Amy said, "it's given us an excuse for a party."

Chapter 46

Alexander saw his bedroom door open. Solstice came out. She was dressed, but she dragged her backpack along the floor as if she was too groggy to carry it. Her chopped-off hair stuck out all over. Tired as she looked, she summoned the energy to give Alexander a dirty look.

That look delighted Alexander. It meant she was recovering from Donny's questions that had made her relive old horrors.

She was on her way to the bathroom when he boldly announced, "I rented a car for our trip. The bike was run off the road once. I'm not taking the chance of anything like that happening again."

She shrugged, her high shoulder seeming to bounce. "Have it your way, Hotshot." She yawned. "Fun on the bike, but cold in January."

Alexander thought she seemed almost her normal self. *Almost*, because he had expected more of an argument. Then she returned to form, saying, "There's no lock on your bathroom door."

"It didn't have a lock when you used it last night, either."

"I wasn't paying attention then."

"Then don't pay attention now."

She let her backpack strap drop so she could cross her arms. "I don't like it. Get me a chair. I want to wedge a chair under the doorknob."

He glared and spoke in carefully measured tones, not loud, but projected, as if to the last row. "You are deliberately being ridiculous."

"So?" She held her ground.

He glared a moment more. Then, with a huff, he went to the kitchen where a door he never used was propped open with a little plastic wedge on the floor. He yanked the wedge out and took it to her.

"Here," he said. Giving in to his annoyance, he carelessly dropped the wedge into the angle of her crossed arms and was amused when she had to fumble to grasp it.

Clutching the doorstop, she looked him up and down. "Almost six-feet tall, right? How much do you weigh? Two-fifty?"

"No! Two hundred." Actually, two hundred ten. He knew she was riding him, but he couldn't hold back his reaction. He was solid, but he could do with a few pounds less. Five, maybe ten. Fifteen?

She pursed her lips "I put this wedge under the door and you could just bust the whole door off the hinges. Do it easy."

"I probably could. If I wanted to. But I don't." He gave her a stern look he could only pull off with her by taking on the role of Judge Danforth from Miller's *The Crucible*. "My bedroom door doesn't have a lock, either. You never would have stayed in there all night if you didn't trust me." He worked up his courage for his next line. "Quit acting like a freckled itch and get into that bathroom before you pee your pants!"

She burst out laughing. "You're okay, Cyrano." She disappeared into the bathroom.

Impulsively, he gave the door a bang with his fist and shouted. "Hey! I may outweigh you by double, but pay attention to which side your bread is buttered on. It can work in your favor."

She opened the door just wide enough to poke her face out. "Which side my bread is buttered on?" She was laughing again.

"You know what I mean. I can protect you."

Something changed in her expression. She gave him a long look and then said, "I know that." She held out the doorstop and dropped it into his hand. "I think I've known that almost from the start."

Chapter 47

At the same time as Solstice was closing the bathroom door in New York City, JJ Gilbert was entering Slim's office at the JumpRope police station.

He looked up. "Back from seeing that retired editor in Connecticut?"

"Yes, and I came here straight from there. Any crime updates for the *Melton Monitor* come in while I've been gone?"

"The only news was what I told you on the phone when you were still away. Nothing since then."

"More about that later then, now, I've now got my own news." She took a seat. "I found out about Carol's current project from the editor. It's about the lives of outrageously wealthy families who are unhappy despite their wealth. Readers eat up books about the one-percenters being miserable. I've brought home a copy of the manuscript along with her notes for families she'd researched but didn't include. I'm still going through it." A light came into JJ's eyes. "Maybe her death was to stop the book's publication."

Slim rubbed his chin. "What would be the killer's angle?"

"Maybe the book would expose something."

"You told me the subject of Carol's first book was a society murder.

Any murders in this one?" JJ hadn't closed the door behind her. Slim could hear a phone ring on the front desk and then the distant sound of the rookie's voice as he answered the phone.

"Not as far as I've read," JJ said. "Some wheeling and dealing, working the angles with lawyers and real estate brokers and banks, but no murder."

"So why would somebody kill to stop publication?"

"Don't know yet, still reading. I've talked to another editor, the one Carol worked with at the company that published her first book. Carol signed a contract with them for the second book and got an advance. I've talked to the editor there and got an okay to put the draft for the second book in shape for publication—depending on their approval of course. Carol had younger siblings. If the book is published and sells well, the money would be good for their college expenses."

Slim nodded. He liked the way JJ's eyes sparkled when she thought she had a great idea. At the New Year's Eve party in Philadelphia, she'd looked terrific. He remembered thinking that maybe he would give her a ride home, only she'd left for another party. Being neighborly, that's all. Watching out for his friend's kid sister.

"Hey," she said, "I heard that the bullets you found matched the dead guy's rifle. The story still under wraps?"

Yeah, sure, she just happened to hear, Slim thought, cursing newshound connections. He kept his voice calm. "I need more answers before I can say anything."

"The subject is the girl that Alexander Fanshawe hooked up with?"

Slim reached for an open bag of cheese curls half-hidden among papers on his desk. "Don't keep reminding me of all that you know, or I'll start thinking you know too much."

She cocked her head. "Have I ever let you down?"

"Nope." He took some snacks, then stretched a long arm across his desk to pass the bag to her.

"Thanks." She dove in with energy. "Been driving since five a.m., not even breakfast on the road."

She started to return the bag. "Keep it," Slim said. "I've got another."

"Okay, great. So what did Donny come home with last night?"

"Jeez, I told you about that, too?" He knew he had. He'd told her when he'd phoned her in Connecticut. She was easy to talk to, Slim thought, probably what made her great with interviews. Maybe he was, too. People spilled stuff before they realized it. Spilling stuff to each other. Should he tell her more about Donny? Sure.

"Donny came back with a yarn about people in Florida. Solstice's story is that they kept her a prisoner, made her work for them."

JJ stopped nibbling to stare at him. "That's usually with females from foreign countries."

"Not always. She escaped and thinks they might be behind the two attacks."

JJ lifted her brow. "Like a contract kill? Why? For getting away?"

"They were into something crooked. Tell you more sometime. Before I heard the Florida story, I'd been hoping to connect the guy who went off the bridge with Carol's murder. I sent his fingerprints to Steve Kroger in Philly, thinking that if he was the one who cleaned Carol's apartment, prints would prove a tie-in, but his prints weren't there."

"Good idea. Sorry it didn't work out." JJ showed a small smile, just enough to reveal that tiny gap between her two front teeth.

Damn, Slim thought, why did he find her smile appealing? He'd been lonely too long, that was the trouble. Narrow face, hair fastened back with a rubber band, a gap between her front teeth. The hell of it was, he liked her; liked her energy, her intensity, her trustworthiness.

Expression thoughtful, she said, "So now you've got two cases. First, an attack in a JumpRope house, where, according to blood evidence, Carol was stabbed before she was murdered in Philadelphia. Second, the accidental death of a guy who may be a contract killer hired by someone in Florida to get rid of Alexander's girlfriend." She cocked her head. "So, you've got two unrelated crimes?"

"That's what it says to me," Slim said.

JJ shook her head. "You're pretty busy for a small-town cop."

"Yep, that's me." He wanted to run over to the Gibeau farm to talk with Vivian Mather about Solstice Windsor, but he figured he could do that after he had something to eat. He said to JJ, "How about if I have early lunch and treat you to a late breakfast?"

She tilted her head. "Trying to buy my journalistic integrity?"

"Can't buy integrity," he said.

"Whoops, that's right. But I'll take you up on your offer." Sliding into her coat, she said, "You going to the party at Pilar's tonight? Meet that New York gal who thinks State Senator Earl Fergusson has the whole world in his hands?"

Slim hesitated. He'd told Holly he was scheduled for work, and couldn't go. But hadn't Alfonso said he would take his shift if he changed his mind?

He gave JJ another glance as he got up, ready to go to the diner. "Sure," he said as he held the door for her. "I'll be there."

Chapter 48

Slim stayed at Krupple's Diner with JJ longer than expected. A lot longer. They'd found a quiet booth as confidential as one would have been at Sean's, not that they needed confidentiality. Their conversation had been about what her four brothers were up to, and gossip about Vivian and Nero. Was she having a baby? Would they get married? Slim had no opinion. There were enough suspicions and theories in police work. Then JJ started telling him more about Carol's book, about the people in it and their tortured but interesting lives. How could people with so many advantages make so many bad choices—or have so much bad luck? It was fascinating stuff, at least the way she told it.

After finishing dessert and their third cups of coffee each, she took hers with sugar too, but no cream, she left to touch base at the *Monitor* and then to try for some shut-eye before the party.

Slim took off for the Gibeau farm, glad he hadn't given Vivian a specified time. He arrived to find her on a stepladder in the kitchen, putting up a wallpaper border. The walls were already finished with a cream-colored paper that looked like suede. She told him that paper was better than paint because it would hide the cracks in the old walls. She said it proudly, as if it was something she'd just learned.

"Can you take a seat until I'm finished with this border strip I've already pasted?"

He'd said sure and sat down, feeling funny about sitting and watching a woman work. Lana had told him wallpaper was out of style, but he thought it looked nice, a border with pictures of different fruit trees, apple, cherry, peach, and then pictures of matching pie slices between the trees.

Food pictures in a kitchen. What could be wrong with that?

Nero's ancient grandmother poured him a cup of coffee, set out sugar and cream. He was completely caffeinated, but he couldn't refuse. It seemed a sign she had forgiven him for that time he'd once nosed around with crime questions about her handyman and she'd waved him off with a shotgun. Tough lady. Maybe another female in the house had mellowed her.

Vivian climbed down from the stepladder. If she was going to have a baby, you couldn't tell. Slim couldn't fathom her and Nero. Everything about her, including the way she carried herself, was citified class. Nero was small-town. He looked good, was a nice guy, and he was a hell of a mechanic. But weren't people supposed to have something in common? Okay, they were hot together, but what did they talk about? He and JJ had just finished talking each other's faces blue. Not that it meant anything. The tomboy and the cop? He smiled at the foolishness.

Mrs. Gibeau put on a heavy old work coat. It looked like something that had belonged to her long-dead husband. She went outside, saying something about the chickens.

After washing her hands, Vivian sat down at the table and began smoothing on hand lotion.

She looked at Slim. "You said you had questions?"

"Yeah, about Solstice Windsor."

"Oh? First I ever heard her full name."

Slim frowned. "I thought you knew each other as children."

"True, but her parents made up names for themselves. I never heard anything but first names." Thinking of the money she'd seen them burn, she said, "They were sort of crazy." Seeing Slim's continued frown, she added, "We moved like gypsies. It wasn't like the town here, where people's life histories are community lore. You only knew what someone chose to reveal."

Slim thought it sounded like the atmosphere in a prison: you form no attachments, expect nothing from nobody. Or maybe more like street people, banding together loosely and then moving on. With Nero's grandmother not there to see, he pushed aside the coffee he hadn't wanted. "I know from Iris that you and Solstice went off together for at least an hour. What was that about?"

Vivian finished with the hand lotion. Her hair was in a braid that hung over one shoulder and she started playing with the end. Watching, Slim recognized tension. Was she preparing to lie?

"Solstice wanted to talk with somebody who knew her when she was a child." She gave Slim a look of speculation. "Did you always live here, go to school here, have family here?" When he nodded, she said, "I don't think you can understand how it was for her. You have people who knew you before you even knew yourself. Family, friends, neighbors, teachers, people who watched you grow up. There were all sorts of shared memories. Keepsakes and snapshots, videos from school plays and graduations. Every one of those things nails down who you are as a person. You are real, not only to yourself, but to the world at large.

"Solstice didn't have that. She floated with nothing solid under her feet, nothing to hold on to or prove who she was outside her own head. What she needed from me was shared memories of herself as a child to prove it had all been real."

Meeting Slim's eyes, she thought of the girl's confession of the time when her body was rented, bought and sold against her will, the fact that she looked so young adding to her value. She set her jaw. "I don't want to break a confidence. What is it that you really need to know?"

Figuring he'd gotten some of the truth, he said, "Her life may be in danger because of her past."

She was visibly startled. "I heard about Alexander's bike being run off the road when she was with him. An accident, wasn't it?"

"We now think it was not only deliberate, it was the second failed attempt on her life. We're looking for someone in her past with a grudge." He considered his options and how to work around Vivian's caution with the information Donny had gleaned. "If I say Florida, would it mean anything?"

"It would." Struggling to conceal her relief, Vivian gave one last tug on her hair and flung the braid back over her shoulder. Being forced into domestic labor was horrible, but it didn't cause the same sense of shame as being a victim of sexual traffic. "Solstice was trapped in a bad situation in Miami," she said.

Slim nodded as her words confirmed what Donny had found out. He told her a bit more and she said:

"The couple you're talking about profited from an old man's death. They wouldn't want Solstice to talk. That's why she's in danger, isn't it?"

"That's how it looks," Slim said.

After Slim left, Vivian cleaned up the wallpapering mess and thought more about Solstice. Vivian was glad the police were on to it, but of course, they would have to find the Florida people first. With their stolen wealth, they could be anywhere.

Or hire anyone to do their bidding.

Vivian hoped Solstice would be on her guard. If Alexander came to his mother's party, Solstice would probably be with him. She would talk with her then.

Chapter 49

Solstice stood in Alexander's apartment and confidently said to him, "I'll go back to my apartment to pack and tell you where to pick me up." She was still refusing to give him her address.

"Then forget it," he said. "If you don't want a change of clothes for my mother's party, we'll get on the road. That suits me better anyway."

"It doesn't suit me!" She actually stamped her foot. With her choppy haircut and petulant mouth, she looked like a mime. *Angry Girl*.

He had something serious to say to her, something he'd been thinking about all night. He decided to save it for later.

"Look," he said, "You slept in Iris's house, you slept in my apartment, you're willing to sleep at my mother's house and you said you trust me. So, let's go to your place and pick up what you need, or we go without it." He immediately wished he could take those last words back. All she had to do now was to say the visit to his mother's house was off.

To his surprise, she grimaced, and said, "All right, we'll go to my place. I'll direct you."

He grinned. "Still not giving me your address, huh?"

"Shut up," she said.

* * *

Her place turned out to be a small walk-up on an old Brooklyn street made up of former one-family homes converted to multiple units. He made her wait in the car while he went inside and checked around and then he waved her inside. He did the same thing at her apartment door, taking her key and going in first.

She made a face. "What's the idea?"

"Attempts have been made on your life." He returned her key and allowed her inside her apartment. "I'm making sure everything is okay."

"No attacks here," she said. "Attacks only happened in your stupid town. Explain that."

He thought that he could, but he reaffirmed his earlier decision to save it.

"I'm getting my clothes," she said, and slid away and into what he guessed must be a bedroom. She shut the door too swiftly for him to see inside.

Alone, Alexander walked around. He looked in her kitchen. Stove, sink, refrigerator; no space for a table. The refrigerator held milk, a jar of pickles, mustard and three apples. A half-used carton of chocolate ice cream and empty ice cube trays occupied the freezer.

The kitchen opened to a living room, only it appeared no living took place there. There was a table, a straight-backed chair and a couch. No TV, no pictures on the wall and no curtains on the two windows that faced the street. The window shades were pulled down to the sill.

He checked out the bathroom. Usual stuff, plus a stacked washer and dryer. A big plus—he wished he had that. He grinned to himself, thinking that now that he knew where she lived, he'd bring his laundry over. Not that he'd do it for real.

On the medicine cupboard's single shelf was a comb, a bottle of aspirin, and—wow—blusher. Girly paint! The blusher looked like a sample that had been opened and used. Probably only in the privacy of the bathroom, which had no window.

The only thing left to snoop into was the closet by the bathroom. He found a raincoat on a hook, an umbrella and a pair of battered canvas shoes on the industrial carpet floor. On the shelf was something that made his heart twist—a collar for a small dog and a leash. The collar had a tag that read *Toodles*. He remembered Solstice telling Donny that she escaped from Florida with a dog. It had since died, but he now saw she'd kept its leash and collar.

Was she still grieving for the animal? Shaking his head sadly, he went to the door of the room he hadn't looked into, so yes, it had to be the bedroom. He heard her moving around. Carefully he turned the knob and quietly released the latch. He peeked in and stiffened in shock.

The bedroom was like a different world. It was painted light green, ceiling and all. There were floor-length drapes on the single window, with what his mother called a valance across the top. The drapes, bed-cover and pillows all had the same wild print, vines with huge green leaves on a white background. There was a tall palm-like potted plant.

A jungle room.

A vision flowered in his mind. His gal, Sheena of the Jungle, swinging through the trees on a vine. And wearing blusher.

The thought made him smile.

He pushed his head further inside. Solstice, her back to him, was sliding what looked like a flesh-toned band around her thigh. There was something shiny fixed to it. He watched her pull out the shiny thing and flick it open, revealing a wicked-looking, curved blade.

He suddenly remembered their first time in JumpRope, after Chuck drove off. He'd told Solstice he would also be staying at Juan's. She'd misunderstood and had jammed her hand into her coat pocket. He'd thought then that she had a weapon. Now he knew he'd been right.

He also remembered times when she'd shoved her hand deep into her skirt or coat pocket. When she was anxious or fearful, she must reach toward that curved weapon. Oh, man, Sheena swinging through the jungle with a knife!

Still unaware, she smoothed down her skirt and turned to her backpack. There were clothes on the bed—underwear, pajamas, sweaters, skirts, her green dress and fancy shoes. It looked like too much to fit into her pack. She reached for what looked like a length of yellow fleece. Was she bringing that too? All at once, he knew what it was.

He must have made some sound because Solstice jerked her head up and saw him.

"Get out!" she ordered. "Get out!"

Instead of backing out, he went in.

"Cute blanket," he said, looking at what she clutched in her hands, a fuzzy yellow blanket with dog faces printed on it. He figured it had belonged to the dog. Remembering the lightness of her backpack when they took the bus, and he said, "You didn't take it before."

"Right. That was before your friend—" she emphasized the word sarcastically "—made me rake up bad memories. But now I don't want it anyway." She cast it to the floor.

"If you thought you needed it a moment ago, you still need it. There's space in the car. I'll hang up your dress and take out the sweaters and skirts to the car. Everything doesn't have to fit in your backpack."

She set her chin. "Does too."

"Sure," he said, and gathered the items he'd spoken of, and reached for and captured the blanket. He put her shoes on top. Arms full, he said, "When I come back, you, and what's left for your backpack, should be ready." It was an order. And didn't that feel good!

When he returned, he found her standing in the hallway with her backpack. Her expression was an interesting combination of angry and forlorn, but she was ready.

They ate lunch at a Turnpike restaurant halfway through their journey. Alexander figured his mother would be in full party mode. All the food in the house would be reserved for the evening. Solstice's snarky shots about his weight had him thinking that wolfing down fast food wasn't the ticket, so he had a modest lunch. Solstice ate like she'd been stranded on an ice floe for a week despite a big breakfast at his apartment. She insisted on paying for her own food and he let her. Let's hear it for independence.

While she was in the ladies' room, Alexander stepped outside and called his mother so she'd an idea of when to expect them. As the phone rang, he looked upward. The sky held lines of grey clouds. The air was still and very cold. Looked like more snow.

Pilar answered, sounding distracted, which surprised him. She was usually in top form during party preparation.

"I'm a bit behind," she said. "The guest of honor showed up to introduce herself. She'd heard I'm a decorator and she's a potential client."

"Difficult to refuse that," Alexander said.

"Exactly," Pilar said. "She and her husband have a second home on Long Island that she wants to have redone. I brought out the portfolio of my work. She looked at that and then walked around, looking and asking questions. I suspect she's difficult to work with."

Alexander smiled. Like working with his mother was a piece of cake. "You've dealt with all sorts of clients."

"True. If she's happy, she'll spread my name. She's staying in the Mather house. She wants her husband to come there. He's ill and she thinks the small-town atmosphere will be good for him." She switched to the topic of the treacherous roads.

Alexander told her he'd rented a car. He realized he should have told her earlier so she wouldn't worry.

"That's wonderful! You two already suffered a mishap on that bike and don't need another. Now all I have to fret about is people getting from their vehicles to the house. It was warm yesterday and snow melted, then, freezing weather and more snow. The drive and front walk are ice rinks. You and Solstice be careful walking to the house. I have bags of that snowmelt that I want you to spread around."

"I'll take care of that when I get there," Alexander said, stepping back inside the restaurant. He saw Solstice coming from the ladies' room and took a deep breath. Time to have a talk with her.

A talk he wasn't looking forward to.

Chapter 50

Alexander had planned to have the conversation with Solstice when sitting in the car in the restaurant parking lot. Then he decided it would be too hard with nothing to look at except her smarty-pants expressions. If they were on the road, he'd be looking ahead.

Once in the turnpike traffic stream, he viewed the grey world all around them. The only colors he saw were of the other vehicles. Keeping his eyes on the road, he said, "The Gastrells know where you live."

For a moment there was a shocked gasp and then she laughed. "Ridiculous! If they knew where I live, they could have arranged all sorts of fake accidents: run me down on the street, shove me in front of a bus, sneak in and rig the gas stove. Instead, they wait until I'm miles away in your dumb town. Explain that, Sherlock."

"It's because the Gastrells don't know you haven't talked about them."

From the corner of his eye, Alexander saw that it looked as if she had her right hand tucked into the pocket of her long winter coat. It was what she did when she was concerned or anxious. He was sure she was fingering that little knife he'd seen. He suspected she'd ceased believing she was in danger. Now, he'd challenged her feelings of safety, so she needed the assurance of her weapon.

"I never let a word slip to anyone," she said. "That is until your red-headed cop pal badgered it out of me. And that was *after* the two attempts on my life in *your* town."

"Yes, in my town where the attacks appeared accidental. If the JumpRope cops reported your accidental death, why would the Brooklyn cops investigate further? The Gastrells couldn't kill you where you live because the Brooklyn cops would find out where you worked and talk to your coworkers. They would hear about the people you were afraid of."

"Only they wouldn't because I never told anyone."

Alexander took a breath and spoke in the voice that had directors who rejected his plays saying he should be an actor, a voice that could have been God in a remake of *Exodus*.

"*The Gastrells don't know that,*" he thundered. He took another breath. "For just a minute, could you please stop thinking of the secrets you've kept and imagine what the Gastrells *feared* you'd said? You're the only living person who knows the truth about their crimes."

After a long pause, she said, "So you're saying that the horrid mother and son assumed I told people about them. And, if I were killed in the city, they assumed that after cops questioned my coworkers, they would know about the people I was afraid of."

"Bravo!" he said, giving her a taste of her sarcasm.

"Except—" Her tone lifted in triumph. "If they wanted to kill me, what gave them the idea I could be here? I could have run anyplace, to California, Idaho, Arkansas, Canada . . . the Gastrells could have spent their whole lives hunting for me."

"Some clue told them where to start looking," he said. "Why did you come to Brooklyn?"

"To get as far from Florida as possible."

"You could have gone anyplace, like you just said, so why Brooklyn?"

She was quiet, and then she said in a smaller voice than before, "The Scholar had a sister who lived there. Before she died, and before he was crippled, he used to visit her."

"Could the Gastrells have known about her?"

"He said his sister had left him items from places they'd explored together. She willed him money, too."

"And if the Gastrells found her name and address in his financial records that would have told them where to look first."

"Could have. They made it their business to know everything. But how could they find me, one person, in an area crowded with people?"

"You've got me there," he said.

"Yeah, it all falls apart now, doesn't it?"

"I'll figure it out," he said.

"Ha!" She shot a triumphant look, like laser beams from her eyes. If he ducked, the beams would zoom out the driver's window and into the car that was passing them. The old lady cuddling a little dog would have twin holes burned in her head.

Dog. He remembered the collar, and the truth hit him like a sandbag dropped from the rigging.

Excited, he said, "From what you told Donny, the dog is the only thing you brought with you from Florida. Did you license the dog?"

"Of course. I'm law-abiding, not some sneak like them."

"Suppose the Gastrells hired somebody to find you," he said. "They could have made a guess that you might have gone to Brooklyn and they knew you took the dog. Their detective could have searched for dogs recently licensed."

"Maybe." Voice fading, she said, "The vet told me he was an Australian terrier. He had silky hair and a stiff tail, and he weighed about ten pounds."

"And when you registered him with that description, you gave your name and address?" He thought of how proud she must have been. A free person, with her own place, her own job, her own dog. *Free.*

"Yes." He knew it was finally all coming together for her. Her voice was so soft he could hardly hear her when she said, "Toodles wouldn't have wanted to get me in trouble because of him." She started to cry.

Alexander felt sympathy, but he was also relieved. They now understood how the Gastrells must have found her, and she recognized the danger. She had drawn away to huddle against the passenger window, her coat collar pulled up to cover her face. He didn't know if she was still crying or not, but he figured it best to say nothing.

They didn't exchange another word as he kept driving. They finally approached his mother's house. He saw what his mother had meant about the ice. Tree limbs and the eaves of the roof were hung with long icicles and the foundation plantings glittered as if decorated for a Christmas card. Patches on the long paved driveway and the walk leading to the front door shimmered like glass.

When he stopped the car, Solstice scampered out while he was still opening his door. When he joined her on the walkway, her feet hit an icy patch and she slipped. His impulse was to reach out and grab her, but a neon NO sign flashed in his head. He couldn't touch her, but she could touch him, right? He didn't know how he found the presence of mind, but he stepped in front to face her, his arms angled out. She grabbed his arms, right and left. He stood like a robot, hoping to God his own feet would hold fast as he accepted her slight but off-center weight and she regained her footing.

She looked up at him. He was supporting her but not touching her.

There was a long pause, the two of them standing like players in a stage set.

"Thanks, Gibraltar," she finally said.

"No problem." He heard his voice sounding deep and confident.

She trusted him. He knew it and she knew it. How could he be anything less than confident?

His one arm dropped as he turned to face his mother's house. The other arm, elbow presented, he offered to her. She clung to it as they made their way over the slippery ground to the door.

He felt triumphant, but then he tensed, thinking that slippery ice was nothing compared with the danger Solstice faced. Two attempts on her life had failed. The Gastrells would surely make another try.

He forced himself to calm down. At least for tonight, in his mother's house, she would be safe.

Chapter 51

Darlene and the other members of the Voodoo Club each brought their own special party foods even though Pilar had said she'd have everything under control. Amy, who had brought spicy pizza snacks, said, "At a party, there's never too much to eat—especially when it's all different."

Alexander and Solstice helped put out the food, Solstice greeting each dish as if it were a treasure.

Darlene found it hard to look at the fragile girl and imagine her being such a threat that people would actually hire a hit man. Toria had told Darlene about Donny's visit to Solstice in New York, and Solstice's frightful story. Darlene wished there was some way she could help. If it was a mystery in a book and not real life, it would be tailor-made for a prosecutor to play detective, track down the evildoers, present the evidence before a jury, and have the judge lock them up. She smiled at the thought of being the prosecutor.

Realizing she was letting her imagination get out of control, she decided to do something useful. She headed into the laundry-utility room next to the kitchen. Her self-appointed task was lining waste cans that would eventually receive the party debris. Acer would be there because it was his job to introduce Robin to the gathering. She didn't want to think about seeing him again, even though she'd worn a dark blue cocktail suit because, well, because Acer had said he liked her in blue.

She decided that maybe he was a better person than she'd originally believed but he was still too much for her. Her insecurities were always revealing themselves in her snippy comments. Robin made a far better match for him. All she had to do was put on a poor-little-me-with-sick-husband act and say she didn't have an escort for this or that and Acer would be right there. Knight in shining armor. And Robin would soon have him in bed with her. He would think it had all been his idea.

Darlene felt that Acer showed interest in her because she didn't fall in line like other women. Yet why did that make her shy of him? In her most private thoughts, she could imagine how wonderful it would be to be held in his arms, to love and to be loved.

She heard the echo of her thoughts. Love? As if that was ever going to happen. Angrily, she jammed a liner down deep in a waste can. Despite the effort she'd put into her appearance, it was far safer and smarter to simply stay out of his way.

She heard his voice and went rigid.

"There you are," he said warmly.

She saw him from the corner of an eye.

Not turning toward him, she kept busy smoothing the liner. "Nobody ever has enough trash bags," she mumbled. Done with the job, she picked up the box of unused bags and clutched them to her breast—an ineffective shield. The utility area was small, and the walls seemed to be pressing in. Acer's solid frame closed off the doorway.

She summoned her nerve to look up at him. He was marvelously dressed, as usual, perfectly styled, perfectly tailored, all set to rule the world. She automatically went into defensive mode.

"You appear pleased with yourself," she said. "But then again, you usually do."

He gazed at her a moment and then said softly, "When will you learn to trust me?"

She moistened her lips. "I don't know what you mean."

"I believe you do." There was only a half-beat, maybe even less, before he said, "Are you and the others in your club still hoping Robin will reveal more about Senator Fergusson?"

Darlene looked away from him. "Toria and I think we should give it up. Some of the others feel differently." She saw a space for the box of trash bags. She was prepared to reach up and shelve the box, but it was too high for a graceful move.

Clutching the box, she turned toward him and said defiantly, "So what if Fergusson's using the town, using Jessi, trying to use you and giving false impressions to the public? He's a career politician—what else could we expect? When he's actually running for a higher office, maybe we can do something. For now, Toria and I will focus on having a nice party." She dared look at him directly. "Which I'd like to get on with if you would move out of my way."

Instead of moving, he leaned one broad shoulder against the door jam. It sounded as if more people had entered the kitchen behind him but Darlene couldn't see who they were because he shielded her view. It was as if in this unlikely setting he had created his own world. One she wanted to escape.

"Are you aware of Vivian's coming child?" he said. "And of her wedding?"

"Rumors," she said. She didn't want to further the conversation.

"It's true," he said. "Vivian and Nero will be here later, but I was at the Gibeau farm earlier and talked with her. She is my heir and dear to me. Before, she never wanted marriage, never even thought of children. Now, she is delighted to be married and start a family. The child will be my heir as well. It's not good to bestow too much on any one individual. Twyla and Ben, the two children you met several months ago, are also my heirs." He paused and then added with a smile in his voice, "Now you, along with my attorney, are the only ones aware of those particular facts. I have been fortunate enough to prosper. Affluence can bring a great deal of pleasure, but no man can live forever."

Darlene hadn't moved a muscle, but everything within her

screamed to run. Why was he always shoving his way in, sharing information about himself that she didn't want to know, information that made her see him as a person rather than empty stuffing in a good-looking suit?

He moved toward her. Gently, he took the box from her hands and easily placed it on the shelf. Hands bereft, she felt disarmingly vulnerable. Struggling to maintain control, she forced a laugh. "To hear you talk, you would think you expect to step off any minute."

"I'm aware of the passage of time." He glanced at his wrist and the watch that embellished it. "Thus, my obsession with timepieces." He smiled into her eyes. "Not my only obsession."

Disconcerted, she looked away again.

He asked. "Will you be attending the wedding?

A change of subject, thank God. Even so, she hedged. "Will it be at one of the churches here, or where her aunt lives?"

"At the banquet hall of Teddy's restaurant in two weeks." He chuckled. "Vivian is an unusually independent female. I would have expected her to want a no-frills private ceremony. She surprised me. Although she felt she couldn't go along with the big Catholic Church wedding Nero's grandmother would prefer, she wants many of the usual traditions. She has asked me to escort her down the aisle."

Darlene heard a catch in his voice and realized the honor meant a great deal to him. This was confirmed when he added, "When it came to the question about giving away the bride, I thought, because she has always been so independent, that she would want to say, *She gives herself.* Instead, she wants me to say, *I give this woman, with the blessing of her family.* The ability to say those words, to speak of her family as if it were my own, is a gift." He gazed into Darlene's eyes with an intensity from which she couldn't retreat. "Sometimes the most generous gifts are those that no money can buy. After I've finished my part in the ceremony, I will step from the altar and find a place to sit. Will you save me a seat?"

Darlene's hands locked together. "But . . . you'll sit with the rest of the wedding party."

"That wasn't my question."

His tone forced her to hold his gaze. She saw a longing in his expression, almost a pleading. For no reason she could fathom, the words of her long-gone widowed grandmother returned to her. Active in church and other community groups, she had once said, *everyone needs to belong to something*.

To belong. Darlene had never before thought that Acer's wealth might isolate him. She knew there were those enamored with his riches, while others, herself included, were suspicious for much the same reason.

He saw her hesitation and said, "At the wedding, before all your friends, will you have the courage to save me a seat by your side?"

Courage. Before her friends. By his side. As if he thought he was someone she would be ashamed of. She saw the honesty in his eyes. Saw him waiting patiently for her reply.

"I could do that, yes." Now, she had trouble controlling *her* voice. "I don't know where I'll be sitting, but yes, I'll save you a seat."

His expression warm, he revealed his appealingly tilted smile.

"Don't worry," he said. "I'll find you."

Chapter 52

*S*mooth jazz piano tunes played background music for the forty to forty-five laughing and talking people comfortably crowded in Pilar's long combination living and dining room. A second table held food and non-alcoholic punch.

A regular bar was on the opposite wall. Former committeeman Max Osterhagen worked bar detail, assisting Francine's husband, Bob. Francine always volunteered Bob for the job because she felt keeping him behind the bar for as long as possible was a good idea. While he was never actually "drunk" (she hated that word) her usual taciturn husband could become the life of the party after a beverage or two.

Jessi Spellman and her husband swirled into the party from the freezing cold with Arnie carrying her because of her fancy shoes and the foul weather. Looking near to bursting with pride, Arnie ceremoniously lowered Jessi to a standing position and accepted her shrugged-off coat, which sparkled with sleet. The coat was full-length faux white ermine worn over a catsup red jumpsuit with wide legs ballooning like harem pants.

"Who's that?" Solstice asked, her pert nose wrinkling.

"A lady who lives here in town," Alexander said.

"Cookiepants," Solstice said.

Alexander snickered. He didn't know what Cookiepants meant, if anything, but it somehow seemed perfect.

Jessi caught sight of Robin and made a beeline toward her.

"Robin! How wonderful to be together again!" Jessi spoke loudly so that anyone listening would understand she was a regular part of Robin's crowd.

"So good to see you, too, dear," Robin said.

They made an admiring fuss over each other's attire and then Jessi said, "Oh, there's Acer! I must talk with him."

Robin observed Wolfgang's reticent response to Jessi. The woman had told Earl Fergusson she had won the JumpRope election because Acer, her dear friend, had bankrolled her campaign. Robin doubted it. This was the second time she had seen the two of them in the same room and sensed zero camaraderie. Robin decided to tell Earl if he wanted to win Acer's favor, Jessi smelled like a liability.

Robin then noticed a tall, rangy man with blond-brown hair who had just come in from outside. She headed toward him. From what she'd heard, he must be the town's police chief. She moved into his path.

"Hello! I'm Robin Harley. You must be the police chief."

"Chief Parkerson at your service," he said, with an easy grin. "You can call me Slim."

Robin cocked her head, her blonde chignon secured with a pearl beaded comb. "Call you any time?"

Slim laughed. "Sure can, but only dial 911 for a true emergency."

Robin might have come back with another comment, but he gave her a nod of farewell and moved off when someone else hailed him. A woman stepped up to Robin's elbow and greeted her.

The speaker was an elderly woman with a fluff of improbable chili-pepper-colored hair. "What a lovely party to introduce you to the neighborhood," the woman said. "I'm Lillian Brent, the secretary for the historical society. I'd love to show you our collection."

"How nice," Robin said. "I'll be sure to be in touch."

"I hope you will," Lillian said. "You'll learn so much about our town. Have you met Alexander, our hostess's son? He writes plays."

"I haven't met him yet," Robin said.

"There he is." Lillian pointed, looking past Robin's shoulder. "That's his girlfriend with him. Solstice, her name is. Don't they make an adorable couple?"

"Goodness, yes," Robin said after giving them a glance. She said she was getting a drink and excused herself.

At the bar, she flirted with both bartenders while receiving her beverage, a safe white wine. Drink in hand, she continued milling around and introducing herself to people. If they had heard about her husband's nurse, she explained that Genna was still under the weather. "Coming here when we did was poor timing," she said. "Winter! What was I thinking? I'm glad we're returning home tomorrow, but we will be coming back soon with my husband."

She saw Pilar's son, Alexander, standing by the smaller food table handing Solstice a glass of punch.

"Are you the playwright?" Robin said when she had moved through the throng to reach him. She eyed the breadth of Alexander's shoulders and deep chest. "My, you look like a football star."

Robin's gaze moved to Solstice. Alexander introduced her. When Robin reached out a hand, Solstice edged closer to Alexander, clutching her beverage.

Robin looked confused for a moment and then, "Oh! Excuse me. Mr. Wolfgang is signaling," she said, and moved on.

Alexander was flattered by Robin's acknowledgment of him as a playwright but he didn't take it seriously. He met her type all the time in the theater and in the advertising business. Filled with personality and spouting empty words to people they wouldn't recognize five minutes later. He was amused by Robin's saying he looked like a football star.

In high school, he'd been asked to try out for the team and succeeded. He was blocky and strong, but he took different classes than most of the other players. They ignored him and the coach mostly kept him on the bench. Alexander didn't care, he considered the experience research. Didn't Tennessee Williams have the character, Brick, an ex-football player, in *Cat on a Hot Tin Roof?* Then came the day when the right tackle was injured. The coach put Alexander in, his purpose to be a rolling dumpster to protect the quarterback. He'd done just fine.

Now, he said to Solstice, "Got a smart-mouth name for that one?"

"Shutterthread."

He tilted his head. "What's that mean?"

"Shutter, like a camera clicking, snap this, snap that, and stitch it all together."

He grinned. "I like it. As good as Cookiepants; maybe better."

Lillian stepped up. "Alexander?" She had hung back until after Robin had moved on and after stopping to chat with Donny and Bethany. Bethany was proudly showing off her baby bump.

Lillian and Alexander were still talking when they became aware that the hubbub was easing off all around the room.

Acer Wolfgang stood by the dining table, facing the gathering. He tapped a spoon against a glass to draw attention, but it was no longer necessary. The crowd had fallen silent.

He spoke, his voice in a normal conversation range, yet carrying well as he introduced Robin as a friend of friends from New York City who was thinking of spending time with her husband in town.

Robin took the floor.

She raved wildly about the community. Everything and everyone was wonderful. Her hands, rings flashing, gestured to emphasize words filled with praise for what she already knew and her enthusiastic expectations of learning even more good things in the future.

When she concluded, there was applause. She then said that Mr. Wolfgang had an announcement.

She stepped back and Acer moved forward again.

Announcing a surprise, he gestured off to one side.

Vivian and Nero appeared. They moved to Acer, standing close together but not touching. Vivian looked radiant. Nero looked uncomfortable about being in the spotlight, but he smiled nonetheless.

Having introduced the pair—Nero, a life-long resident, and Vivian, new to the community, but with family roots—Acer said, "I'm pleased to announce that Vivian and Nero are to be married."

During another round of applause, Holly, who as mayor would perform the ceremony, reached for Toria's hand. "Soon us," he whispered. Toria looked down at her engagement ring on the hand that Holly held. Then, smiling into his eyes, she brought their hands up together and pressed them to her heart.

The crowd quieted. Acer gave the wedding date and said, "The ceremony will be at four o'clock in the afternoon at the banquet hall of Teddy's Bar and Grill Restaurant. Everyone in town is invited to the ceremony and to the reception at Teddy's that will immediately follow. I ask you all to spread the word. Come to attend this wedding and rejoice with the bride and groom."

Chapter 53

Slim had been talking with friends and moving around the room when he saw JJ. He moved toward her.

"Hey," he said. Her hair was fluffed and she looked good. "Did you hear the confirmation of the gossip mongers? They were right about Vivian and Nero."

"Small towns." JJ grinned. "Non-stop mongering. As bad as reporters."

"Almost as bad," Slim said. "Look over there at our guest of honor." He directed her attention to Robin, who stood against the wall near the bar, texting on her cell phone. "Think she's messaging hubby to say she can't wait to get back to his bedside?"

JJ snorted, just as she used to do when she'd been a kid. "She came rushing up to introduce herself when I first came in. I doubt she's the type to spend time in a sickroom. That's why she has that nurse, so she can stash him and forget him."

"Reporters," Slim said, "always looking at the dark side."

"And cops aren't?"

They bantered a bit more and then moved to congratulate Nero and Vivian.

Slim gave Nero a handshake. When he gave his best wishes to Vivian, she said to him, "I can't help but be worried about Solstice. Have you learned anything more about those people in Florida?"

"Wish I could tell I have, but no," he said.

Vivian nodded and said she was going to go find Solstice.

Slim went to get JJ a drink and to refresh his own. Back with the drinks, he looked across the room at Jessi and Robin. Following his gaze, JJ saw the two women facing one another, gesturing and talking, party noises swirling about them.

"Jessi wants to impress Robin," JJ said.

"Jessi wants to impress everybody," Slim said.

"Jessi's the cutest," JJ said.

"Robin's the tallest," Slim said.

"Doesn't count with women as it does with men," JJ said.

"So why has Jessi got those stilts on her feet?"

"Fashion. Besides, Jessi's the youngest. That's what counts with women."

"Sure," Slim said. He glanced around.

"What?" JJ said.

"Thought somebody came in, but they didn't. Felt a draft from somewhere." He touched the back of his neck and shifted his bare arms. With all the people, the temperature in the room had risen. He had shed his jacket.

JJ gazed for a moment at his arms, strong-looking, corded with muscle. She lifted her eyes. "If the draft was behind you, pal, you're blocking me from it."

He grinned, "Yeah, I guess." He had a lean frame, but he was broader and certainly taller, although she was a tall girl. He remembered way back, attending a basketball game with two of her brothers to watch her high school team win the regional championship. Kid sister of his pals. Nobody to get interested in.

"It's fascinating how Robin rushes up to people," JJ said. "'Hi, I'm Robin!' Like she's a one-name celebrity. Beyoncé. Adele."

"Lassie," Slim said.

JJ snickered and punched his arm.

"Ow!" he said, but he was laughing.

"Looks like you two are having fun," said Pilar, coming up to them.

"Great party," Slim said.

"I'm glad you're enjoying it," Pilar said. "I'm telling people that if they want to step outside for some air, they should go out the front where it's been cleared. I've also asked Alexander to salt icy spots out back. Then people can go out that way, too. Max will be helping, so it won't take long."

"Max Osterhagen?" JJ asked. "The one on committee before Jessi pulled her tricks?"

"Yes, Max." Pilar made an airy gesture.

JJ wondered if there might be something going on between Pilar and Max. She was thinking of a way to ask a leading question when Slim said to Pilar, "Great news about Nero and Vivian. Can't figure out the New York guest of honor, though." He gestured to where Robin and Jessi were now seated with the mayor and Toria. "She's going to park her husband here and run back and forth?"

"For a while perhaps, but she's a busy person. She's fixing up a vacation house that she wants my help with, then there's her interest in politics, and of course her business enterprise. I suspect she'll tire quickly of traveling and find a place for him more convenient to the city."

JJ sniffed. "At a distance, he'll be easier to forget. She told me about him and her concern sounded phony."

Pilar smiled. "Phoniness goes with her business. Like me dropping French words—très élégant. Moneyed people appreciate flair from interior designers. It's the same in the fashion world."

"That's her business?" questioned JJ. "Fashion?"

"Yes. Don't be misled by her cool surface manner," Pilar said. "She can be quite warm. Acer told me she's credited with pulling her husband out of a terrible depression after a family tragedy."

"Oh?" JJ's sharp-featured face became sharper. "What happened?"

"It was to the husband's family, the Harleys. His first name is Owen. Years back, his only child, a daughter, ran off, and they finally learned she was dead. The sorrow brought the mother to her own death. Owen was in a tailspin until Robin. She'd been a model for one of his style magazines. She gave him a new lease on life. Not that she didn't benefit. He got her started with her own fashion house."

After Pilar left, JJ said to Slim. "Fashion and style magazines. That's what my friend Carol wrote for, but unpublished book is about wealthy families that suffered disasters."

"Got any of the families' names?"

"I haven't had time to look at everything." She looked thoughtful. "One of the Philly cops wondered if her missing paperwork might be important, remember?"

"Yeah, and you got to know one of the cops a little better than the others."

She grinned and then turned serious again. "When I get home, I'm reading everything I have that was Carol's."

"You're like a dog with a bone." Slim ran a long-fingered hand through his rumpled hair. "You're back to the ideas we deep-sixed, taking this fashion stuff to weave a new web to explain Carol's death. We're at a party, kiddo. Relax and enjoy."

Chapter 54

Vivian found Solstice in a chair in the living room where the people standing around and talking made it a secluded corner. Vivian joined the girl on a matching chair. Alexander appeared, easily shouldering his way through, bringing a replacement beverage for Solstice and a dish of food and a napkin, which he placed on a table by her side.

"Something for you?" he asked Vivian. She smiled and shook her head, lifting the drink she already held. He nodded and returned his attention to Solstice. "I'm going to the garage for more deicer. The weather has gotten worse, but people might want to go out back for fresh air. Will you be okay?"

Solstice awarded him a saucy grin that matched her gamine haircut. "Thanks, I'm playing catch-up with an old friend."

As he withdrew, he paused to look back at her over his shoulder. He reminded Vivian of a burly shepherd keeping a watchful eye on his lamb.

People closed around the gap left by Alexander. "This is my second plateful," Solstice said. "I don't know when I've seen so many good things to eat. Remember how it used to be back then?"

It hadn't been the same for Vivian, but the comment had taken her where she wanted to go. "I wanted to thank you for some of the things you remembered. That time you came to the farmhouse, you wanted me to remember things about you as a little girl that nobody else knew. Afterward, I realized that the things you knew about my father helped me."

Solstice paused in eating a fancy little sandwich. "Everybody knew he was wonderful."

"I didn't," Vivian said. "He could be loving and caring, and then he would change. I didn't know then that he'd been damaged in the war or what he suffered. He would ride off and leave me, and I thought that his love wasn't real."

"I didn't know about any of that," Solstice said. "He was nice, and he was fun. He gave me rides on his motorcycle." She took another bite of her sandwich. "Boy, did that make my mother mad. She hated his motorcycle. Called it a filthy hog. Guess because of the picture on it."

"A decal of a pig," Vivian said.

Reflectively, Solstice said, "I used to wish your father could be my father, too."

Vivian smiled. Hearing good memories about her father was a balm. And now she had something to say to Solstice about her past that would be good for her to hear.

"I know what it's like not to believe or trust that someone cares for you," she said, "but thinking of times back then made me remember something. My father would pick up general delivery mail. There were people who must have cared about you because one time I know somebody sent your parents money. It probably happened more than once."

Solstice, busy with her plate of food, didn't reply.

All around them were the jumbled sounds of people talking, their voices blending, words punctuated by occasional laughter. Although no one was smoking inside the house, there was still the scent of tobacco, probably carried on clothing. With it were the mixed fragrances of fresh flowers, foods and perfumes. Rising above it all was the compelling aroma of freshly made coffee.

After scouring her plate clean with a scrap of bread from her last sandwich, Solstice said, "You're wrong about money. Nobody would have done that. My parents said their parents were wicked. That's why we lived the way we did. There were letters sometimes, but my parents burned them."

The same as they did with the money, Vivian thought, but she didn't say it.

"I was always hungry," Solstice said. Her brown eyes looked huge in the room's dim party lights. "I could beg food, but the baby, my little brother, was helpless. There couldn't have been any money. If there was, our lives would have been different."

Vivian dropped the subject. Her hope of showing the girl that someone had cared had only stirred up sad memories.

The group that had been enclosing them moved on. Glimpsing the small food table with no one around it, she called it to Solstice's attention. "Enough talk about the past. There's more food over there. Maybe there's something you'd like that Alexander missed."

It was the right thing to say because Solstice responded with a giggle. "Yeah, he might be smart, but he sometimes misses things."

With Solstice gone, Vivian walked around and found Nero. He sat near the wall in chairs pulled from the dining table. She sat next to him, pleased with how well he was handling himself in the crowd.

Telling him about her conversation with Solstice, she said, "It's so wonderful talking with someone who remembers my father out west. She reminded me of times when he was fun, joking around, giving us kids rides with him on Porky."

"Porky?"

"My father was a nickname guy. He called the white van our group traveled in *Blossom*. His motorcycle was *Porky*."

"It probably was a Harley," Nero said. "As a kid, you probably didn't know, but your dad used a spin on the official nickname, H.O.G. The nickname started with a group of Southern riders who won motorcycle races. They were the Harley Owners Group, and that became known by the acronym H-O-G."

Vivian frowned. "Solstice said her mother hated my father's motorcycle. When she called it a hog, I thought it was because of the pig decals, fierce-looking pigs with tusks and helmets."

He nodded. "That fits."

"It does, but . . ."

"But?"

"I was asking Solstice about who could have sent money to her family when she was a kid. She didn't believe there was money, but she said there were letters. Her parents burned those, too." Vivian's frown deepened. "I didn't know Robin's last name was Harley until I heard Acer introduce her this evening."

"You're thinking Robin has a connection to the company?"

"No," Vivian said. "Acer said the family is in publishing, no connection with motorcycles. It's the fact that Solstice mentioning how her mother hated my father's Harley. Suppose the danger to Solstice isn't from people in Florida. Maybe it has to do with people who kept trying to get in touch with her parents when she was a little girl."

"And now you think those people are after her?" Nero said. "The ones who sent letters and money?"

Vivian frowned. "That doesn't make sense, does it? I'm worried and not thinking straight."

She saw Robin talking with Toria, Holly and Jessi. She didn't see Solstice but figured she'd returned to the secluded chair where they'd talked before, but when she looked, someone else was there.

"Solstice has to be somewhere," Vivian said, standing to have a better look around.

Solstice had drifted to the table along the living room wall where Iris was putting out more food. "Don't be afraid we'll run out," Iris said with her bubbly laugh. "And best of all, the Colonel and I will soon be bringing out desserts, so save some room."

Solstice liked Iris. She was fun, and shopping with her had been fun, too. When she selected the green dress, Iris had encouraged her to buy two necklaces so she could give it a different look when she wore it again, and here she was, wearing it with a different pretty necklace. By herself, she would have never thought of buying jewelry. She'd never had any before.

Plate in hand, she selected Swedish meatballs.

Robin appeared beside her and picked up a plate. "Such marvelous food!"

Solstice mentally shrugged. It was a nice party, the only one of its kind she'd ever been to, but she bet Robin had been to tons of fancier ones where the guests didn't bring out food from the kitchen, the servants did. She read the labels on some of the dishes. *Mini quiches. Prawns with dill cocktail sauce.*

Robin started prattling about people she'd met that evening.

Conversation for the sake of it, Solstice thought. Robin poking her beak in somebody else's business and fluffing her feathers. She wanted Robin to go away, but she probably wouldn't, so she'd just add crackers and dip to what she already had and come back later.

"This looks good." Robin drew a spoonful of salmon in a white sauce.

Solstice didn't know how it happened, but as she reached for the crackers, Robin was bringing back her spoon, and somehow their arms collided. The spoon spun from Robin's hand and clattered to the floor, but not before white sauce spattered down the skirt of Solstice's green dress.

"Oh, I'm so sorry!" cried Robin. "Here, let me help. "

She whipped the printed scarf from around her neck and dabbed at Solstice's skirt, and then she cried, "Oh, now I've only made it worse!"

"And wrecked your scarf, too," Solstice said setting down her plate.

"What a mess I've made!" Robing thrust her scarf into Solstice's hands. "There's a bathroom down the hall. Go blot the worst from your dress and from my scarf. I'll go find some laundry product for stains." She gave Solstice a push toward the hallway. "Maybe slip off your dress," she said over her shoulder as she moved away. "That way we can clean it better. I'll be with you in a jiffy."

No way would she take off her dress, Solstice thought as she started down the hall. That would reveal the hip-length camisole that allowed her to reach through the open skirt pocket to touch her finger knife. She hoped Robin found a good laundry product because plain soap and water wouldn't lift off the oily sauce. It surprised her that Robin even knew about products for stains. Maybe she hadn't always been rich.

The hall was a long one and the bathroom was halfway down, almost opposite the master bedroom. As she was turning to go into the bathroom, a figure abruptly came up behind her and an arm went hard around her shoulders, trapping her arms against her body. It happened so fast she couldn't figure out at first what was going on, except that she was trapped, held, squeezed, touched . . .

She was about to scream but it only came out as a squeak when she felt something flat and cold against her throat and a voice growled into her ear. "This is a knife, little girl. Shut up and do as I say, or I'll use it."

Chapter 55

Surprise and the man's superior strength left Solstice helpless to struggle as she was pulled backward, feet dragging on the rug. One shoe came off. Within seconds they were across the hall and in the master bedroom.

When the man paused to open the door to a patio that led off the bedroom, Solstice started thinking again. She managed to get both feet under her, but instead of struggling to pull away, she did the opposite, surging against the man just as he succeeded in swinging the door wide. The move loosened the pressure of his arm against her chest.

Ignoring the threat of the knife; she was dead anyway if she failed, she slid one hand along her thigh to her weapon as she jammed her shoeless foot against the open door frame and shoved back against the man with all her might. He stumbled. They fell together on the freezing bricks of the patio, Solstice on top.

An exterior light flashed on. With a piercing scream, Solstice whirled her body off the man and brought up her right hand. Before he could stop the movement of her arm, the curved blade of her little knife slashed him across the face under his left eye. Bellowing in outraged pain, he smashed her to the bricks. Pivoting, he loomed over her, knee squashing one of her legs and holding one hand against his bleeding face he groped for his fallen blade while she, still screaming, managed to make a shallow but long slash across the side of his neck.

Alexander was heading from the garage after putting away the rest of the deicer when he heard what sounded like a scream. It seemed to come from outside, but he couldn't figure out the direction. For an instant, he thought it was a trick of the wind, but no. It was a woman's voice.

The only area the sounds could be coming from was around the side of the house, where the bedroom wing ended with a patio outside.

Starting to run, Alexander went past the kitchen and utility area, slipping on ice-slick pavers by the trash cans. His footing became more secure when he reached frozen grass.

The automatic light on the patio was on.

He saw two figures grappling. A guy all in black and—

Another scream.

Solstice!

Running as fast as he could, Alexander saw the guy on his knees over her. She laid face-up on the bricks, screaming and struggling, feet kicking. There was a flash of something in the guy's hand.

A knife!

Alexander was now close enough to see more clearly. The man's heavy jacket was open. The flaps got in the way as he stabbed under his own body, trying to sink the knife into Solstice, who kept screaming. She wriggled like a fish, eluding him. His knife point snapped off when he stabbed bricks instead of her. Dropping the broken knife, his hands had gone for Solstice's throat when Alexander plowed forward.

He felt like he was in that football game again, storming toward the opposition, only this time, he would be committing a big-time foul. He grabbed the collar of the assailant's jacket with one hand and the seat of his pants with his other hand and powerfully lifted him off Solstice and flung him forward with all his might.

Alexander's momentum kept him moving. He managed to jump over Solstice instead of tromping on her. He tumbled to the bricks and righted himself immediately, prepared for whatever the assailant did next.

Which was nothing. The way Alexander had grabbed the man's open jacket had yanked his arms behind him. Helpless to free himself, he'd slammed head-first against a hefty jar that in summertime held a potted plant.

Alexander heard Slim's voice from somewhere and saw Donny. Figuring that Solstice's attacker would soon be under control, he pivoted on the sleet-slick bricks toward her, seeing her curled into a shivering ball, her party dress rippled from one shoulder.

By that time, the rest of the people in the living room who had felt the steady draft from the open door and then heard screaming, rushed down the hallway to the master bedroom and poured out to the patio. The sky above and all around was a murky fog of sleet and snow hovering against an uncaring blackness, but the patio was now even brighter thanks to the master bedroom light having been switched on.

Robin shoved her way through the crowd and outside. She looked to the fallen man who had blood streaming across his face.

"Gregory!" she screamed. "What has that little bitch done to you?"

Her attention switched to Solstice and to the knife lying beside her, broken in two parts.

Robin swooped down, grabbed the damaged, but still dangerous knife by its handle. She swung it toward Solstice, who quickly slashed her curved blade across the back of Robin's hand, severing the tendons. The knife dropped. For an instant, the ruined back of Robin's hand showed bone and yellow fat, then blood sluiced forth, gushing over the bricks. Robin sank to her knees, her other hand clasped over the gaping wound as she screamed like a banshee.

Then Slim was there, hauling a keening Robin to her feet. He gave a glance at the ruined hand and quipped, "There goes the violin lessons."

"Violin!" gasped a wide-eyed Iris, who had braved the snow with the others of the Voodoo Club. "Violin lessons! It's Mar-see-ah's warning come true!"

Nobody paid any attention.

Alexander hovered over Solstice. "I'm here—it's okay. Are you hurt? Did that guy—"

She interrupted him with a sob. "I had to do it. I had to cut them, I had to. I had to cut them." Her voice broke on another sob.

He realized she meant her small and clever hidden knife. She'd used it to slice Robin and the guy. *Good job, baby!* He wrestled off his jacket to put it around her as he said, "I'm not touching you, this is just my coat, just my coat, not me touching you."

As if from a distance he heard Slim bark, "Get the knife, Donny. It's there in the blood. And pry that broken piece from the brick before somebody steps on it."

"Got it," Donny said. Bending, he gathered the knife and its broken tip with a gloved hand and dropped them into an evidence bag,

An EMS crew and more police officers arrived because someone had called 911. A commotion arose as Robin's injured hand was bandaged. She kept wailing and repeating she didn't know what was going on and calling out for someone to help her.

"Cuff her when you're done," Slim said to one of his men.

Robin continued wailing and repeating her protests of confused innocence as Alexander left with Solstice in his arms.

On the patio, Gregory struggled to get away, his arms still trapped in his jacket. Donny yanked him to his feet. With his jacket and shirt front pulled open, the indigo blue spider web tattooed across his chest was revealed.

Darlene, standing nearby, had heard Robin call the name *Gregory*, and now, she'd seen the man's tattoo. A web? *Gregory*? She remembered the conversation at the Fergusson event about the Internet. Gregory the webmaster. *Yes!*

Vivian, who'd been watching with the others, caught a glimmer of something when the man's hands were cuffed. She realized that what she had seen was the edge of the gold-faced watch. She blinked, casting her thoughts back to the previous day and the female who had accompanied Robin to the Mather house.

"Nurse Genna?" she murmured, in stunned disbelief.

Slim gave orders as to the handling of the prisoners. Hospital and then the county lockup. The bulk of the crowd, driven by the cold and the sense that the excitement was over, trooped back inside to the warmth, their clamor of voices fading.

Bob Smithers, who had happily gone into entertainment mode, said to Pilar, "You really know how to throw a party!"

"Shush!" said Francine. She dragged him inside.

Jessi stood on the bricks, swathed in the white faux fur that Arnie had hurried out to her. She glared fiercely as Robin was placed on a stretcher and carried under police escort to the waiting ambulance.

Her nose in the air, Jessi said to no one in particular, "That horrid woman! True quality can't be faked. I knew Robin was a pretender."

There were sounds from the street as an ambulance and a police car pulled off into the relative darkness of Pilar's country road.

Holly, accompanied by Toria, looked at Slim. "You understand what's going on?"

The chill finally seeping through the excitement, Slim rubbed his bare arms, then scowled and ruffled his hair. "A hell of a lot of unanswered questions, but I think I should have paid more attention to one of JJ's theories."

Chapter 56

Alexander carefully placed Solstice on the guestroom bed. Pilar, who had followed, said, "She's wet and chilled through." In the background came sounds of people talking as they were leaving.

Solstice lay curled up, her eyes shut, her freckled face pale. The only thing moving was her fingers, working around the edge of the sheet as if feeling for something.

"What is it you want?" Alexander asked.

"Toodles's..."

Understanding, he lifted the fuzzy yellow blanket from where she'd folded it on a chair and gently spread it over her.

With her eyes still squeezed tight, Solstice turned it, feeling the binding until she found a frayed corner. She brought it close to her face, against her lips, her fingers in the loose strands.

"Could you bring her something hot to drink?" Alexander asked his mother. There was something he needed to do, but not with her there. As soon as Pilar was gone, he said to Solstice, "I need your little knife." He knew how important it was to her. "If Robin knows you cut her, she may demand a search. If the police take it, you may never get it back. I'll return it later. No one will know it exists."

Solstice sobbed her protests, but he kept reassuring her. Finally, working under the covers, she removed the finger knife and scooted it into view, eyes still squeezed shut as if pretending she wasn't surrendering it.

He marveled at the knife's small size, its cleverness. The curved blade was short, but he'd seen the damage done to Robin. As he took it to the main bathroom in the hallway outside the guest room, he realized that in making sure the weapon wasn't taken from Solstice, he was hiding evidence. The thought horrified him. He was law-abiding, not some creepy scofflaw. For a moment he stood as if paralyzed, then he remembered the broken knife in the bricks. Robin could have accidentally sliced herself on the protruding blade.

Yes, he thought. It *could* have happened that way, but he knew it hadn't. Protecting Solstice was what mattered. He'd talk to her later, tell her she must not say anything about cutting anyone.

After washing the finger knife and dunking it in bleach from the cabinet under the sink, he tumbled it into a cabinet drawer that contained manicure implements: clippers, nippers, various curved scissors and files. Now it was simply one more instrument of fearsome design to groom fingers and toes.

Returning to the guest bedroom, he found his mother sitting on the bed next to Solstice, who huddled in a fetal position, her eyes squeezed tightly, all her spark and spunk chased away.

Pilar said, "Her feet are freezing, and her dress is wet and torn."

"Leave her alone for a bit," he said. Not only did Solstice not want to be touched, he was sure she also feared the discovery of the fastening for the knife on her thigh. As always, when he wasn't quite sure how to behave, he fell back on what he thought of as a scholarly manner as he loftily addressed his mother.

"It's not every day that an attempt is made upon a person's physical being," he said. "Solstice is terrified. She's not deliberately behaving in a contumacious manner."

A muffled word came through the blanket Solstice held over her face.

"Did she just call you Webster?" asked Pilar.

"As in the dictionary," he said, his face turning warm. Solstice had actually said, "Stuff it, Webster."

"She must be feeling more herself," Pilar said. The sudden ringing of the phone took Pilar from the room. In a moment, she was back.

"It's Slim," she said, holding the receiver out, and he saw it was muted. "He still outside. He wants to talk with Solstice."

Alexander stared, incredulous. "Now? He's crazy."

He took the phone, paused a moment, eyes closed, and then flicked off the mute button. Making the most of his deep voice, he said, "Yes?" After a pause, he spoke again. "Our doctor said she's not injured, at least not physically. What? Oh, the doctor was at the party. Yes, my mother does know a lot of people." There was a longer pause as Alexander listened and then said, "Being attacked and nearly murdered has, shall we say, an unsettling effect. She has been sedated and is soundly sleeping. Perhaps you could speak to her tomorrow? Later rather than earlier?"

There were a few more words, and then Alexander clicked off and returned the phone to his mother.

"You should be on the stage instead of trying to write for it," Pilar said.

Alexander showed no expression. "It's been suggested," he said.

Chapter 57

Solstice huddled in the bed after Alexander and his mother left. Her mind kept replaying what had happened earlier: the brutal man grabbing her, dragging her, then the horror on the terrace, him pressing her down, trying to stab her. Then, that woman, Robin, jumping forward. She had a knife, too. Why were they trying to kill her? The only answer was that the Gastrells had hired them. The police took them away, but who would the Gastrells send next?

She was so tired. All she wanted to do was sleep and forget, but what happened kept playing in her brain. She wished she had something else to think about. Something that had nothing to do with knives and fear.

The door opened and Alexander stepped in. "I'm staying with you, tonight," he said.

"No!" The word shot out automatically.

He kept talking, using his British voice from a play he'd said he liked, *My Fair Lady,* about a professor and a flower girl. "I won't be touching you," he said. "I shall be dressed in my pajamas and sleeping on top of the bedspread and under another cover."

"No!" she repeated.

It was as if he hadn't heard her. "I will stay on my side of the bed and I will not touch you, but I am staying with you. Like it or lump it."

"Not bloody likely!" She knew British words, too. She whirled her body and jammed her feet out to position herself crosswise on the bed.

In a calm tone, he continued. "After I change into my pajamas and brush my teeth and get another blanket, I will be back."

When he returned, his footsteps were quiet.

Furious that she couldn't stop him from doing what he wanted, Solstice had scooted to the far side of the bed and was now like a caterpillar clinging to a cliff edge. She pretended to be asleep. He sat on the edge of the mattress, his back to her as he took off his slippers. She angled her head and opened her eyes a crack and saw that his pajamas were light blue with dark blue piping around the collar.

Slippers off, he lay down carefully on the counterpane, his weight making her body tilt toward his. He switched off the lamp, and she heard him say softly, "Good night, Fair Lady."

Slim was in his office at the police station, dragging through the reports required after the arrests of Robin Harley and her co-conspirator, Gregory Sparrow. It was two a.m., but he kept working because he wasn't willing to face the paperwork in the morning. His cell rang. The display read *JJ*.

Jeez! Already nagging for copy?

He picked up and said, "It better be good."

"Is the answer to one of your problems good enough?"

"Sure, sure, get on with it." He remembered saying he should have listened to her more.

"This is about my friend, Carol Vetter, and her writing about the fashion world."

"Right. At the party, you said you had the draft and notes for of her second book and you were going to finish reading it tonight."

"Right. Did your prisoners admit anything?"

"They claim it was all a misunderstanding."

"Trying to kill Solstice was a misunderstanding?"

"Yeah, you know how it goes. Robin and her Sparrow."

JJ laughed. "So you thought they would sing like birds?"

"Not funny. When I left, they were waiting for Robin's lawyer, some lady she called and left a message for. Guess she's still asleep in her bed in Manhattan. Where I should be."

"In bed with the Manhattan lady lawyer?"

This time he did laugh. "I'd want a good look at her first."

He heard JJ snicker. Then she said, "Carol decided that one of the families she'd left out of her book still interested her."

"So, she did more research?" Slim slouched back in his chair and put his feet up on a pulled-out desk drawer.

"She did, and her notes tell me why her blood was found in an empty house in JumpRope. She came here to meet Vivian Mather."

He sat up. "You're sure?"

"Of course I'm sure. In her notes is the name, 'Vivian Mather.' She came to talk with Vivian, only she was lured to that empty house where she was stabbed."

"You're guessing that last part," Slim said.

"It's a good guess. I'm also guessing that Carol managed to drive herself back to her apartment in Philadelphia. Her attacker followed, finished her off, and left with her writing records."

Listening, Slim shoved his desk drawer shut and stood. What he was hearing made him want to move around. He looked up at the high window in his office. The height was to dissuade a break-in for sensitive police records or evidence, but he had never liked it. As tall as he was, he couldn't see anything out of it except the sky. Black sky now.

Slim heard JJ tell what she knew as if it was a story: Owen Harley, a man in the fashion magazine world, had a wife and a daughter. The daughter ran off with a failed musician twenty-eight years ago. She was of age and refused to come home. Eventually, she died. Her mother died soon after. Carol had wanted to interview Harley about the old tragedy, but his second wife nixed the idea.

Breaking off from her storytelling mode, JJ said, "Want to guess the wife's name?"

"Too easy," Slim said, thinking maybe this was starting to come together. "Robin Harley, second wife of Owen Harley."

"You win the prize. Carol learned that Robin knew all about her husband's search for his lost daughter but since he was ill, Robin said it would be too upsetting for him to rake up the past."

"Only Carol kept pushing, right?" Still on his feet, Slim walked from his office and past the holding room where benches and cuffs on the wall took care of anybody brought in who'd been causing trouble and wanted to cause more. At the main desk, Alfonso snored in a chair. Small department, usually no strain, but the commotion at Pilar's had scrambled things and left Alfonso, who'd been on duty all day, remaining on for the night shift.

"I'm still reading Carol's notes," JJ said, her voice clear over Slim's phone, "but I've learned that years back, the Harleys hired a private investigator to keep track of their daughter, Heather. He kept on the job until the girl died. Carol found this out from the investigator's widow, who had saved her husband's reports to the Harley's. The wife allowed Carol to copy them."

"And they mentioned Vivian Mather?"

"Close. The name mentioned was David Mather. He and a group of friends, all war veterans, apparently wandered from place to place out west. For a time. Heather and her musician guy traveled with them. Carol learned that David was dead, but that he was Vivian's father."

Slim was now at the plate glass door that led from the police department end of the building. He cracked it open to the fresh, cold air.

"So then," he said, "Carol wanted to meet Vivian."

"Yes. Vivian traveled with her father when she was young. Carol figured Vivian would know things about Heather, things that Robin, didn't want her to know. Carol wanted to find out what it was."

"Okay," Slim said, summing things up in his mind and saying it out loud. "Carol went to meet Vivian, only she somehow had the wrong address. She was attacked, leaving her blood in the empty house, so police here were involved. Although wounded, she managed to get back to Philadelphia and was killed there, so the Philly police were involved. Now our county prosecutor, who ignored the blood in the house, is involved because of last night's trouble caused by people from Manhattan."

JJ laughed. "Police from our town, from Philadelphia and Manhattan—sounds like a cop shindig is next. And don't forget what you told me that Donny found about people in Florida. That's somehow a part of this."

Chapter 58

When Solstice opened her eyes, it was early daylight. The walls were peach-pink. She didn't know where she was, but she felt safe. *It must be a dream*, she thought. Her fingers found the frayed edge of the blanket that reminded her of Toodles's curly coat. She had never felt safe before, only now she did. So it must be a dream.

In her real life, she was afraid all the time. Her parents were always moving to escape her mother's wicked parents. After her mother was gone, her father went away after leaving her with wicked men. They thought her name was *Esstu* because that's what they thought her father said. The good thing about it was, when awful things happened to *Esstu* it was like the real Solstice stayed untouched inside of her, even after she was sold to the Gastrells.

By the time she escaped to Brooklyn, she felt she should be okay, but now the Gastrells were after her. Yet even with that danger, she somehow felt unafraid. It was so wonderful except . . . except there was this weight across her middle.

She tried to move, but then she stopped.

It was a man's arm. She wasn't dreaming. She knew whose arm it was, Alexander Fanshawe's. She remembered that after the terrifying events from the night before, Alexander said he would stay with her. She'd kept on telling him no, but that didn't stop him.

She had clung to the side of the bed, experiencing feelings she couldn't explain, then she must have gone to sleep for real. Now she was awake and Alexander Fanshawe's big stupid arm lay like a log across her, but she still wasn't afraid. She remembered what he'd said as he turned out the light, "Good night, fair lady," his deep voice soft and soothing.

As she remembered, she started to cry. She didn't know why. The harder she tried not to cry the more the tears keep coming. Her face was streaming, her nose was running and she was shaking. Then her nose stopped up and she knew she was making noise.

"Oh, God!" Alexander cried and jerked his arm away. "I'm sorry, I'm so sorry." He sprang from the bed. Her body rolled toward the hollow where his weight had been.

"I didn't mean it," he said. "I was asleep, I didn't know. I'm so sorry." He kept apologizing and Solstice kept crying,

Felling more helpless than ever before, he finally stumbled to what had been his boyhood bedroom. It still had play posters on the wall. He'd hung them when he'd first started dreaming he could be a playwright. Seeing them there had encouraged his belief that it could happen. Ha! He was nothing but a failure all around.

He'd really messed up with Solstice. He heard the echoes of his promises not to touch her. He had betrayed her. She was so fragile, and she awakened to find his arm pressing down on her. She must have felt trapped, as she'd been trapped in so many ugly situations in her past.

He went into the bath near his bedroom and showered, refusing to think about those dreadful moments in the room with Solstice. Instead, he thought that if Robin Harley and her knife guy had been sent by the people in Florida, they would be replaced. Just as the man who'd shot the gun and had tried to run them off the road had been replaced by Robin and her henchman. But why had a society woman like Robin gotten mixed up in it?

Acer Wolfgang had introduced her as the wife of friends, or at least friends of friends. Was he involved, too?

Realizing he could drive himself crazy with speculation, he got dressed. What were the police doing? He hoped they found some answers. He decided to help his mother clean up the party mess. A good distraction.

When went out, he was surprised to see the living and dining areas were spotless. In the kitchen, he found his mother sitting at the little table for two with a cup of coffee. The newspaper was on the table, but her attention was on the computer tablet he'd given her for her birthday.

He moved to get himself a cup of coffee. "I was going to help you clean up, but you've done it already."

"Max stayed last night to help," she said.

Alexander froze.

Stayed? Max? Did that mean Max stayed long enough to help, or *stayed-stayed*, like all night? Realizing he risked letting his coffee overflow, Alexander stopped pouring and set his cup on the counter. He added milk from the pitcher sitting next to the coffee and took a spoon from the antique pressed-glass spoon holder. As he stirred the contents of his cup, his thoughts stirred as well.

Max didn't seem the type his mother favored.

Alexander knew he was a widower, and he had the impression that the wife's death wasn't recent. He'd helped with deicing the walkways. As they worked together, Alexander had seen no hints of the confused torment that usually inspired the brand of nurturing that he thought of as his mother's *entertaining*. Max had seemed stable and nice, a really cool, older guy, but what Alexander said to his mother, was: "So he's a wounded soul who needs healing because Jessi swiped his committee spot?"

"Why, no, not all." Pilar sounded surprised. "We simply get along very well. He's such a comfortable man."

Comfortable, Alexander thought. That sounded harmless like it had nothing to do with bed. All at once, he wondered what he was thinking. His mother was an adult. She had the right to do what she wanted and the right to choose who she wanted to be with, bed or not. He was an adult too. It was time to act like one. Besides, he wasn't so perfect. He'd hidden evidence from the police and lied directly to a cop about a doctor seeing Solstice. He'd had his reasons, okay? And he'd do it again.

He sat down with his coffee. "What does the paper say about last night?"

"Nothing in print, but a little bit in the online edition. Reporters and TV people have been calling since dawn. I told them all I knew was that there had been two arrests. I said I knew Robin Harley in the context of her being a guest, and we'd only just met. I said the man who had been arrested wasn't a guest and I knew nothing about him. The morning TV showed an aerial view of our house. The newscaster reported an emergency call from the pictured address and that there had been two arrests and that was it."

"Did they ask about Solstice?"

"Yes, I don't know how they knew her name. I said she had also been a guest, and I had no comment about my guests. I said they would have to speak with the police."

"They accepted that?"

"What could they do?" She shrugged. "Some came in person, two with camera crews, and stood on the lawn. I told them that if they didn't leave, I would call the police and have them arrested as trespassers."

"Good," nodded Alexander. "You did good."

"The online article was written by JJ Gilbert, who was here last night." Pilar passed her tablet to Alexander. "See for yourself."

Alexander read the headline: MANHATTAN SOCIALITE MASTERMINDS ATTEMPTED MURDER.

His gaze dropped to the brief article:

Birds of a feather flock together as New York fashion house entrepreneur, Robin Harley, and her webmaster, Gregory Sparrow, were apprehended by the JumpRope police last night on suspicion of attempted murder. The investigation is ongoing.

Alexander looked up. "I hoped it would tell if the police have a line on the Florida people who are behind it."

Pilar frowned. "Florida?"

Realizing she knew nothing about the Gastrells, Alexander related everything Solstice had told Donny, and nothing of what he secretly knew about her life before that. He ended with, "Her life's in danger because she's the only witness to their crimes."

There was a moment when he thought he saw that look in his mother's eye when she suspected she hadn't told her the whole story. He hadn't not about the sex gang. But then she said:

"The poor child. How brave she's been." She shook her head. "Slim called and expects to be here late in the afternoon to speak with her. He said he's working with police from other jurisdictions. That all makes sense, now. He's bringing Vivian Mather. He thought it would be good to have a person here who's known Solstice for a long time."

Nodding, Alexander turned his gaze to the kitchen window. The sun was bright. Icicles dripped from the branches of the big tree that shaded the house in the summer. He wondered where Solstice would be then. He had imagined they'd go on trips together on his motorcycle when the weather turned nice, only now she was done with him. *Goodbye Girl*, he said in his mind, meaning the Paul Simon screenplay that became a Broadway musical. Musicals had happy endings, not strange sorrowful endings like in real life.

Pilar said, "I think Robin came here earlier yesterday to familiarize herself with the house and then told that man the best route to sneak in. The scarf Robin had been wearing was on the bathroom floor. I suspect she lured Solstice there and then returned to the party to cover herself while the man did her dirty work."

Alexander spoke with a growl. "Fancy clothing, fancy airs, but Robin is nothing but a criminal working with other criminals to kill an innocent person."

"Agreed," Pilar said. "This morning Max saw a car parked by the side that probably belonged to the man. We alerted Slim. He said officers from the prosecutor's office will be here to move that car and the one Robin drove here for the party."

Alexander smiled to himself. Max *had* been there all night. Good. Despite her show of calm, his mother had probably been a nervous wreck after what happened. He nodded to himself. He was glad his mother hadn't been alone.

Pilar smoothed her hair, tucking a blond-streaked strand back into the dark chignon at the graceful nape of her neck, as she said:

"Go see if you can persuade Solstice to stir. I'll prepare breakfast for the two of you."

Thinking there was probably no longer "two" when it came to him and Solstice, Alexander slowly rose to his feet, prolonging the moments until he had to see her.

The matter was taken from his hands.

Fully dressed, Solstice appeared in the entry from the dining area. She didn't look good, Alexander thought. Her freckles stood out in a face that was too pale despite blotches from crying. Her eyes were swollen. Her gaze slid past him as if he was a stage prop.

She moved into the kitchen. Focused only on Pilar, she said in a scratchy voice, "He thinks it was his fault, but it wasn't. Alexander didn't do anything wrong." Tears threatened as she stood awkwardly at a distance from the table, looking only at Pilar. "I can't talk to him."

Alexander was afraid to move; afraid he'd break the spell in which he'd heard her say he hadn't done anything wrong. Only he had, hadn't he? But it sounded as if she'd really meant what she said.

Pilar responded in the way of hers that told Alexander she somehow knew exactly what to say. "

You're perfectly right," Pilar said. "Of course you can't talk to him." Without removing her attention from Solstice, Pilar signaled Alexander to go away.

Death Spins an Indigo Web

Alexander crept through the utility room and out the back door. He wore no coat, and the early morning air outside was freezing, but he was warmed by Solstice's puzzling, but wonderful words: *Alexander didn't do anything wrong.*

Chapter 59

At nine o'clock that morning, Slim was in the Melton County Prosecutor's building, waiting to talk with the county detective he knew best, Isaac Ellis. Nobody knew when Ellis would be in.

So far, what Slim had learned was not encouraging. With money, contacts and fancy footwork, Robin's lawyer had gotten her out of lock-up. That lawyer would only work with Robin, so Robin had hired someone else for Sparrow, who refused to say anything until his lawyer arrived. That was supposed to happen a bit later that morning. In preparation, Sparrow had been moved from where he'd spent the night, to a conference room. He was alone there, hands cuffed behind him, with a bored county cop outside the open door.

Since Slim was waiting around for Ellis, he told the guard he might as well go get a cup of coffee and he'd stay. The guard accepted and went off.

Slim was still standing there alone when JJ appeared.

Your office said I'd find you here," she said.

Slim explained the situation. "I'm waiting for Detective Ellis. You might as well leave. I have no idea when he'll show up."

They talked a moment, then JJ went silent, she frowned, then closed her eyes as if thinking hard She opened her eyes, gave Slim a smile, then said in a carrying voice, "Robin Harley is one impressive woman."

Confused, Slim made a shushing motion and pointed into the room where Sparrow sat alone.

JJ took a half step closer and said, "He can't hear me, can he?"

Her voice seemed deliberately loud. Slim caught on. Clever JJ. She was pretending she'd knew something about Robin, had talked with her, which Slim knew was impossible.

"No, you're good, he can't hear us," Slim said, hoping Sparrow could hear them just fine. "What's up with Robin?"

"Look at the situation," JJ said. "Robin Harley has money and a fine reputation. Gregory Sparrow has his own website business, but basically, he's a nobody."

"He's done minor stuff over the years," Slim said. "Nothing like attempted murder as he's done now, with witnesses. Robin's attempt was witnessed as well."

"That's part of the misunderstanding," JJ said, her nod and smile telling Slim he was playing the game just fine. "Robin claims she has a blood phobia and panicked. Spilled blood and seeing Sparrow grabbed by cops and not understanding the reason drove her temporarily nuts."

"Come on, I talked to witnesses," Slim said, playing along and thinking how believable JJ sounded. "That pair came to JumpRope with Sparrow dressed as a female nurse with a fake sore throat to disguise his male voice. It also gave him an excuse to lay low until Robin gave the signal. I saw her using her phone. When we checked, the number she contacted was his."

"You've got it wrong," JJ said, "Robin honestly believed Sparrow wasn't well and she was checking on his welfare. She had no idea he was involved with criminals. She's squeaky-clean and knows nothing of that type of thing. If Solstice, his intended victim, hadn't fought back and wrecked his plan, he would have dragged her off and killed her. By the time Robin returned to the Mather house after the party, Gregory would have been there, playing innocent, his dirty work all done."

"If Robin wasn't involved, why go along with Sparrow's pretense of being a woman? Robin introduced him to Vivian Mather as a female."

"Robin was too timid to come alone," JJ said. "She trusted Gregory Sparrow as a good friend but believed staying in the Mather house with a man might have made her look bad."

"Like telling the world she fooled around?"

"No! Robin would never cheat on her husband. She and Sparrow were simply friends, but she didn't want to risk people coming to the wrong conclusion. He was the one who came up with the nurse scheme. She went along with it, having no idea he was using her for his own purposes."

"So, Robin claims to be completely in the dark," Slim said. He paused as if thinking, then said, "Yeah, with her wealth and standing, I can see how she can pull that off."

"If Gregory Sparrow is smart," JJ said, "he'll tell his side of the story before Robin tells hers. He can say he was supposed to grab Solstice and hold her and wait for Robin's instructions. He didn't do real harm to Solstice. You've got him for assault, but if he comes clean, then no matter what Robin's lawyer tries to say, his having made a deal first gives him the upper hand."

JJ left. By the time the regular guard came back and checked on his prisoner, Slim heard Sparrow yell that his lawyer better show up soon because he had a lot to say.

Chapter 60

The prosecutor had wanted Solstice to come to his office so he could preside over the unraveling and tying up of what had been a complicated situation.

Instead, Pilar called in a local physician, for real this time, to examine Solstice. His report stated that although she was tired and confused by the previous night's ordeal, she was able to be interviewed—if it was conducted in a home environment where she would feel safe, rather than in a legal office that would only frighten her and possibly do great harm. Keeping her safe also meant no publicity of any kind at this time.

Accepting, the prosecutor decided that Detective Isaac Ellis from that office would accompany Slim to the Fanshawe home.

Slim and the detective arrived at the Fanshawe house along with Vivian Mather, who carried a pricey-looking handbag that looked big enough to carry a Kevlar vest and a couple of traffic cones. As he knocked, Slim thought of the many times he'd had to knock on a door to bring bad news, but this time, he had news that was good.

Pilar greeted the three of them, ushered them in out of the cold, and took their coats. Slim introduced Detective Ellis. Pilar led them into the Fanshawe's long, rectangular living area. The room was arranged with two facing couches, one under the window, and two easy chairs flanking the couches, with a coffee table in the middle.

Alexander and Solstice appeared and stood behind Pilar. They merely nodded when the detective was introduced. They wore that scared yet defiant look Slim was familiar with: braced for bad news and prepared to argue about it. With a hidden smile, Slim knew they were going to love his news, but it was going to take him a few minutes to get to it.

Pilar invited everyone to take seats. Slim and Ellis chose the couch under the window where the light would be behind them. Vivian moved toward one of the easy chairs. Alexander and Solstice followed Pilar to the other couch. Alexander, bearded and broad-chested, sat between the two women. Pilar, calm as always, placed a graceful hand on her son's knee. Solstice sat on the end close to Vivian. The house was warm, but Solstice had a fuzzy yellow blanket pulled tight around her shoulders.

Having received permission for the recorders placed on the coffee table, Slim got down to business.

"I have things to share," he said in a relaxed tone, "but first, Ms. Windsor, we need to hear step by step about the attack made on you. Start with the time before you left this room last night."

Solstice gave Alexander a glance, then began with the mishap of Robin jogging her arm and sauce spilling on her dress and Robin's scarf, and Robin sending her to the bathroom to wait for her return with a cleaning solution.

"Setting her up," Alexander said.

Solstice nodded. "I was heading for the bathroom when a man with a knife grabbed me and dragged me down the hall. I kept struggling. When we went through the master bedroom door to the patio, he tripped and we both fell outside on the bricks."

Her voice was faint but clear and steady. "I hit my head." She touched the back of her head. "Things got blurry after that."

"The man's cheek was bleeding," Detective Ellis said. He was a bronze-skinned man in his thirties. "Do you remember how that happened?"

"Maybe it was from my fingernails." Solstice glanced down at her hands. "I just don't remember."

Ellis asked about Robin's cut hand.

Solstice said she only remembered hearing Robin screaming.

Slim knew Ellis asked questions the prosecutor might ask to try and weaken the prosecutor's case against the accused. However, Ellis had privately told Slim that Robin's blood was on the broken knife tip and both her prints and Sparrow's had been on the handle. It was clear that Robin had tried to attack Solstice, and ended up injuring herself.

After more repetitive questions for the record, Ellis thanked her and sat back, satisfied.

Slim checked his recorder and then said, "This incident and what led up to it involves not only our people but also law enforcement in Philadelphia and New York, specifically Manhattan."

"What about Florida?" Alexander demanded.

"I'm taking events in turn," Slim said. He continued, using the information revealed by JJ, and even more from Gregory Sparrow's confession. "The first event was blood found in a vacant house in JumpRope. The victim was Carol Vetter, who was writing a book about wealthy families that had suffered a personal loss. When an interview concerning a family whose daughter had run off, was denied to her, she pursued the story on her own. She found reports to the Harleys written by the private investigator hired by the family years before to find the girl. The investigator's widow, assuming that the writer worked with the family, gave her copies of the report, but then the widow spoke with a family member who was desperate to keep things quiet."

"Which probably tipped them off that the writer was actively going after the story," Alexander said.

"Got that right," Slim said, and went on. "Neil Bannister was hired to make sure the writer didn't find information the family member didn't want to be disclosed."

"The people in Florida, that's who's behind it," Alexander said. "They hired Robin Harley. They thought she'd never be suspected because she's rich."

"You're half right," Slim said. He deliberately hadn't mentioned Robin's name before to keep the story moving.

"What do you mean half?" Alexander said. "You saw her and that guy. You know what they did."

"True," Slim said, "but let me get on with it." From beside him, he heard Ellis chuckle. Slim didn't necessarily trust county guys, but Ellis had always seemed okay although he sometimes jumped in took over when he felt he could make himself look good.

"Keeping events in order," Slim said, "we learned that the writer had come to JumpRope to talk with Vivian Mather."

"Me?" Vivian's mouth dropped.

"Yes, the investigator's reports had your father's name. Through research, the writer had discovered that David Mather was your father. The writer hoped you might know something about the Harleys' runaway daughter. She was lured here, believing that she'd made contact with you. That led to her death,"

Slim moved his gaze to Solstice. "The man who murdered the writer was Neil Bannister, who tried to shoot you on New Year's Eve, and then tried to run you off the road, dying in that attempt."

"A killer versatile with weapons," Ellis interjected. "Knifed the writer, shot at you with a rifle and tried to smash you with his car. If he'd lived, he probably would have tried a rope or poison next."

Slim frowned at Ellis's flippant tone. He figured the man was feeling smart because the prosecutor had chosen him to take his place.

Slim said to Solstice, "Gregory Sparrow, the man who attacked you last night, was taken into custody and questioned. Adept in using the Internet, he's Robin Harley's webmaster for her fashion concerns and also her lover. At Robin's behest, he was the one who deceived the writer into thinking she'd made contact with Vivian Mather. He also hired Neil Bannister to murder the writer. He also found someone else who sought information about the Mathers. A person with the email handle S².*

"That's me," Solstice said in a small voice.

"Right," Slim said. "Gregory Sparrow informed S² that the Mathers were dead, but fearing S² might discover that David's daughter, Vivian was still alive, he hacked into S²'s email to keep aware of her activities."

"What?" Alexander was clearly shocked.

"Yes, that's how he learned your plans to come to JumpRope at the end of December."

"What about Florida?" Alexander said.

"Okay," Slim said. "Here it is. There is no Florida connection."

"No! That can't be—" Alexander began

Ellis overrode him, not addressing Alexander but Solstice. "The county has more resources than a small police force. We learned that the Gastrells, the people you named as possible perpetrators of the crimes against you, sold the Miami, Florida house, where you'd been held, the house willed to them by the previous owner, Darius Floye."

"That's a big lie," Solstice said, spots of color mingling with her freckles. "They stole it from him."

"Regardless," Ellis said, "after the sale of the Miami house, the Gastrells moved to Las Vegas. This past September, they toured Europe and are currently in Florence, Italy. They left this county before there was trouble for you."

"Traveling on stolen money," Solstice said.

"And using it," Alexander said, "to set up the plot against Solstice from a distance."

"They could have," Ellis said, "only they didn't. There's more information that will explain that."

"Okay," Slim said. He was working his way to the good news, if he could only get there. "Owen Harley and his first wife, the girl's mother, sent money to the daughter, her name was Heather, when they knew of her various locations, even though she'd turned her back on them. Then—"

Ellis interrupted. "The Harley family could track their daughter thanks to their private investigator. He's gone, but his reports told us what we needed to know."

Slim was tempted to interrupt and take the story back again. Everything Ellis knew about the Harleys and the search for their daughter had come from him through JJ's work.

Then he started thinking.

So what if Ellis was so eager to keep his hands on the reins? Why not let Ellis tell Solstice the good news. The man was working on his career, while Slim was happy right where he was. It was good news no matter who told it. He heard Ellis continue:

"The Harley's investigator discovered that their daughter, Heather, had given birth to a child. When the child was about seven years old, Heather died. The child, and the child's father, dropped from sight. Then the first Mrs. Harley died.

"Now, here's the main point." Ellis paused dramatically, then spoke directly to Solstice. "Owen Harley never gave up hope that someday his lost granddaughter would be found. His second wife, Robin, was determined to keep that from happening. She stood to inherit Harley's total estate when he died, but that would change if the granddaughter appeared. Sparrow believed he had discovered Heather's daughter, and Neil Bannister took a photograph. When Robin saw that you had large brown eyes and freckles, like old pictures she'd seen of your mother, she knew you were her husband's long-lost granddaughter, and to preserve her full inheritance, you would have to die."

To the room that had now fallen silent, Ellis's dark eyes sparkled as he gazed at Solstice. "Solstice Windsor, your last name, Windsor, apparently came from your father, but since there is no record of your parents ever marrying, your last name is Harley. And—" Another dramatic pause, and then, "You, Solstice Harley, will be welcomed with open arms by your grandfather and become the sole heiress to his fortune."

For a moment, there was nothing but silence in the room.

Then Solstice exploded. "This is all lies!" She strained forward, her eyes wild. "My mother's name was Solstice, not Heather. I'm Solstice Windsor, not that stupid other name. Vivian said something to me once about someone in my family who cared about us, but that's not true." Her face was flushed, her hands clenched. "My mother's parents were horrible. If they'd been nice, my mother would have taken me home. It's all lies, nothing but lies. I'm not believing a word of it!"

With that, she flung herself from the couch and stumbled off, the yellow fleece dragging on the floor behind her as she rushed toward the bedroom hallway.

With a cry, Alexander was up and after her.

So were Vivian and Pilar.

Alone with Ellis, Slim shook his head, thinking that maybe it's just as well that Ellis had butted in. Who could have guessed that what he'd thought was good news could turn out so bad!

Vivian, who was behind Pilar and Alexander, paused at the open door to the guest bedroom. Solstice lay curled on the bed. Alexander stood helpless. Pilar said to Vivian. "Go to her. You two have a shared history. You will know what to say."

The words *shared history* echoed in Vivian's mind. She looked at Solstice's huddled form and remembered the girl's parents, so wrapped up in each other that nothing else much existed. Vivian knew children need to believe in their parents. She had only recently become certain of the love her father had for her and knew the difference it had made in her life. For Solstice to be told she might have had a better life if her mother and father had not refused it, that was too much to accept.

Vivian moved around the bed to be closer to Solstice. She remembered that in the car, the detective had spoken to Slim about things that had been discovered about Heather Harley's background.

Speaking now in a near whisper, Vivian said to Solstice. "Let me tell you things I've learned. Your mother, Heather, graduated from college and started to work with her father's style magazines. She fell in love with a musician, Keith O'Toole, who would become your father. He, for whatever reasons, had no attachments to his own family. His music wasn't the success he wanted. He had no regular job and no home, living instead among various friends. Heather's parents, your grandparents, didn't think Keith was the person who could give Heather the life they wanted for her. Maybe they were wrong, or maybe they should have handled things differently, but the end result was that Heather and Keith ran away together.

"Your mother was a trifle stubborn," Vivian continued with a smile in her voice. "I guess you inherited that from her." Vivian imagined a faint reaction to that, and she was sure of it when Solstice said, "She had freckles, too."

"Yes, she did."

"She had pretty red hair, not mousy brown hair, like me."

"But you are as pretty as she was," Vivian said, pushing from her mind how wasted the young mother had become from the weird diet she and Keith O'Toole had insisted on.

"The trouble was," Vivian continued, "She and your father experimented with different drugs and herbs . . . that strange tea they made harmed them, left them confused. They probably started out thinking her parents had been wrong, but over time, in their minds, they saw her parents as evil. They didn't intentionally deceive you. They told you what they'd come to believe was true."

The room was bright enough, Vivian thought, but there was still darkness in it. Pilar had left the room to speak to the chief and hadn't returned. Alexander still stood stiffly, his hands together, as if no move he could make would be the right one.

"You've always been strong," Vivian said to Solstice. "You've been alone and stayed strong. I'm thinking it will take a new kind of strength to believe that someone you don't yet know, your grandfather, could care."

Solstice gave no sign she had heard. Vivian returned to the subject of the girl's parents, drawing a more forgiving picture of the couple than they possibly deserved. After what seemed a long time, she felt Solstice relax, and finally, she realized Solstice had fallen into an exhausted sleep.

After settling the girl more comfortably on the bed and tucking the raggedy-fringe blanket around her. Vivian turned to Alexander, still hovering anxiously.

"She has a lot to absorb," Vivian said to him. "Give her time to come to terms with all that's happened. Let her sleep."

Chapter 61

It wasn't until early the next morning that Alexander, who'd been checking on Solstice throughout the night, found her standing at the window, looking out at the dawn sky, the sun a rose-gold on the horizon. She wore her long skirt and a sweater. The yellow fleece lay sprawled on the bed.

He hesitated, not knowing what to say. He said. "Are you hungry?"

Not answering his question, she said, "I'm twenty-two years old. I know what I can do and what I can't do. I know what I can have and what I don't dare ask for. This town, with its silly name, made me laugh, and that was good. You helped me meet Vivian again and that was good, too. I was looking forward to her wedding. She was proof that good things could come from the past, but I was kidding myself if I thought there was a future for me."

Alexander stared at her. She sounded different. Even the set of her uneven shoulders seemed different, her back was straighter; everything about her seemed determined.

She directed her words to the window. "I want to go home."

"Home where?"

She whirled to face him and spoke with her teeth clenched. "To my apartment in Brooklyn! Where else do you think, you loonygump?"

He was so accustomed to her smarty-pants name-calling that he'd stopped paying attention—sort of—but even in this, her manner had changed. Her tone was ferocious.

Bewildered, he said, "But you've learned you have family, at least a grandfather."

"He wouldn't want to see me."

"It sounds as if he does, and you know he cared about your mother, so he—"

She cut him off. "I sorted it all out. I had a lot of things to think about and I didn't like any of the answers."

"Maybe we could talk about it a little. Maybe together, we . . ." Feeling totally inept he let his words fade.

She continued on her own train of thought. "My mother, this college graduate who went to work for her father, held all the promise in the world. She's the one my grandfather remembers. She's the one he was so desperate to get back. He would want to look at me and see me as he once saw her. The nicer he is, the more he would never want the real me, never want to see what I've been turned into. No one would. How could they? I can't have a normal life with anybody, not after . . . after everything. I'm all nasty and dirty—"

This time she chopped her words off and would have run. Alexander wasn't sure where she thought she was going, but she had been going somewhere if he hadn't stepped directly in front of her, blocking her with his body.

She actually bumped into him and bounced back. "No!" she said and put up her hands as if to shove him aside.

He wouldn't let her do it. He couldn't touch her, but he could be a wall.

She tried to get around him, but he moved to block her path again.

"You're not going anywhere until we talk," he said.

She looked up at him. Her back was to the daylight, her cropped brown hair a nimbus around her head. Her face was shadowed, but he could see the glisten of her large eyes, the sheen of moisture on the curve of her lower lip.

Before she could challenge him, he said, "I know." He took a breath, his chin held an uncharacteristically determined jut. This was do or die. Maybe it was both. "I know about the name, Esstu."

"What?" Her voice rose in alarm.

"I know about *Legal but Don't Look It* and *Daddy's Girls*. I know you were forced into it."

Her eyes went even wider. "No! Vivian would never . . ."

"I heard nothing from Vivian. I found it on the Internet."

She just stared, so he kept talking. "You kept calling me names, so I wanted one for you. I was fooling around. Your username was S^2, so I spelled it phonetically on a computer. I keyed in variations. What came up was your photo, Esstu, at the so-called *Gentleman's Escort Service*." Remembered fury vibrated roughly through his voice. "I saw how young you were, how scared you looked and knew some animals were using you . . ." His voice did strange, gravelly things as if he was being strangled, and he couldn't go on.

"When did you know?"

He struggled for control. "When we came here to JumpRope the first time. You were at Iris's house. I took my laptop when I went with the Colonel to the museum."

"You knew all this time? Yet, you still . . ."

Her voice trailed off. He knew he better say something fast. What came out was the honest truth. "Liked you? Yes. Cared about you? Yes."

"You never touched me," she said in a tone of wonder.

"You didn't want me to, so I wouldn't. I never would have because you didn't want it. But it helped that I understood the reason why."

For a long time, the two of them stood exactly as they were.

The clock ticked on.

Alexander didn't think he'd ever felt so suspended, so fearful.

More minutes ticked by.

Then she moved. Closer to him.

"But I can touch you." She was looking up at him.

"Yes." His voice was hoarse.

She placed her hands on his chest, moved them higher to touch his beard, all the while looking at him. She moved her fingers through his soft, curly beard hairs.

He'd never felt anything like her touch, so tentative, so light, zephyr soft. Without realizing it, he was holding his breath. Her fingertips moved down along his chin whiskers, tangling gently, toying with what felt to him like individual strands.

She closed her eyes and moved a fraction closer.

He saw her smile.

"Toodles," she said in a whisper, still fingering his beard.

Toodles? Her dog?

He was confused, but her expression told him that what she'd said was a good thing.

She opened her eyes and kept her body close to his. "Except you're a person," she said softly, as if continuing a previous conversation. Again, he knew it meant something good to her, and that was good enough for him. Everything didn't have to be sorted out all at once. When he took a breath, he became more aware of the delicate pressure of her slight frame. He released a breath, and then took another. Held it, wanting nothing to break the moment.

Her hands left his beard and slipped downward, down to where he held his hands obediently to his slides. Her hands slipped within his. He had to breathe then, and he had to gasp with the shock, the surprise, the marvelous sensation of her hands in his, her fingers innocently touching his sensitive palms.

She took his hands and brought them around to her back.

He left his hands as she had put them, mostly suspended, barely in contact with her slender waist. He remained baffled and motionless, like a clay figure, molded by her touch.

He ached for understanding. *What did she want him to do?*

She moved her hands up, inside his arms, around his broad back, clasped him.

Hugged him. Her head tucked under his chin, her hair touching the trimmed ends of his beard. Then she drew back enough to look up at him.

"You comfort me," she said. She smiled and her embrace tightened. "I won't break."

He hesitated, feeling all at sea. She nodded and gave him a little nudging, instructive squeeze with her both arms tight around him as she rested her head against his chest.

He hugged her, softly at first, as if she *would* break, then firmly, like coming home after a long time apart. This time his breath was an inimitable hitching, almost sobbing sound, but he didn't care. Didn't care about anything except standing here with this weird and wonderful girl, this woman, who was hugging him as he was hugging her, both of them swaying slightly together as if rocked by the gentlest breeze.

He closed his eyes, but through his lashes, he could see the light all around them, the warm eastern sunlight as the curtain rose on a bright new day, touching them with gold.

Chapter 62

𝒥umpRope residents eagerly flocked to the wedding of Vivian Mather and Nero Gibeau, the biggest wedding ever. Peculiar that it wasn't in a church, but guests were fascinated to see Teddy's entire restaurant with its charming Teddy bear murals given over to a single event. One banquet hall was prepared for the wedding. The adjoining hall would serve for the reception. The guests were either gathering in the bar where the mural on the wall showed a Teddy bear jumping rope and reading a newspaper or moving to take seats in the wedding hall.

Everyone in town was invited, although of course, not everyone came, but the timing of the event was excellent.

First, it fell during the winter doldrums.

Second, it occurred when people yearned to gather and discuss every known detail of the recently solved JumpRope murder mystery in which the criminal mastermind had been a glamorous ex-fashion model, who had recently enjoyed high status in Manhattan's social scene. Plus, there was a newly discovered heiress in their midst. Quite a photogenic little thing, although you might not take much notice of her in person.

The *Melton Monitor* reported that the criminal mastermind, Robin Harley, had also been accused of drugging Owen Harley, her elderly husband, to hasten the time when she could inherit his fortune. *Monitor* feature writer, JJ Gilbert, who had broken the story, wanted to add it Carol's book as an Afterward. However, when the book editor saw the *Monitor* article, she got excited. She said the Harley story was worth a book of its own. It had everything, including sex, thanks to the fact that Robin Harley had enticed her lover, Gregory Sparrow, to take part in the murder scheme that not only took the life of author Carol Vetter, it nearly destroyed Owen Harley's granddaughter, Solstice, the newly discovered heiress. The editor wanted JJ to author the book. JJ was considering it.

People wondered how Pilar Fanshawe's next *JumpRope Jive* would cover all that had happened, if it was ever published. Pilar had authored the newsletter in partnership with her son, the striving tedious playwright, but Alexander presently had other interests. Wonder of wonders, he was reportedly dating the heiress.

Pilar, dressed in a cream-colored cocktail suit that would have been plain had it not been for the antique necklace of cabochon-cut rubies and matching clip-on earrings, moved from Teddy's bar to the wedding hall, escorted by the pleasant-looking mustached widower, Max Osterhagen. Alexander accompanied Solstice, whose recent reunion with her grandfather had gone smoothly. Her long dress flattered her slender form and her short hair, now expertly styled, retained the tousled, gamine look. They too were moving toward the wedding hall with other guests.

Jessi Spellman was not among them. She disliked events where she was not the star, and at a wedding, the bride would hog all the attention. However, now that she had become acquainted with cultured people worthy of her notice, and she knew that the Mather family had money, it crossed her mind to wonder which designer would have created Vivian's gown.

Vivian Mather had no interest in designer attire. The most beautiful dress she had ever seen was worn by a princess in a picture book she'd once read to Solstice. It had been purple and had long sleeves with slits so the wearer's arms showed through. Vivian had described the gown to her unconventional Aunt Elizabeth, who thought it sounded wonderful and promptly assigned a dressmaker to fashion it from beautifully draping silk velvet. Instead of a veil, a Juliet cap was made of the same purple velvet as the dress, with a cascade of ribbons down the back. Nero's grandmother, Yvette, along with Aunt Elizabeth and Vivian's Cousin Grace, handled the wedding details. The older women expected they would never have another wedding to plan, so they made the most of it. Vivian was appreciative. If her Aunt Elizabeth had too wild of a brainstorm, Yvette and Grace would dampen it down.

Which meant the reception wouldn't include stilt-walking clowns or lion tamers.

Vivian laughed as she thought of Nero's expression if something like that happened. He thought it was so much fun teasing her because she could never lift a single eyebrow. Well, she had a surprise for him, but it wasn't about eyebrows.

Nero's wedding attendants were the older veterans, Holland Kingston, Sr. and the Colonel, who had supported him with their friendship when he'd been a falling-down drunk. Bob Smithers, who would serve as his best man, had enough faith in him to give him a garage job when he'd proved he was off the sauce for good. Nero also asked Father Thomas Capodanno to give a blessing. Father Tom was the chaplain at the veteran's group where Nero had sessions that were making a positive difference. Not only had the man become a friend, but at age thirty-five, he was also the only one of the group besides Nero who was young enough to read in dim light. Plus his Catholicism pleased Nero's grandmother.

Vivian's attendants were her Aunt Elizabeth and her Cousin Grace.

The banquet hall's multitude of chairs was arranged with a central aisle. White, purple and blue flowers were everywhere, and the ladies in the town organizations had covered the Teddy bear mural in the wedding hall with flower-bedecked drapery. Bridal attire pasted on jumping rope bears had seemed too fey for a dignified occasion.

For music, Elizabeth had engaged a string quartet and a trumpeter. She liked the way a trumpet got people's blood moving. When the quartet played a bright and sprightly musical piece, signaling the seated assembly that something was about to happen. From a side door, Holly, who was to perform the ceremony as mayor, came out to take his place on a platform that was exactly the right height for him to look out comfortably upon the crowd. He gave a smile to everyone, and his gaze settled on Toria for a longer, warmer moment. That moment caused a little ripple around the room as people wondered if the next nuptials in town might be theirs.

Father Tom, Bob, the Colonel and Holland Kingston, Sr. walked out and stood to one side. Nero appeared, tall, dark and handsome and looking almost unbearably happy as he stood in his cutaway, with a boutonniere that was a white rose with a cluster of violets.

Amy Newton gasped and in a voice that might have been louder than she intended, exclaimed, "Nero looks like a movie star!" Her husband, Chuck, patted her hand and gave her a tolerant smile.

There was a fanfare trumpet tune and Vivian's cousin, Grace, started up the aisle. Elizabeth, who hadn't wanted to roll up the aisle in her wheelchair, was positioned behind a screen on the platform where the ceremony would take place. She would appear when Grace was in position. Holland, Sr. would take charge of her chair at the recessional at the close of the ceremony.

The two children Acer Wolfgang had befriended, Twyla, and her cousin, Ben, were flower girl and ring bearer. They came next, she in white velvet printed with orchid designs, he in a purple little boy's short pants suit. They looked adorable, Hummel kids come to life.

The women who were the children's mothers sat on the bride's side in the same row as Darlene Gage. A vacant chair sat on the aisle to Darlene's right, her purse upon it to save it. Darlene looked quite wonderful, but she was visibly tense.

There was a pause, a flourish from the trumpet, and the crowd stood as the music became a joyful march, not the usual wedding march, but something else that was familiar, signaling that the bride would appear.

And there she was, Vivian on Acer's arm, the ribbons streaming from her Juliet cap shimmering over the waves of her long dark hair.

Lucky man, thought the assembled men of Nero as they gazed at Vivian.

Francine, thinking that at least Vivian didn't *look* pregnant, muttered to Iris, who stood at her side, "At least she has the class not to wear white."

Guileless Iris whispered back, "You're always right! With her coloring, white wouldn't have flattered her nearly as much."

The guests resumed their seats. The ceremony began and moved to where Holly asked, "Who gives this woman?" Acer responded with warm pride, "I give this woman, with the blessing of her family." He took Vivian's hand and placed it in Nero's hand.

Stepping back, Acer turned from the bridal party and toward Darlene. She was seated where he had seen her on his way up the aisle, with the empty chair beside her.

Darlene watched as he approached. There was a smidgen of hesitation in his sea-blue eyes that showed, even then, that he was not quite one-hundred percent certain of her. She smiled. A real smile, suddenly glad to reassure him. He took the seat beside her and after a heartbeat, he reached for her hand, which she allowed. It was his left hand. She could feel the scars. *We all have scars*, Darlene thought and relaxed.

The ceremony moved to the exchanging of the rings. Nero placed his ring to Vivian on her fourth finger of her left hand, looking into her eyes as he spoke the words that expressed this symbol of his love. She was ready with her ring for him when he jogged a single questioning eyebrow. It stopped her. She couldn't help it—she tried to mirror the gesture. And failed. He mouthed the word, *practice*. She nearly laughed, but with effort, suppressed it as she slid the ring on his finger and repeated the symbolic words.

Slim, slouched comfortably, his long legs stretched out under the chair in front of him, wondered what had gone on when Vivian had almost broken up. Slim found them an interesting couple and felt an unexpected sense of anticipation as they moved together for a kiss.

Their lips met. Looking at one another they drew apart. And then, as if drawn by magnetic force, they moved back together. To the delighted murmur from those assembled, their lips met a second time.

Double tap, Slim thought, shifting in his seat. Damn, if that pair didn't leave him feeling itchy and wishing he had somebody of his own. He thought ahead to the reception. JJ, who was currently on an assignment, would meet him there in an hour. That would be good. He briefly visualized her face, her eyes bright, her grin showing that little gap between her front teeth that he was finding increasingly appealing.

Yeah, that was all good.

In the reception room following the ceremony, the guests waited expectantly. Acer, performing as the Master of Ceremonies, announced, "And now, for the very first time, please greet Mr. and Mrs. Nero Gibeau."

There were cheers of congratulation and good wishes as Vivian and Nero walked together through a flower-trimmed arch.

Live music began. The formally dressed musicians had once been a ragtag group of youngsters playing in New York City's Bryant Park for change thrown into a hat. Now, thanks to the efforts of Elizabeth Mather, they swung professionally into a lively version of a song made famous by Patsy Cline, *Back in Baby's Arms.*

Stunned, Nero said to Vivian, "You remembered!"

She smiled. "You once said Cline's music was a favorite. I said her songs were sad. You said, 'Not *Back in Baby's Arms.* You can really move to that.' It was our first date. Of course, I remembered!"

With that, she was in his arms as they moved together in a swinging two-step in one of the many happy moments of their wedding day that they would treasure forever.

After

MAR-SEE-AH SPEAKS

Mar-see-ah did not accept social invitations from clients but when the members of the Voodoo Club invited her to Vivian's wedding and they said that almost the whole town would be there, she couldn't resist peeking in.

Standing in an alcove she wondered briefly about the dismissed threat of the so-called, "Florida people." She put aside future concerns in favor of watching the couples she recognized joining the newlyweds on the dance floor.

She saw the members of the club that she knew, all except Darlene. Then she saw her standing with Acer.

They had paused at the edge of the flower-trimmed-arch, watching those on the dance floor move to the lively rhythm.

Acer gave a half bow and took Darlene's hand in his.

In answer to something he'd said, Darlene smiled.

Together, they joined the others in the dance.

A good ending, Mar-see-ah thought. *Perhaps a good beginning for them as well.*

JPI

We Are Mysteries

An anthology of WhoDunits and HowDunits
by 34 mystery writers.

JERSEY PINES INK

https://www.jerseypinesink.com

JPI

We Are Horror, Fantasy and Speculative Fiction

A collection of 42 entertaining mystery and speculative short stories

JERSEY PINES INK
https://www.jerseypinesink.com

JPI

We Are Romance.
and Supernatural Mysteries

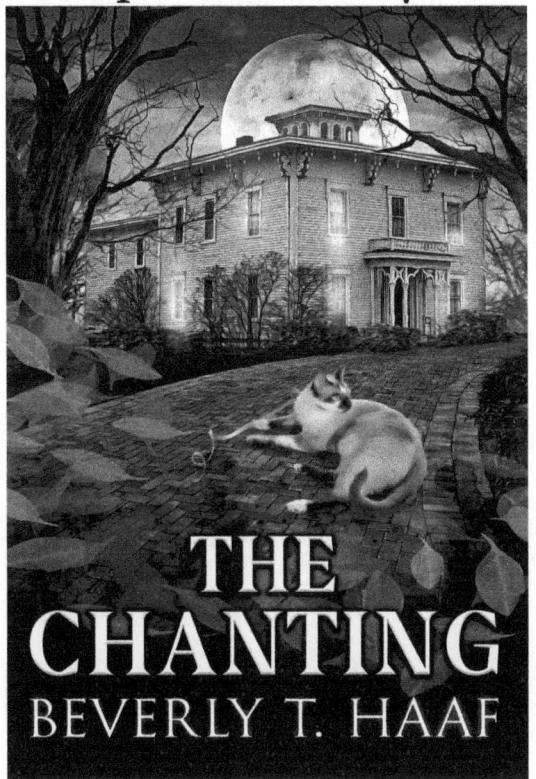

A woman, a child, and a man . . .
Will the spell of the mysterious yellow house
draw them together or tear them apart?

JERSEY PINES INK
https://www.jerseypinesink.com

Upcoming books from JPI
Jersey Pines Ink
https://www.jerseypinesink.com/

A Drop In The Cup, A Collection of 42 Speculative Short Horror and Fantasy Stories by Diane Arrelle

WhoDunit, A collection of 42 entertaining mystery and speculative fiction short stories

The Chanting, a Supernatural/Romance Novel by Beverly T. Haaf

Ready for your reading pleasure now

Series: ***JumpRope Chronicles*** by Ivy C. Leigh

Death Behind the Lilacs

Death Counts the Golden Coins

E-Book ***Jump Into***

Seasons on the Dark Side, a Horror Short Story Collection by Diane Arrelle

Crypt Gnats, an Anthology of Horror Stories You've been Itching to Read, edited by Dina Leacock

https://www.jerseypinesink.com

Milton Keynes UK
Ingram Content Group UK Ltd.
UKHW011808041223
433765UK00001B/316